PRAISE FOR ESTATE SALE

"Buyer beware: Mia Dalia's *Estate Sale* is a cursed kaleidoscope of gothic proportions, equal parts *Needful Things* and *The Confessions of Aleister Crowley*. Reading this prismatic black magic, sprawling historical horror epic may just end up cursing you ..."

CLAY MCLEOD CHAPMAN

AUTHOR OF *WHAT KIND OF MOTHER* AND *GHOST EATERS*

"*Estate Sale* is a sweeping historical horror story rooted in global upheaval and a dark quest for occult secrets. Mia Dalia has penned an epic tale of undying love with bloody repercussions that echo across the centuries. This is one debut novel you don't want to miss."

DOUGLAS WYNNE

AUTHOR OF *SMOKE & DAGGER* AND *HIS OWN DEVICES*

"Dark, brooding, and wonderfully creepy, this stunning debut brings to mind the best Gothic works of the past century while charting a territory that is entirely its own. A must for horror fans!"

JETHRO WEGENER

AUTHOR OF *LOST CITY OF TERROR*

"I loved it. A clever, erudite, and thrilling book! Mia Dalia's *Estate Sale* is an original and terrific take on the classic "cursed objects" trope. Blending real historical figures and events and pure occult tales, Mia Dalia weaves a convincing and powerful narrative, which is also a dark portrait of a woman of her times. A must-read for all lovers of literary horror!"

SEB DOUBINSKY

AUTHOR OF *CITY-STATES* SERIES

ESTATE SALE

MIA DALIA

LETHE
PRESS

ESTATE SALE

Mia Dalia

First edition first (self-)published in 2023
This edition published in 2025 by Lethe Press

ISBN 9781590215579

Library of Congress Number (LCCN) available on request

Cover art: Justin Sanz.
Interior illustrations: Chelsea Sanz
Interior design: Inkspiral Design

FOR CHELSEA,
FOREVER

CHAPTER 1

BEFORE

THE FIRST THING she remembered was fire. That couldn't have been right, of course. She was seventeen by then, with a standard collection of memories accumulated by a person of that age. Yet, when she looked back to the beginning of her life, all she saw were flames.

It was as if the fire in its mindless rage had obliterated all that came before it. All the happy sunny years of her youth. All the lovely contentment of carefree life. And from its ashes, like a phoenix, Anastasia emerged, suddenly no longer a child.

Her father was broken by it. He had spent too long building and cultivating his estate and was too old to rebuild. The revolution changed the world around him into one he could no longer understand or comfortably exist in.

"These peasants," he grumbled. "They are not thinking clearly. They shall starve without us."

Anastasia didn't know if that was true. She never gave any thought to politics. A dreamy child, she'd always been indulged by her elderly parents to whom she came late in life as a welcome surprise. As a young girl, she enjoyed French and literature, and geography, things that fueled her dreams. She never thought it would end.

Anastasia didn't know if the people working for them all this time hated them or not. *But they must have*, she thought, watching her family home go up in the fire started by them. *They must have.*

Her mother, a naturally reticent withdrawn woman, barely reacted at all; she seemed stunned.

"She is in shock, Nastya," her father said. "We must let her be."

But let her be where? Where would they all go? What would they do? How would they live?

Anastasia never thought of their life as a play with many different acts in it, but ready or not, the stage was set for act two. The stage was covered in ashes.

CHAPTER 2

AFTER

THE CHAIR

(JUNE 1ST, 2000)

I'VE NEVER KEPT a diary. Never wanted to. But then again, I've never experienced writer's block either. The desire to write, the need to do it doesn't go away, but the words don't come. More like the ideas don't come. The words themselves show up and sit on the page uselessly, refusing to add up to a coherent thought. Can't plot, won't plot ... But the keys still call to my fingertips, hence this enfeebled attempt to jog something into action in that blocked brain of mine. Just write, they say, and the story will come. Bullshit. Oh, and walking doesn't help either. So let this great experiment commence. Entry one, over and out.

(June 3RD, 2000)

Well, here we are again. These words remain the only ones written by me thus far. That and what I scribbled on our mortgage check. I've read King's book *On Writing* but taking advice from someone seemingly supernaturally charged (contracted?) to write doesn't appear to be of any great help. It's like taking Oprah's advice on popularity. I'm off to take a walk around the neighborhood. Later, Diary.

(June 10TH, 2000)

An estate sale makes you expect an estate. The place I went to just now was decidedly not one. Or maybe it was, and the original features had become impossible to discern through time and dilapidation. Either way, that was some Grey Gardens situation if I ever saw one. The age and the size of the house probably qualified it for some grand descriptor like an estate, a mansion. A manse even. (Now there's a word you don't see outside of a book. Imagine *that* in a realtor's listing.) But the state of the place ... sheesh.

How'd they even know the old lady finally died? No one around to visit. No one around to smell the dead body. What a tragic end to a life. Then again, who knows, maybe her life was tragic all the way through, making this the most fitting of ends. Trapped under a collapsed bookcase. Murdered by books. That's one of the rumors.

My inability to write books might turn murderous. No, that's stupid. A stupid parallel. One must respect the dead. Or at least death itself. Glibness is too easy.

Anyway, I bought something at the estate sale. Yes, yes, I know I shouldn't have. Not with the alarmingly dwindling advance for a story I can't seem to write, not with the mounting stack of bills. I've heard it all from the missus already, and you, Dear Diary, don't get to judge.

It was cheap, anyway. And I really did need a chair. Or no, I really did *want* a chair. I can differentiate need from want. Well, now I have one. If only all dreams were this easily achieved.

(JUNE 15TH, 2000)

THE BLANK SCREEN of the computer has defeated me once more. I stared down the blinking cursor, and the cursor won. I'm so mad. So frustrated too. Now I'm staring down this new chair of mine, and the chair seems to be winning too. It's a handsome one, that's for sure. Doesn't really seem that striking in our place, not after the missus spent my first advance moolah on that fancy mid-century decor she adores, but in the old house, its original home, the chair stood out for being so oddly pristine amid all that ravage of age and time.

"No one's ever sat in it," said the person presiding over the sale. "Why is that?" naturally I inquired. She said the old lady was weirdly superstitious about it.

With a name like that, like the old lady had, she had to have been from the old country. First-generation, I bet. Superstition in the blood. Yeah, well I got a nice, practically new chair out of it, though. Tall, slick, comfortable, surprisingly supple tasteful upholstery. It even rocks. In fact, why haven't I sat in it yet? It might be the only way for me to rock these days. Buh-dum-dumtz. Self-pity party of one, reservation at the self-deprecation restaurant. Enjoy.

(JUNE 16TH, 2000)

I WROTE. I freaking wrote today. And wrote and wrote. Don't know where it came from. Woke up and the story was just there, in my mind, almost completely formed. I barely made it to the computer, and it just began pouring out of me. I ended up skipping a meal and then completely forgetting about a double date we were supposed to go on with some friends. Worth it, though.

This new story is a strange one, not quite in line with what I've written until now. Maybe I'm finally making an entrance into genre fiction. Why not? That sort of thing is popping and hopping right now. Guess reading King paid off, after all. Subliminally? Slick, psyche, slick, you warped fucker.

THE MISSUS IS pissed. Says I'm locking myself away from her. I'm not, not really. It was only to get some peace and quiet. This story is good, I know it, I feel it in my bones. Just have to get it all down on paper, as it were. I've reread some of the earlier chapters while comfortably rocking in my new chair, and they barely need any editing at all. The manuscript is practically print-ready, saving this writer from the much-hated process of rewriting.

I've been thinking about the old lady who died. Mrs. Koshmaroff. Guess someone knew her well enough to post an obit. I read it. She made it to ninety-nine. Nearly a century, so much of it spent alone. What that must have been like. The crushing weight of loneliness all those years. I can't imagine, I barely get any alone time.

Turns out the old lady was married to a writer once upon a time. The guy wrote short fiction for those old school publications like *Amazing Stories* or whatever. Science fiction, mostly. Dabbled in horror. There might have been a novel or two also. His greatest claim to fame was one story adapted for *Twilight Zone*. Wonder if he made a living out of that. Must have. Enough to buy that old house, which must have been quite something back in the day. Anyway, back to writing.

I'M GETTING CLOSE. I can see the finish line from here. Try explaining this to a woman whose birthday you missed. Yeah, that's right, I did it, and honestly, I don't know how I'd managed to forget it. The reminder on my computer was all set. She claims I didn't come out of my office (we call it that aspirationally, the space is smaller than a Norwegian prison cell) for two days. Apparently, I had locked myself in, and all she heard through the door was typing and chair rocking. It doesn't seem right, but then again, I can't honestly say that it's wrong.

I'm just going to apologize. Grovel if need be. Overspend on a gift. Whatever it takes to get back to writing in peace. I believe this ending is going to be a doozy.

FROM THE *RUE Morgue* magazine (October 31st, 2021):

The late great author Finn James vanished without a trace over two decades ago, leaving behind the manuscript of his timeless masterpiece *Futures Writ in Blood*. The manuscript was found in his office, which was mysteriously locked from the inside, thus not only providing us with the definitive scary story of the 21st century but also with what is sure to be an enduring puzzle to boggle the minds of readers for years to come.

James' place has recently been converted into a museum, which you can visit, just like the author of this article did, and see if you can solve the mystery for yourself. To me, it looked like an ordinary, if much too small, office with a bookcase, a desk, and a desk chair—all mid-century knockoffs. A somber reminder that Finn James never got the chance to enjoy the success of his famous novel, its multiple reprints, and its Oscar-winning movie adaptation. All the furniture appeared well-used, except for a nice and seemingly authentic antique rocking chair in the corner of the office. You can practically picture James rocking away in it, contemplating the ingenious, twisted ending of his final work. James' wife refused to comment, but the chair is said to creak at times for no apparent reason. Spooky indeed.

FROM THE OBITUARY of Paul Koshmaroff (August 17th, 1957):

Mr. Koshmaroff, the scion of a great Russian family with ties to the late Tzar, settled with his wife in the proverbial all-American small town after extensive traveling, and had dabbled in the occult for years, which was said to have inspired his short fiction and later novels. Mr. Koshmaroff's mysterious disappearance was never solved.

(DATE UNKNOWN)

DEAR DIARY, WHEREVER you are. Remember me? Finn? I'm still here. I can't stop writing now, thoughts pouring out in what I imagine to be invisible ink and settling down on pages no one will ever read. I'm still here. Dreaming loud nightmares. Screaming silent screams. In this chair. Rocking away. You'd notice if you ever sat down. But then again, no one ever sits in this chair.

CHAPTER 3

BEFORE

As it turned out, their second act would play out in the recently renamed Petrograd. Anastasia didn't like the new name, patriotic or not, it sounded coarse compared to its much grander previous moniker.

The city was a beauty under any name. For a wealthy but provincial seventeen-year-old girl it was the ultimate cosmopolitan experience. She drank it in like zavarka, the strong black tea her mother swore by, the one that had only recently become widely available.

"The best thing the Red Army ever did for me," her mother would proclaim.

They had to buy a new samovar, of course. Who knew what became of the old one, a glorious family heirloom left behind like most other things in the fire. Its replacement was serviceable but plain. It fit their new lives, which were much plainer, much less ornamental than the previous ones.

They survived courtesy of Anastasia's uncle, a stern, barrel-chested man with an imposing mustache. Her mother's brother. A military man recently retired on account of his ruined back, Uncle Oleg never had much time for frivolities. This included fine things, women and, by extension, his delicate sister and her dreamy daughter. Nevertheless, as a man of duty, he honored his familial responsibilities and so, stoically, he took them in. His house, if not his heart, was certainly large enough to accommodate them.

Now that she was a proper city girl, Anastasia could no longer ignore politics. They were everywhere. The protesters were taking to the streets, screaming for bread, screaming for justice, determined to make their voices heard. Politics were discussed everywhere: in her home, in the cafes, on street corners.

"First they lost faith in him," her father would say to his uncle, referring, she knew, to the Tsar. "How could they not? The way he disregarded the Duma. The way he cowered. The way he carried on tolerating that horrible mystic. But now they are misplacing their faith in this terrible dream that'll be written in blood."

Her uncle would invariably agree with her father. They were both staunch royalists, but, as informed and reasonable men, they could read the writing on the wall. And for anyone who couldn't, the shouting rioters hammered in the message loud and clear. A new world was coming. From fire and blood, a new country was to be built.

"Oleg is having financial difficulties," Anastasia overheard her father saying to her mother one evening after supper. "He doesn't want us to know, he's too proud, but we are a heavy weight upon him. One of the factories he's had a vested interest in has been shuttered. And another might be soon."

She didn't know it then, but a plan was set in motion that night. A plan to find a suitable husband for her, one who would provide the rising tide to lift all their boats. Or, at least, prevent them from sinking.

Once she found out about it, Anastasia didn't know quite what to think of the idea. On one hand, she had read enough romances to think of it as a possibility of a grand adventure of the heart; on the other, though she no longer felt like a child, she wasn't sure she was ready for marriage yet either.

Maybe it won't come to pass, Anastasia told herself. After all, she'd have no dowry now. Surely her prospects were limited. Surely her parents didn't know enough people in Petrograd yet. They barely left the house lately, mired inside— the men with their vodka and politics, her mother with her tea and her sad thoughts.

Time passed slowly, then faster, and then it was her birthday. She was turning eighteen, and her uncle promised her a party. It would be more of a small gathering, of course, for practical reasons, but still she looked forward to it immensely. An entire day to feel special, the cake, the gifts.

Anastasia didn't know most of the people who came. They must have been friends of her uncle's. She hadn't seen any of her own friends since they moved to

Petrograd. She tried to stay in touch through letters, but either the postal service was exceptionally unreliable or they had begun to forget about her. Making new local friends had proved challenging. City people were prickly, cautious, difficult to get to know.

"Nastya," her father's voice cut through her maudlin thoughts. "Meet Pavel Ivanovich Rostov."

She looked up from her cake and saw a tall man with piercing eyes who was trying to form his naturally stern-featured face into a friendly expression.

"It is my pleasure, Anastasia," he said and kissed her hand. "Happy birthday. I brought you a gift. I hope it pleases you."

It was a bird. A beautiful bird with a green-feathered body, yellow head, and red epaulets on its shoulders. The bird was sitting on its perch in a large, elaborately decorated cage that looked very heavy, despite the fact that Rostov appeared to be holding it effortlessly with one hand.

"A bird," she exhaled, quietly delighted. A beautiful bright thing amid the dreariness of it all. A striking reminder that there was still joy to be found in this strange and uncertain world.

"Wherever did you get such a thing?" asked Uncle Oleg, approaching and peering in closer to the cage to study the bird.

"On my travels to the Americas, my friend," Rostov answered. And then to Anastasia, "It is a double yellow-headed Amazon parrot. He is from Mexico, and his name is Diego. He'll love you and only you forever. Oh, and he talks. Teach him anything; he's got a beautiful voice."

As if on command, Diego piped in. She didn't understand a word, but the notion of a talking bird the likes of which she had only ever read about thrilled her. Finally, some company.

"He mostly speaks Spanish now. You'll have to teach him some Russian."

"And French," Anastasia offered, charmed.

"*Ah, oui bien sur mademoiselle parle français,*" Rostov switched seamlessly. His accent, Anastasia noted, was impeccable.

"*J'ai peur que mon français ne soit pas aussi bon que le tien,*" she stumbled shyly.

"Nonsense," Rostov told her with utter seriousness, "I'm sure your French is just as good as mine."

"I don't get a lot of chances to practice. I haven't had a tutor since we moved here," she explained.

"Well, I'd be delighted to be your practice partner," he said. "And in time, I'm sure Diego would help too."

After that day, Rostov became a fixture at their house. Showing up with gifts, in his impeccable suits with his nicely cut hair, flattering her, speaking French to her. He even brought treats for Diego. As far as she could tell, he was, all in all, a perfect gentleman. But still, it was difficult to consider him as a future husband. And she knew, *she knew*, though no one would overtly speak of it, that this was her parents' plan all along.

For one thing, Rostov was so much older. Not as old as father or Uncle Oleg, but older, maybe forty if she had to guess. For another, there was something about him that scared her, something beneath his flawless manners and perfect clothes. There was a wildness in his stare when he didn't guard his expression. And then there were rumors ...

She picked up on them here and there, amid the parlor whispers at gatherings and overheard intimate conversations of her parents.

"The man is a fiend," said her mother once to her father. Anastasia had never heard her mother refer to anyone that way. It frightened and excited her. "A fiend. I've heard all about him. He was friends with the mad monk himself."

"They weren't friends, Sonya, darling, they *knew* each other. That is all. Many people knew Rasputin. They were both frequent guests at the Winter Palace. And at Tsarskoye Selo. Just socializing. It was nothing."

"But I heard he also belonged to that weird sect. The Khlysts. You know what those people got up to."

"Now, now, dear, that's just hearsay. A man like that, a man with money, a man who travels and has connections ... there will always be rumors flying around. Just that, rumors. And at any rate, whatever his interests are, that's his private business. The man is wealthy, smart, decent. He adores Nastya. And we can't wait much longer. Oleg's just about bankrupt and won't admit it. The Romanovs are dead. The world as we know it is long gone. We need to make sure our daughter will be safe. Rostov will take care of her."

And thus, her fate was sealed. Amid the crumbling empire, guided to the altar by fear of others rather than love of her own, she became Anastasia Rostova.

Married life, in a way, reminded her of being back in her parents' house. Before the fire. The same feeling of being taken care of and provided for, the same carefree life.

And then there was Pavel, as he insisted she call him. Never Pavlik, no diminutive would ever suit him. Her husband. How strange that sounded. A perfect gentleman, he maintained a separate bedroom. They ate most of their meals together. She accompanied him to the opera, to the parties, gilded in the finery he bought for her. They spoke French. They played with Diego, who trilled back delightfully, their perfect feathered polyglot.

Anastasia expected, nay, *dreaded* ... more. The things she'd glimpse servants do after dark in stolen private moments, the things her mother had ever so vaguely discussed with her, but so far, Pavel had made no demands of that nature on her. She didn't know if she was entirely pleased about that. Did he not find her attractive? Desirable? Was she merely a companion, a decoration upon his arm?

He first came to her bedroom on the eve of her nineteenth birthday party. The lavish affair with multitiered cake and hired musicians went on well into the night, before finally winding down. Anastasia, half undressed, cake-delirious, and danced out, was still reliving it when she heard the soft knocking on her door.

She opened it, and he came in, looking uncharacteristically hesitant. She took a step closer.

"If you want me to stop, say it," he said, and kissed her. It was her first proper kiss. The kiss from the books she'd read—so much more than a perfunctory peck he'd usually bestow upon her. Her husband carefully took off the rest of her clothes. Her party dress had been cast to the floor like a skin shed. He didn't stop. She didn't tell him to. He moved slowly and then faster. The shape of his broad shoulders obscured all the light.

It wasn't magical, and it wasn't dreadful. If Anastasia had to put a word to the act, she'd say she found the experience interesting, after the initial discomfort. Something she wouldn't mind doing again, to see if it could be improved upon. Pavel was kind, at least. There was that.

In the morning after he'd left, always an early riser, Anastasia lay in bed and studied the bloodstain on the snow-white sheet. *How strange*, she mused, *that this is me now.*

From that point on, they slept together at least once or twice a week. It did improve, or maybe she got used to it. Either way, she didn't think the fault was with Pavel, for he was a picture of consideration. She imagined it was her, still trying to get comfortable in this new skin, the skin of someone's wife. The adult. The mistress of the house.

More like a mansion, Anastasia had to be honest. There was no need for false modesty. Their place was huge, gorgeous, surrounded by equally impressive buildings, and in close proximity to the Winter Palace, with its baroque splendor and gilded trim.

She would walk past the imposing building, which had gone from being a residence to the Russian Imperial family to becoming a state museum and a symbol of the Bolsheviks' power in just a few short years, and think about how quickly everything can change. Then she would go back to her beautiful house and try to forget the troubled, impermanent world.

But the city rumbled too loudly, and blatant displays of wealth became more and more dangerous. One night at supper, her husband brought up the idea of moving.

Moving? Again? She didn't want to. She was comfortable here. Almost happy.

"My business and my studies would be best attended elsewhere, *ma chérie*," Pavel told her, reasonably.

Anastasia still didn't know much about either his business or his studies, other than it took up an inordinate amount of time and required inviting many people into their house. People she would be introduced to, only to, soon after, forget their names. Most of them appeared older and wealthy, like Pavel, and some had an esoteric peculiarity to them that defied easy categorization.

Once, after an especially spirited gathering, she asked her husband what they studied.

"Our fields of research are quite recherché, darling," he replied mildly. "I don't think you'd find them interesting."

Anastasia had learned to sense a finality in his voice and did not pursue the subject. Her curiosity was idle at best; most of the time she was perfectly content with things as they were.

But the topic of relocation continued to come up and soon evolved from a casual discussion into an actual plan. Pavel was good at subtly getting his way, she'd noticed that about him. A very persuasive man.

Once again, she would have to leave everything behind. There was always someone in charge, it seemed, someone charting the course of her life. First her parents, now her husband. But there were no alternatives that Anastasia was aware of. And who knew, maybe it would turn out to be a good thing in the end. At any rate, it would be different. A new adventure.

"We're going to Paris, Diego," she said, lightly tapping on the bird's cage.

The parrot tucked his head to the side the way he did to show he was paying attention and said nothing.

"Paris," she repeated dreamily, this time to herself.

CHAPTER 4

AFTER

THE QUILL

THE LAST WILL and testament of Silas Sloan was read aloud on a gloomy October day in a small, bland office by a small, bland man named Jackson Craven. Darcy thought the name suited the man as she studied his out-of-date brown suit and a small dewdrop circle of sweat ringing his balding pate. What hair he had left formed a horseshoe of grey-tinged beige tufts that were valiantly hanging on for seemingly no reason other than stubbornness.

I bet this man has never done a brave thing in his life, Darcy mused. She'd never be like that; not her— she was destined for something ... well, she wasn't sure what, but some version of greatness She believed it fully, felt it in her bones with the arrogant conviction of youth. A conviction that neither her mother nor her stepfather, seated on her left and right respectively, seemed to share but would never say so out loud.

The will read much as expected. All of Grandpa Silas' earthly possessions were to be inherited by his only daughter, Jennifer, Darcy's mom, with the exception of a sizable stamp collection going to an old friend no one had ever heard him mention. Easy enough. And disappointing. Darcy wanted to inherit something of her own. She liked the concept; she even liked the sound of it. It would have made her an heiress, if only in some small way.

Of course, being an heiress to the late Silas Sloan's estate was no great prize. The death of his wife, Mae, Darcy's beloved grandmother, a few years ago, seemed to have unleashed in Silas a previously unknown—dormant? nonexistent?— passion for hoarding. He didn't call it that, of course. Silas Stone was no hoarder. To hear him speak of it, he was a collector. He prowled antique shops and estate sales looking for and acquiring items that matched some specific attributes from some specific inventory he kept in his mind.

The charming and always neat cottage, maintained to perfection by his houseproud wife right up until her dying day, turned into a ye olde curiosity shoppe quicker than anyone had anticipated. And then the place became downright dangerous; with towering stacks of worthless treasures doing their best impressions of the leaning tower of Pisa along the walls and across the rooms. The newly constructed mazes eliminated daylight and created claustrophobic labyrinths that Darcy wouldn't want to venture into, Ariadne's string or not. Her mother would go there, now and again, out of daughterly obligations and safety concerns, but nothing ever changed. Silas remained undeterred in his treasure hunt, and his Great Wall of Garbage construction. When a part of this wall collapsed, burying him under it, it was a death as appropriate as deaths came. The smell was another story, but Darcy wasn't there for that.

At sixteen, she was deemed mature enough to hear all the gory details, though. What she didn't hear, she'd overhear; her morbid curiosity welcoming the information. Darcy wasn't goth and would punch anyone who mistook her heavy makeup and penchant for black clothes for it, but she did have a certain fascination with death. She hoped it was a friendly ankh-wearing teenager from the *Sandman* books, but after her grandmother's passing made the concept all too real, she was no longer sure.

Granny Mae was her favorite relative, by far and away. Her best babysitter. Her best friend, even. Together they did all the things her mom was always too busy for. Granny Mae taught Darcy to read and write, to dream and draw. She nourished her love of old movies and new cookie recipes. While Darcy's mom was studying to get her degree, working, dating, and eventually marrying, Grandma was always there, always present, always caring. Sure, Grandpa Silas was always there too, but more as a distant, bemused onlooker, puffing on his stinky cigars, lost in his history tomes.

Grandma's death was sudden and hit Darcy like a ton of bricks. What did a myocardial infarction even mean to a twelve-year-old? Nothing. An imaginary concept. It felt surreal then. But not anymore. Now it felt normal, just sad. The wound had scabbed over, leaving an ugly scar behind.

Besides, Darcy had a superpower and could bring the dead back to life. Well, not really, but it seemed that way when she drew. Art gave her the sort of freedom she failed to find anywhere else: in school, at home, outside. Nothing compared to being able to create an entire world fueled entirely by her imagination and rendered exclusively by her hand. Nothing.

Darcy had tried different styles and methods over the years but always came back to comics. There was simply no better medium for her. She didn't care for the muscle-bound, perfect specimen of the traditional superhero comic books, either. Darcy wanted to create something different. She always preferred the offbeat characters of Vertigo comics and tried to reflect that in her art. The goal was to have her characters be flawed, relatable, likable. And so, she created DynamoGirl, an average teen who discovers she is the direct descendant of an ancient race of superpowered beings that had once visited Earth. Empowered by this knowledge, she learns to harness and master skills that had lain dormant within her DNA for centuries. Mentored on her journey by a kindly, wise witch, modeled lovingly upon Darcy's grandmother, DynamoGirl was an average kid by day and monster slayer by night. And the monsters came out of every shadow and every corner, activated by DynamoGirl's presence.

Okay, so maybe not as original as she might have hoped for, Darcy reflected in her more self-critical moments, *but original enough.* The rest was all in the execution. That, Darcy knew, *was* original. Her inks were fresh and crisp, her shadows ominous, her use of black was straight out of the Mike Mignola playbook. DynamoGirl was going to be a hit. It just needed funds.

Funds that her mother and Barry were annoyingly tight with. Freaking Barry. Who even got named Barry anymore? It was so seventies and not in a good way.

Barry started coming around when Darcy was nine, quickly becoming a permanent fixture in their lives. Darcy didn't like him from the get-go. It was nothing he did, per se. In fact, if viewed objectively, he tried really hard. Barry had *tryhard* written all over him. He brought Darcy gifts that screamed "a nice lady in the toy store picked this out based on age-appropriate recommendations." He bought pizza. He tried to show interest in her schoolwork.

Darcy wasn't having it. She knew a dud when she saw one. Barry was old, a lot older than her mom; he smelled old and covered it up with an overpowering cologne. He had a gut that was carefully hidden under tailored suits during the week and only made appearances on the weekends, straining Barry's pastel golf shirts. He talked and laughed too loudly. No, Darcy wasn't fooled by Barry at all. Her mother, though … hook, line, and sinker. The two of them were married within a year. The newly assembled family went to live in Barry's admittedly nice large house, where Darcy had her own room with an en suite bathroom. "A height of luxury," her mom joked. A bribe, Darcy knew.

There had been many bribes since, but less and less so over the years. Because of Darcy's attitude, she'd been told. Her ingratitude. Her barely-passing school grades. Consequently, now she was one of the only sixteen-year-olds she knew without a car. And her stepfather was a car salesman. The lead car salesman at Shaw's, no less. What a freaking joke.

When Darcy was spending most of her time with her grandma, all the business with Barry and Mom and school didn't really matter. But then a stupid fateful infarction robbed her of the only person she could honestly say she loved and honestly believe loved her. It figures it would have been Grandma's heart—it was always too huge, too overworked.

From then on, Darcy was stuck in Barry's mansion full time. Or Barrylair as she drew it in her comics, a place where the main monster lived. DynamoGirl had slain him many times over the years, but he knew the secret to immortality and thus always managed to resurrect himself.

Darcy was there now, in her room, idly drawing, not quite sure in which direction the story was heading. She often used people she knew in real life for her comics. Grandpa Silas had made it into her books as a remote wizard, whose pointy hat stirred clouds and made them appear as smoke. She supposed she'd have to kill him now. It'd be no great loss; he was a minor character at best. But it nagged at Darcy that he left her nothing at all. It was like an official declaration of her inconsequentiality. Sure, she didn't much care for the old man, but it still stung to know the feeling was mutual. She didn't want to overthink it but couldn't help it.

The thought wouldn't go away. It stoked the ever-present fire of anger within her until she decided to do something about it. Take matters into her own hands. Get her own inheritance.

After all, it was what DynamoGirl would have done.

Of all the dumb TV shows Jenny had used to pacify her brain over the years. *Gilmore Girls* took the cake. The sheer idiocy of the concept—it wasn't just unrealistic, it was insulting to her, personally. To think that a mother and her daughter could have this great, best-friend-like bond if they were close enough in age. What a load of crap. Jenny and Darcy were the living proof of that.

Sure, Jenny knew that she ought to regard Darcy as the greatest thing that had ever happened to her and not a dumb high school mistake ... and she did. At least to others. But within the safety of her own mind's confines, in moments of wine-fueled honesty, Jenny would willingly admit that her motherhood experiment had largely been a failure. She loved Darcy, of course, but she just couldn't seem to like her very much.

As a newborn, Darcy's cries made Jenny want to crawl out of her skin. There was something visceral about it, a force driving her *away* instead of *toward* a screaming infant. Jenny was too young to overthink it then, but she had done so often in the years since. It didn't speak well for her, she knew, this absence of natural maternal instinct. She was glad for all the times her mother stepped in to help. But then, of course, it also contributed to the distance between Jenny and her daughter, who would always prefer Grandma.

Darcy's father, the beautiful, floppy-haired English boy from an exchange program, came and went, never learning of all he'd left behind. Jenny dreamt about him for years; his accent, his soft hands. Until she realized her subconsciousness was conflating his image with that of a popular rom-com actor. Funny thing, the way the mind worked. The way we recreated memories upon recall, each time fine tuning them into an alternate reality.

It made Jenny interested in psychology. She went to college, where she didn't exactly advertise being a mother. Back then she was Jen, wild and free. A persona she was all too happy to embody.

Jenny came later, because of the inherent easy charm of Barry and Jenny. Barry, of course, came later too, and their connection was all about easy charm.

By then, Jenny had been out of school for years and had come to learn that the job market left a lot to be desired for a social worker. Too much stress, not enough money. She was tired of fighting and ready for life that felt like less of an uphill battle, and Barry swooped right in. Jenny went to Shaw's to maybe buy a new car and walked out with a ticket to a new life.

Sure, Barry was quite a lot older, but there was something nice in that too. A certain welcome steadiness Jenny had never known in any of her previous relationships. It wasn't an unbridled passionate lust that brought her Darcy; and it wasn't any of the inconsequential college flings or dead-end affairs with losers and commitment-phobes of subsequent years. Barry knew what he wanted, how he wanted it, and what he was willing to do to get it. Jenny picked up on that from the first time she heard him place an order at a restaurant. She liked it.

He was a self-assured man with good manners, good social standing, good income. He was even good to Darcy, and that was no easy task. In the fuck-marry-kill dating game of life, Barry was the guy you married. And so, Jenny married him.

Best thing was that Barry, while fine with a stepchild, didn't want any kids of his own. He said he was too old for them. Jenny's tied tubes—oh yes, she learned her lesson, the hard way, but she learned—high-fived that choice eagerly. So that part of her life was easy too. Darcy, though, unruly and difficult to begin with, had steadily become all but impossible since her grandmother's death. None of Jenny's life experience, education, or professional training seemed to help in establishing a more or less normal, loving, respectful mother/daughter relationship.

They didn't bond over a shared mutual love of movies and books and didn't have witty mile-a-minute-as-if-scripted-by-someone-mid-coke-binge dialogue. They didn't seem to like each other at all. There was either angry screaming or dagger-laden silences between them. There were never any earnest, honest discussions or lachrymose confessions. Nothing. In fact, most of what Jenny knew about her daughter came from sneaking into her room and spying on her. Jenny wasn't proud of it but managed to rationalize it all the same. She read Darcy's diaries, browsed her book selections, checked out her art. It was possibly the worst way to go about getting to know one's own child, but there didn't seem to be any alternatives. For a generally smart girl, Darcy's school performance was disastrous. Her art, seemingly the only thing she was interested in, was disturbing and dark. She didn't appear to have any friends. And she certainly didn't think of her mother as one. So fuck *Gilmore Girls*. Lying liars, all.

THE SPARE KEY to her grandparents' cottage was under the same garden gnome as it ever was. One thing you had to love about old people was their consistency. Of course, Darcy thought with a sudden sharp sadness, there were no old people to love here now. All that was left were mountains of junk.

Mountains of Madness, she edited herself, enjoying the Lovecraftian reference. This was her grandfather's madness. What was he looking for? What did he think he could acquire that would compensate for the loss of his wife, his loving, faithful companion of forty-some years? These old newspapers? These stacks of water-damaged magazines? This collection of TVs that looked like a weird technological progress display in some museum of anthropology?

It boggled the mind that he had managed to accumulate all that in just a few short years. He must have been busy. To be fair, Grandpa Silas was in good shape all his life; tall with a military straight posture and strong, always so strong. He was fond of walking and moved so fast that whenever they were going somewhere together, Darcy would always struggle to keep up. To Darcy, he was like an oak tree, and it should have taken something as monumental as lightning to strike him down. Or, more reasonably, it should have been his smoking. Not a collapsed tower of haphazardly stacked, overloaded book boxes. It was an almost beautiful death, though, if she thought about it. Poetic in a way.

But Darcy wasn't here for books. She had enough books. And a well-used library card. What she wanted was something special. Something expensive. Something that said, "Grandpa loved you, Grandpa cared," especially since Grandpa himself, it seemed to her, forgot to do so.

She hadn't visited in a long time. Most of Darcy's memories of the house held her grandmother in it. This barely seemed like the same place. Both too empty and too full at the same time. It felt wrong somehow. She decided she never wanted to come back.

Getting around the house, squeezing through the artificially narrowed corridors, was making Darcy claustrophobic. At last, she found her way to Grandpa's desk. It appeared to have a small clearing around it, and Darcy paused, gratefully, leaning on it and taking a deep breath. It was a large, heavy desk from the time before particleboard. The dark wood top was all but buried under a random collection of office supplies and books. Grandpa didn't believe in computers. But apparently, he believed in writing letters. Or writing something. There was a fancy, antique-looking quill on the desk, set in an equally ornate inkwell.

What were you writing, Grandpa? Darcy tapped her fingers on the desk. Maybe it was nothing; maybe, like so many things in this house, there was no purpose to the quill being there. At least it was beautiful, so unlike the rest of the junk around it. There was a decorative aspect to it.

Darcy picked the quill up and studied it. She touched the writing tip, and it was sharp enough to draw a tiny bead of blood. The ink must have evaporated from its container (*inkwell,* she corrected herself), but that was probably an easy fix. The feather (was it a real feather?) caught the thin light struggling through the dirty curtains and glowed iridescent. Darcy found herself charmed. She thought of the crisp, sharp lines she would draw with this quill. It would take her work to the next level, she imagined.

She put both objects in her canvas messenger bag and made her way out, carefully replacing the spare key beneath the gnome. The gnome looked at her with no apparent judgment. Darcy smirked, turned her back on the happiest place she had known in her sixteen years, and left.

———— ◆ ————

As JENNY WAITED for Barry to come home, she ruminated on her father's death. It was sudden but not surprising. He really wasn't the same man after her mother's passing. He distracted himself with all his hoarding, or *collecting*, as he insisted, but it didn't seem like his heart was in it all the way. It appeared to be a distraction at best or a compulsion at worst. But either way, it wasn't living. His living was over and done with when his beloved Mae left him.

Those two … A storybook romance, if there was ever one. You'd think some of that romantic juju would have passed on to their only daughter, but no, it must not be genetic, for Jenny was a resolute pragmatic, through and through. A pragmatic thought currently guiltily swimming in her wine-lubricated brain was that she was happy to have been spared dealing with a protracted decline of an elderly parent.

Jenny wasn't cut out to be a caretaker; her failed attempts at motherhood had taught her as much. She didn't relish the thought of watching her wonderful friendly giant of a father forgetting her name, forgetting his name, forgetting how to use the bathroom. That would have been a terrible way to go. For him. For her. In a way, what happened was for the best. He died doing what he loved, *if* hoarding could be loved. It was quick too. She told herself it was quick, anyway, to ameliorate any potential moral qualms. And now he could be with his beloved wife in whatever happy afterlife they both believed in and Jenny didn't.

When her mother died, it was more of a tragedy. There was a brutal suddenness to it. And then there was the terrible effect it had on Darcy. The kid practically went feral with grief. They tried three different therapists, each more expensive than their predecessor.

Jenny did not want to relive those times, but they haunted her mind anyway. There were moments she was genuinely worried Barry would move out. She would have, probably, given half a chance. But Barry, bless his stolid ways, stuck around. So did she. And surprisingly, so did the last therapist—a real sharpshooter, not what you'd expect from someone named Lucy. Eventually, Darcy settled down into a surly, unpleasant but tolerable teenagerdom. And that was that.

At least her daughter wasn't close with her grandpa. His death did not unmoor her again. Though she did seem upset at not being mentioned in the will. The thought had probably never even occurred to Silas. He left it all to his only child, knowing that, eventually, it would pass down to her only child. But *eventually* was too far away for a sixteen-year-old. Jenny would know. Sixteen was a stupid age, any way you sliced it. At sixteen, you were smart enough to know some things but too dumb to know how insufficient that knowledge really was.

Darcy will learn, too, she thought, taking another swig of wine. She was a smart kid. If she applied herself, she could even pass that driving test one day. Jenny didn't want to chauffeur a sulky, withdrawn, and moody kid around all her life.

FINDING INK WAS harder than Darcy thought it would be. Eventually, she figured out where to buy some, black as night, and when she finally got to drawing with it, it did not disappoint. Sure, it took a while to get used to the quill and avoid ink splotches, but the lines … the lines this thing drew were pure poetry. Sharper, crisper, more precise than anything Darcy's other pens, pencils, and brushes had ever produced.

Darcy drew all weekend, only emerging out of her room for food. These brief outings were arranged strategically to avoid both her mother and Barry. It wasn't difficult. She was good at being a ghost. So was DynamoGirl, it was her new superpower. When activated, she became a mere outline. Rendered by Darcy's new quill, it looked awesome.

Now that there was a new superpower, Darcy thought there ought to be a new villain to counterbalance it. She flipped through the mental catalog of the people she knew, and, somehow, the sweaty, balding pate of her grandfather's lawyer swam to the surface of her mind. Yeah, that guy. That profoundly average beige-brown man.

She remembered him well enough to draw him, which was funny for a guy so utterly unmemorable. The artistic embellishments came easily. His supersuit was brown too. His powers ... Well, Darcy wasn't sure yet, but for one thing, he could put you to sleep just by talking. And he could muddle your mind so that you wouldn't be able to make any decisions. Now he just needed a name. Mr. Average? Mr. Banal? No, not quite right. Mr. Beige? Yes, that was perfect. Someone so profoundly blah. It reminded Darcy of a Tarantino flick where the criminals gave themselves colors for nicknames. That was a good movie. She'd watched it twice.

For Mr. Beige's first outing, he took on DynamoGirl herself. After spiriting her away to his criminal lair, all beige and brown, of course, he tried to deactivate her powers by making her forget who she was, using what he referred to as talk therapy.

Darcy knew all about talk therapy. Once upon a time her mother and Barry were all about it. Took her to three (no less!) three different shrinks. The first two were idiots, but the third one was okay. In retrospect, maybe even more than okay. She made Darcy feel heard, really heard, for the first time since Grandma Mae's death, but in the back of her mind she was always thinking, *This isn't real, this woman gets paid for it.* So it wasn't a total success. But by then Darcy was out of tears anyway; her tough-teen carapace was beginning to develop. She knew she could put on performative normalcy just as nicely as the next person. And that was that.

Mr. Beige was talking DynamoGirl's ear off until she cut him down with ... with what? A machete? A cutting remark? Aha, the steel blade of truth, a special power, cuts through the bullshit like hot knife through butter. After that, it was easy. Cut once, duct tape his mouth shut twice. There, a perfectly useless waste of a man put in his place. All in a day's work. To add insult to injury DynamoGirl redecorated his entire evil lair with a technicolor flourish. When Mr. Beige came to and saw this, it blew his mind. Literally. His head exploded. Providing all the more bright red colors for his walls.

Nice. Darcy smiled to herself. *Ready to print.*

———————◆————◆———————

Jenny had dropped off Darcy at the library, came home, and proceeded with her latest snooping mission. Her daughter's love of books and reading had always made her happy, though Jenny was all too aware that it was just another way in which they differed. To think, they were both essentially raised by the same people, and yet they were so dissimilar. Wasn't psychology grand? The way it weaved and dodged and avoided all reason. The more you looked for patterns, the more you wondered if perhaps there were none to be found. Some things were just random.

Credit where credit's due, Silas and Mae were very good grandparents, Mae especially. Was Jenny herself the confusing variant in this equation? Or was it simply that grandparents could love fully like people given a do over while parents are too busy figuring it all out for the first time?

Whatever the case may be, despite having mostly the same caretakers and environment, the things Jenny rebelled against as a kid, Darcy took to like fish to water. No boys, just books. Mommy's opposite and Mommy was grateful for it. Of all the things to worry about, becoming a grandmother before forty wasn't on Jenny's list.

Darcy had never so much as mentioned a boy. Jenny made sure to give Darcy the birds and bees talk as early as the best parenting advisers on daytime TV recommended and then continued to do so at frequent intervals until Darcy finally said, "Eww, mom, I'm not like that." which was surprisingly tactful for a kid who surely meant to say "Eww, mom, I'm not like you."

And so, Jenny was perfectly fine with a daughter who at sixteen was usually either reading or drawing or throwing a tantrum, as long as that was all she did.

The library was the best babysitter for her baby. Darcy could be left at the library for hours on end, but they agreed that Jenny would come to pick her up at four. There was time.

Today's snooping wasn't exceptional by any means, but then Jenny noticed a new object on Darcy's desk. A freaking quill of all things. Oh boy, did she birth a weirdo into the world. What modern teenage girl used a quill? It took a moment, but Jenny actually recognized the object as one last seen on her father's desk. It looked strikingly out of place there too, amid all that mess.

Late in life, her father had taken to bragging about his latest finds and acquisitions, and he was thrilled about that one. Got it from the Koshmaroff estate sale, Jenny shuddered to think. She remembered the old lady from her career girl days when, as a social worker, she had to check up on the elderly. She only went there once, and you couldn't pay her enough to go back to that house or talk to that woman again. The place creeped her out—it felt like being watched by unseen eyes. The old lady Koshmaroff seemed offended by the implication that she might not be able to take care of herself or that she might need this stranger's help. She was perfectly polite but reserved in a way that unsettled Jenny. Forbidding, that was the word for it. Like an ice sculpture unwillingly animated into tolerating a stranger. No warmth twinkled behind her eyes, no other quaint clichés of the elderly were apparent. *If winter was a person*, it came to Jenny in an uncharacteristic fit of poetic abstraction, *she would have been Mrs. Koshmaroff.* Soon afterward, Jenny happily retired into the comforts of being a housewife and had forgotten all about the encounter until her father had brought the memories back up.

She couldn't imagine wanting a single thing from the Koshmaroff's estate. But this quill, she had to admit, was beautiful. There was a certain elegance of bygone craftsmanship to it that you seldom saw in modern things. Darcy must have been using it for drawing. The kid even got proper ink for it. How enterprising. Jenny was amused. And then, after looking at her daughter's latest drawings, impressed.

There was a new refinement to it. No longer could it be dismissed as childish doodles. The outlines were striking, the shadows haunting, even the facial expressions were much more sophisticated. The new medium agreed with Darcy.

"Should have gotten the kid a quill years ago," Jenny mused out loud. She brushed her hand across an action panel on one of the pages, marveling at the quality. The paper's edge caught her fingertip, slicing it. A tiny cut, but it stung enough to put in her mouth, a childhood remedy that still held true. The smarting subsided quickly.

Jenny never got into comics, not as a kid and certainly not as an adult. She didn't even care for the newspaper funnies that Barry adored. And so, she found the adventures of DynamoGirl as nonsensical as any other comic book out there, though she read them anyway for insight into her daughter's life.

This silly costumed creature was Darcy's alter ego. It saddened Jenny to consider that her shy, reticent daughter lived a life that was practically on the other side of the moon from the one she so clearly wanted—the excitement and adventures of DynamoGirl.

Look at this latest story. A new supervillain to defeat. Jenny nodded along, reading the pages. The writing still left a lot to be desired, but the art was really quite good. Mr. Beige, for one, was drawn in such a lifelike manner. His face was expressive. His death was expressive. Who was it that he reminded her of? Oh no, that was going to drive her crazy until she remembered.

Jenny snooped some more in all the usual places and then went to have a light snack before picking up Darcy from the library. As she was getting into her car, it finally came to her. Mr. Beige looked just like her late father's lawyer.

DARCY LOVED THE library. It was her favorite place away from her room. She loved the quiet, the smells, the sound of pages turning. The promise of endless adventures held within the books lining the shelves. And as far as adults went, the head librarian, Maud, was awesome.

Not since Darcy's grandmother had she had an adult take such interest in her and her reading. Maud was always there with a terrific recommendation and new books set aside. Always happy to discuss what Darcy had been reading. She never talked down to her or made her feel like a stupid kid. It was almost like having a friend. Conditional and limited, but still ...

Maud didn't look like a librarian. She looked like a friendly diner waitress. Jolly and roly-poly, she favored pastels in her clothing. Her reddish hair was usually gathered in a bun with pencils sticking out of it. She likely had a couple of decades on her mom, but wasn't anywhere near as brittle and uptight. And there was such warmth to her, that it made the two women incompatible in every possible way. The most librarian thing about Maud was her name.

Darcy loved chatting with Maud and always stopped by her desk first. But there was no happy greeting for her today. The Maud that said, "Oh, hello, Darcy." was a ghost of her former self. Pale, sad, she looked like she'd been crying.

"Are you okay?" Darcy asked without thinking. She didn't want to pry, but how could she not.

"Jackson passed away," Maud said simply.

"Jackson?" Did Maud have a cat or a dog? Darcy had no idea; their conversations were usually pretty limited to books.

"My husband, dear, my husband Jackson. Twenty-eight years together, and he's just ... gone."

"I'm so sorry," Darcy offered automatically. That was what you said. Instead of asking a million actually pertinent questions like when and how and why.

"Should you be working?" she inquired instead, politely.

"It helps." Maud sighed. "I was going crazy sitting around the house with nothing but memories for company."

"My grandmother died," Darcy told her. "She had a heart thing. It was so sad." That was what you said too, wasn't it? As an adult, you had to offer commiseration. Sympathy. "My grandfather died too," she added, almost as an afterthought. "Just recently."

"Oh, I know, dear. My husband was your grandfather's lawyer. I'm so sorry for you."

Don't be sorry for me while I'm being sorry for you, Darcy thought. *That's too many emotions to juggle.*

"What happened?"" She couldn't help herself; all those gory fascinating details.

Maud sighed again. "It was a brain aneurysm. Just one of those things, I'm afraid. It was quick."

Darcy thought about it throughout the afternoon and on her way home, while her mother tried and failed to make conversation. Jackson Craven had met a fate strikingly similar to his comic counterpart. A brain melt. How weird. Maybe Oscar Wilde was right. Life did indeed imitate art.

DARCY CELEBRATED HER seventeenth birthday at home with her mother and Barry. There was cake. She didn't care for it. And then there were car keys. Something she very much cared for.

She had finally passed her driving test a month earlier and now had a new car waiting for her in the driveway. Okay, not new, a certified pre-used vehicle, but still ... It was blue, had a radio, and would take her anywhere she wanted to go.

Barry droned on about the safety features and gas mileage, but Darcy barely heard a word. She was elated, dangerously close to happiness. Now she could finally add distance to her dreams. Of course, she deserved a car. For all she knew it was bought with the money that she should have rightly inherited from her grandparents, but this was neither the time nor the place to bring it up.

"Thanks again, you guys," she said with as much cheer as she could muster and dug into the too-dense chocolate cake to show her gratitude.

Now THAT HER daughter finally had her own set of wheels, Jenny's days had opened up in a way that offered almost too much freedom. She could drink any time she wanted, knowing she wouldn't have to drive. But there was also a new set of worries. She didn't think Darcy was a particularly good driver. The kid had her head in the clouds. The few times they were in a car together, Jenny felt unsafe. She mentioned this to Barry, but he said, and he was right, of course, that there was really nothing they could do but hope for the best. He left out the other part of that saying because Jenny was never good at preparing for the worst. In fact, that's what alcohol was for, keeping that line of thinking far, far away.

Still, Jenny couldn't say she was surprised when Darcy crashed her newly acquired car six months later. She was only surprised it took that long, and grateful it wasn't too terrible of a crash. The tree seemed to have gotten the worst of it, though the car was certainly damaged.

Darcy was okay. Barry wouldn't have put her behind the wheel of a car with less than top-rated safety features. Darcy was bruised, her skin and her ego both. And whiny. The whining was a direct response to Jenny and Barry taking her driving privileges away.

The goal was to teach the kid something about responsibility. All she had to do was complete a driving safety course and earn enough money to pay for half of the repairs. It seemed as fair a deal as any, but she wailed like she was a toddler. The noise Jenny hated then and now. Darcy hurled accusations like daggers. Darcy turned on the waterworks like Niagara Falls. Darcy screamed that she shouldn't have to work outside of school when her own mother didn't. Okay, that one actually stung, Jenny had to admit. But they remained resolute in their decision, firmly sticking to their *tough love* parenting. Some law had to be laid down. The kid was nearly an adult and nowhere near adultlike, and they simply had to do something.

Jenny wanted Darcy to learn a thing or two about discipline, she just didn't want to be the one to deliver the message. She thought it sounded much more authoritative coming from Barry. It was unfair to her husband, she knew, to put him in the path of Darcy's hate. Jenny would just have to find a way to make it up to him.

———◆———

Barry was being a beast. Darcy never harbored any love for the guy, but lately, she had begun to outright hate him. She didn't mean to drive the car off the road. *Of course* she didn't. She loved her car. It was just one of those things. Darcy simply got distracted by something she saw or thought she saw—she was no longer sure; she had such an active imagination—and lost control of the steering.

She was an artist, someone prone to getting lost in her thoughts. They didn't understand.

She said she was sorry. They didn't care.

And now she was supposed to get a job. In this stupid dinky town. Doing what? Slinging burgers?

"Nothing wrong with that," said Barry. It was what he did when he was Darcy's age. And look at him now.

Yeah, just look at him now. The guy sold cars. Huge fucking deal.

Darcy tried pleading with Barry, which usually worked, but not this time. She knew her mother was behind this newly found resolve of his and hated the power these people got to have over her.

She drew and drew, her trusty quill in hand. Her latest supervillain had a tailored look to him, but when his suit jacket came off, his gut came out, taking over and making him do evil things. The Gutman, she named this new villain. He paralyzed DynamoGirl, the powerful rumblings of his gut producing a set of invisible chains he threw around her, and then he stole one of her secret power objects.

The Gutman was to going to meet a terrible end. Darcy contemplated several and finally settled on a plunge into a boiling vat of chemicals à la Joker. She'd been reading a lot of Batman comics lately. Though the effect in her story was different. The acids in the vat reacted to the acids in the Gutman's gut in such a way that they left him completely crippled on one side of his body. From then on, he was Mr. HalfAGut, a pathetic shadow of his former self.

Nice. Darcy looked over the final page with a self-satisfied smirk. At least there's some justice to be found, if only in ink.

———◆———

BARRY HAD A stroke a month later. Darcy heard her mother's screams cut through her umpteenth rewatching of *Ed Wood*.

What is it? she thought, unwilling to abandon Johnny Depp at his campiest best. *Messed up a nail, did she?* But the screaming continued, shrill and annoying, and Darcy had no choice but to dutifully hit the pause button on her remote and trudge downstairs.

Her mother was on the floor, holding Barry. Barry seemed to be alive but far from lively; his coloring was terrible. "He just collapsed," her mother wailed. "We were just sitting and talking, and he ... he just collapsed." A teary gasp interrupted a wail. "Call 911."

Darcy did. It was the least she could do. *Talking.* Yeah, right. They were probably trying to get it on, and the excitement proved too much for poor old Barry. Gross.

Later, she found out all the grisly details. A blood clot had formed in Barry's heart and traveled to his brain to block a vessel there, causing a cardioembolic stroke. Yikes.

Death didn't freak Darcy out; she was used to it by now. But this half and half state her stepfather seemed to be in was profoundly disturbing.

He didn't die, but the stroke was debilitating. It was his weight, his age, his lack of cardio. So many reasons that it was a surprise it didn't occur sooner. Blah, blah, blah.

The heart, as far as Darcy could tell, was nothing but a problem waiting to happen. Infarctions, blood clots, cardiac arrests. So many euphemisms for a crappy ticker and an entire lexicon to cover the damage that could befall it.

Strokes, in particular, were weird. In Barry, it seemed to have mainly affected the left side of his body, resulting in a droopy countenance and all but useless left arm and leg. A situation entirely too close for comfort to Darcy's drawing of Mr. Gutman getting his comeuppance. It had to be nothing more than one of those random freaky things, of course. Darcy knew it. She was a rational person. But she couldn't look at Barry and not feel the uncharacteristic stirrings of guilt for a man who, if she were being honest with herself, was mostly only ever kind to her.

Darcy didn't like the feeling and began avoiding Barry altogether.

JENNY COULDN'T HELP noticing the irony of it all. She, who had failed to properly care for her daughter time and again, who had so fortuitously avoided becoming a caretaker for her elderly parents, was now stuck taking care of a man who was only ever meant to take care of her. It was in his wedding vows to her, for crying out loud. Barry promised he would always take care of her. He was still doing it in a way—his clever investments over the years and his insurance policy added up to a current continuation of their financially comfortable life. But now she knew the money was finite. Unreplenishable. And meant to also stretch to cover the new and bewilderingly unpredictable expense of taking care of an invalid. There was a terrifying uncertainty in her predicament. *Their* predicament. Maybe it wasn't irony exactly, but it was something.

Jenny lit a cigarette. She had picked up smoking again after all these years. It didn't seem to matter as much these days, plus it went nicely with her cocktails and helped her relax. She knew Barry minded, but what could he say now?

Jenny tried taking care of him with as much cheer as she could muster, but she felt her good graces ebb with every passing day. She wasn't built for this. She didn't want this. But she couldn't leave this either. Couldn't leave *him*. She'd be destitute, not to mention shunned by the small-minded townspeople for abandoning her husband when he needed her most. Jenny was stuck and hating it. She smoked, inhaling deeply, like it was a self-inflicted punishment. And in a way, she supposed, it was.

Darcy was no help at all. She got back to driving, taking Barry's car. Jenny didn't have the energy to fight her on that. Darcy was never home anymore. She couldn't bear to be in the same place as Barry, it seemed. As if you got to choose those things, Jenny wanted to scream at her. As if life ever went to plan. As if this was ever meant to be fair. But she didn't, of course, because what good would that do? The kid would learn in her own good time all the shitty lessons life had to offer.

DARCY TRIED TO fix things the only way she knew how. It was crazy and superstitious and stupid, but she thought she could undo what happened somehow through art. And so, she drew all three of them, her mother, Barry, and her on their happiest day together that she could remember.

There was a week they spent at the beach, when Barry took them to Ocean City. The place was so joyful and sunny that it had cast a spell on them. "Be good," it seemed to say. "Smile. I insist and will give you plenty of reasons to." They shopped on the boardwalk, played arcade games, ate giant slices of pizza and spicy curly fries from huge paper buckets. There was ice cream for dessert every day. Barry tried teaching her how to swim. Even her mother seemed content, her complaining down to the minimum. There was just something about the ocean, the sand, the sunshine. Some magic. You couldn't help but be happy there.

Darcy drew all of them, goofing around at the minigolf place. Building a ridiculously lopsided sandcastle that got done in by the flooding of its own mote via an errant wave. Taking in the sunset on the boardwalk.

Why didn't they go back? What on earth did they decide was more important than that? Oh yes, the bitter realization came to her. Grandma died the following year. Maybe good times came at a high cost. Or just couldn't be sustained. What did she know of happiness anyway?

Apparently, she didn't know much about magic either. Her trick didn't work either. The happy memories lay flat on paper, perfectly inked but lifeless. Her mother was still an angry, sad booze-soaked mess, Barry was still a cripple. Life was no comic book, and DynamoGirl could do nothing to help.

THINGS REMAINED BLEAK as one tedious day bled into another, and then, for the first time in a long while, Darcy had a glimpse of hope. It was shaped like an acceptance letter from CalArts. Her artistic skills must have outperformed her underwhelming academic records. Somebody somewhere was impressed. Somebody wanted her. They said yes to her. All she had to do was say it back. Of course, she wanted to go. She couldn't remember ever wanting anything so much.

California was as far as she could get from her suffocating house and her stupid small town without driving off into the ocean. It was perfect. And very expensive. Darcy knew she had to have a money talk with her mother and dreaded it. She would have preferred discussing it with Barry, but he had all but withdrawn from the daily affairs of managing their family. Her mother tended to leave him permanently planted in front of a large TV with ready-made microwaveable meals in their disposable trays, and he got used to the situation. Nowadays, it seemed that all Barry wanted was an easy vacation from his bleak reality that the television so conveniently delivered.

So mother it was. Darcy had been on her best behavior for weeks now. She even forced herself to help out with Barry. He was kind to her, asking about her life in his new slurred speech, trying to banter with her. It was horrible.

And finally, when she couldn't put it off any longer, Darcy asked her mother directly if they could talk that evening. It had to be done. There was too much at stake.

CALARTS. JENNY PACED the living room, smoking furiously. *Fucking CalArts.* It couldn't have been some small, local school. Jenny was sure her daughter's lackluster academics didn't merit more than that, but she supposed that her art, which, admittedly, had gotten quite extraordinary lately, must have won the Californians over.

Did Darcy know how much the yearly tuition there cost? Jenny knew. She had phoned the school and found out. She'd been preparing for this conversation ever since she found the acceptance letter on one of her snooping missions. She had to hand it to Darcy, the kid knew how to keep her secrets.

Even though she'd been anticipating the conversation, Jenny was enjoying the armistice preceding it, milking her daughter's sudden helpfulness for all it was worth. For a while, it was almost nice, a glimpse of what life could have been like, with cooperation replacing animosity.

But tonight was the night. Tonight, she had to say no. To crush a dream. Jenny didn't want to, fully aware that it was a shitty thing to do, unforgivable even by her low mothering standards, but there was just no way to make CalArts work. Not without making drastic changes to their lifestyle. It wouldn't be merely giving up regular mani/pedis or takeout either; this was more along the lines of selling the house and moving to live out their days in some crappy condo. She flashed back to the only time they visited Barry's parents in their own crappy condo in a retirement village near some Floridian swamp. It was wrist-slashingly depressing. She was glad Barry didn't get along with them, and there was no need to go back.

Sure, there was a small inheritance left to Jenny by her parents, but that was firmly stashed away in a rainy-day high interest fund. And it wouldn't go that far by California tuition standards anyway.

Sorry, kid. Jenny shook her head as she put out her cigarette in the overfull ashtray. *There was just no way. Dream smaller.*

Darcy didn't want to dream smaller. That much was clear from the beginning of the conversation and the speed with which it devolved into a shouting match, their voices bouncing off the art-covered walls of Darcy's bedroom. Jenny had to admit there must have been some love between them, because no one she didn't love could have wounded her with their words the way her daughter did.

The things she said, the things she must have held onto all these years, stashing them like ammo for later use. It was brutal. She pushed every button. Jenny tried to remain an adult in the situation, but it only went so far.

"You already can draw," she said. "There's nothing more they can teach you about that. The rest you can learn locally." She wasn't denying her daughter a chance at higher education. She just couldn't sponsor the luxury version of it.

"You want to keep me here. So I can be just like you. A disappointed disappointment of a person. A useless fucking lush. This was all *you* could do with your life, but I want more. I *need* more." Darcy screamed until her face turned beet red. They'd had fights over the years, but Jenny had never seen her like that.

"This is nothing," Jenny said, pointing at Darcy's art. "This is nothing in real life. It means nothing and goes nowhere. Life has designs for you, and you can't avoid them. Did you think I wanted to have a kid in high school? Did you think I wanted to have a husband in a wheelchair? Did you think I wanted a daughter like you?"

That last one was a stab too far. Jenny knew it as soon as she said it, but there was no unsaying it. Her words had hit the artery. She couldn't backpedal and was afraid to press on. She grabbed Darcy's drawings instead as if they could offer her some clues on what to do next.

On top of the stack, there was a picture of all of them on the beach. She was blanking on the name of the place, but she could still remember the day.

It was a good day, such a good day. One of the best they'd ever shared as a family. Jenny was so touched that Darcy remembered it too *and* took the time to render it with such care and skill that it brought tears to her eyes. She didn't want her daughter to see her like that so she turned around and walked downstairs.

Darcy followed her, screaming, "This isn't over. Give me my drawings back. Don't walk away from me."

Jenny stopped in the living room. It was early May, but you wouldn't know it by the weather. The morning had been so brisk that Jenny had started up their fireplace. A real wood burner, as Barry liked to point out with pride, not one of those fake gas numbers. These days, he didn't seem to care, focusing mainly on

TV. But he did turn away from the screen as best he could toward the drama unfolding in real life.

The fire was roaring now. It seemed as angry as they were, perhaps at being woken up after it was all settled in for a long, restful slumber. Jenny didn't know what possessed her at that moment; her hand moved as if it belonged to a stranger, flinging the papers she held into the fire.

It seemed strangely appropriate just then, like a metaphor for their lives.

"MOM!"

Jenny would never forget that scream. Not in a million years. The anguish in it. The crushing knowledge that she was the cause of it. She was a bad mother indeed. The worst.

The act was certainly a conversation stopper, though. They silently watched the fire hungrily consume the beautiful drawings. And then Darcy turned around and stomped off. Jenny heard her rummaging in her room upstairs before emerging shortly after. The next sounds were that of the front door slamming and of Darcy starting a car and driving away. *I'd leave too if I could*, Jenny thought. *I'm sorry. Forgive me.*

She looked at Barry, but he could offer her no comfort. Forgiveness didn't seem like an option either.

Jenny poured a drink and lit a cigarette. Self-hatred washed over her like a tidal wave. She sat on the couch and stared at the fire. The fire stared back.

RICK ADAMS, THE fire investigator on the scene, agreed with the sheriff, who agreed with the local firemen's chief. This was no arson. No signs of accelerant; no signs of foul play. Everyone knew Jenny smoked like a chimney. She must have fallen asleep with her cigarette lit.

What a waste. Rick remembered Jenny from high school. She was the prettiest girl in his class. Way out of his league. Until she got knocked up and became the local cautionary tale. He knew Barry too, a nice guy, a standup guy, always donated to local charities. Rick's wife had bought a car from him; got a good deal and everything.

Rick looked at the ruined house. So much tragedy for one family in such a relatively small span of time. And what about the kid?

To be fair, Darcy was no longer technically a kid, having just turned eighteen. She made the shortlist of suspects during the initial phase of the investigation, but she was in the local 24-hour diner all evening and all night. Both waitresses and the cook remembered her.

Darcy was tough to miss; she turned out to be a stunner just like her mom, although shyer about it. She drew all night, they said. With a quill and ink, no less. Tough to forget a detail like that. Drank coffee, ate pie, and drew. Strange kid, but as solid an alibi as they came.

The house was a write-off. Nothing left worth saving. The sort of spooky freak thing that made one count their blessings and mind their manners. *What a shame*, Rick thought, shaking his head. W*hat a shame.*

So THIS WAS what freedom felt like. Darcy liked it. All of her family was dead. All of her inheritance money was in her bank account. CalArts, tuition paid, was waiting for her with open arms. Of all the things the fire stole from her, she missed her books the most. But it was nothing money couldn't buy. So long as Darcy had her beloved quill, she knew she could reimagine this world into whatever she wanted. So long as she wouldn't think of her mother and Barry dying in a fire, so long as their charred corpses would stop hurling accusations at her in her nightmares, she would be okay. She had read once somewhere that guilt was a wasted emotion. Darcy would remake herself into a brave and guiltless creature. Like DynamoGirl, she would overcome all the ugliness of the past that had held her down for so many years. Her heroine did recently acquire the power of flight. *Onwards and upwards,* Darcy told herself, smiling as she adjusted the rearview mirror. Adventures ahead. Oh, what a beautiful world she would draw.

CHAPTER 5

BEFORE

Now that she was here, Paris reminded Anastasia of her family's old maid's cooking. Mother had gone through several cooks until finally settling on Sveta. The choice had to have been made based largely on aesthetics. Mother never did eat much; she picked at her food, grazed at it, rearranged it on the plate. It's no wonder Sveta's cooking appealed to her—it was pure presentation. Beautifully presented meals that ranged in flavor from bland to barely palatable. All for show.

Much like Paris. This beautiful city, all glitz and glamour, appeared to be trying too hard, as if to disguise something unpalatable beneath. She expressed this idea to Pavel, and he was amused by it.

"Do you know what is beneath this city?" He laughed. "The catacombs. Old bones. Unpalatable indeed."

She had heard of the catacombs. It sent shivers down her spine. What a horrible thing to have the dead so close.

Amused or not, her husband did not share her opinion of Paris. He seemed to enjoy the city. Of course, he had been there before. He'd been everywhere as far as she could tell, but now that they resided in the city permanently, it was something like a new start. Pavel relished it.

"Literature is alive here," he'd say to her.

There was indeed a preponderance of literary salons. It seemed like almost everyone was writing a book. Those who weren't were making art. Or maybe it was all art, just different expressions of it.

Anastasia didn't know much about the new authors. She enjoyed her classics. The Brontës, Austen, Tolstoy, Dostoevsky, Gogol. The short-lived dead British women and the long-lived dead Russian men. Those were the storytellers of her life.

Pavel's reading had always been more wide-ranging and less discriminating. He'd go through phases, which she idly tracked. His latest had been English mystery novels, tales of a detective with a funny name and his amiable sidekick. Then there was some new book he had been raving about lately, *The Mysterious Affair at Styles*. He'd read it in a day and proclaimed the author to be a genius.

"She's got a career ahead of her," he told Anastasia excitedly. "Just you wait and see."

Pavel would leave the books for her, but she never found them alluring. Besides, unlike him, she couldn't read in English.

He took her to salons full of witty and droll people intent on outperforming one another. She found them tiresome.

As a couple, they enjoyed a certain popularity. There was a freshness to their émigré status, a charm to their accents. And of course, Pavel's money paved a lot of roads. But Anastasia didn't want to be paraded around like a prized poodle, didn't want to answer their prying questions, and didn't want to try to fit in with these people.

She found them all rather flimsy, pretty and superficial, with nothing sturdy to support the specious façades. And so, she made no friends out of the countless acquaintances she was introduced to.

Anastasia kept to herself. She wrote to her parents. By now, Uncle Oleg had indeed been bankrupted and had become a bitter old man, grumbling about the rioters and the Bolsheviks. She could imagine it, her family, all three of them, sitting around, reminiscing about the happy days of yore. They wouldn't come to Paris, claiming it was too late in life for them to go anywhere. It was as if the weight of their private disappointments had pressed on them too heavily to move at all. She had guessed that by now their only means of support was coming directly from Rostov's accounts, but she never asked. They never talked about money. It sufficed to know that there was enough of it, without going into too much detail.

Pavel had found a new passion recently. In horror, of all things. He had developed a taste for what appeared to be some sort of modern-day penny dreadfuls. Books with grotesque covers and ominous titles littered his study. Whenever Anastasia visited him there, the macabre images seemed to stare at her. She would avert her eyes whenever she had to share something important.

"I'm pregnant," she told him one day, interrupting his reading and note taking. He looked up at her slowly with an expression she had never seen on his face before. It was something like happy disbelief, as if a bet he had placed long ago and forgotten all about came through and won him millions. Books forgotten, he rushed to her side.

"My darling," he whispered, wrapping her in his arms.

All Anastasia could see was the cover of his latest book, abandoned splayed on his desk: the tentacles reaching out of the darkness. She thought it to be an inauspicious image for such an occasion.

"I've decided to try my hand at writing," Pavel announced over breakfast one rainy morning.

Anastasia paused, her hand halfway down to dip a bread soldier into a soft-boiled egg.

"Oh?"

"I've been reading enough books, so I thought, Why not write one?"

"Surely it's not that easy, or everyone would be doing it."

"*Au contraire, ma chérie.* Not everyone would have the time or the inclination or the imagination, whereas I do, and I shall."

Pavel seemed in too good of a mood about this, and Anastasia didn't want to question him further. After all, what harm could this new hobby of his do?

"Writing," she told Diego later, when they were alone. "My husband is going to be a famous writer."

"*Au contraire, ma chérie,*" said the parrot. "*Au contraire.*"

One had to wonder about that bird.

"They are all such snobs," Pavel said a few months later, throwing himself onto the divan like a petulant child.

Anastasia had stopped going to the salons by then, citing pregnancy-related tiredness, but her husband still went. And it seemed his literati friends didn't care much for his literary output.

"They are all doing the same or similar things, and no one even wants to try something different. And that horrible fat woman ..."

Anastasia knew just who he was referring to. A severe-looking salon owner with a man's haircut.

"She is an ugly person inside and out," Pavel grumbled. "Picasso's portrait doesn't do her justice."

"Why not go elsewhere?" she suggested idly.

"I thought there was prestige to be had at her place. The crème de la crème gathers there. But you're probably right. I should shop around for a new scene."

He reached down to the floor and picked up the book dislodged from the divan's cushion by his downward plunge. It was a collection of stories By M.R. James. Anastasia had tried it once, but it had only put her to sleep and brought her terrible dreams.

"How are you, darling?" Pavel asked, shifting gears. Always considerate, her husband had been downright solicitous during the past few months. There was still wonderous disbelief in his eyes when he looked at her growing belly.

"Oh, fine, just fine." She smiled.

"I have such plans for this child, *ma chérie*. Such plans. Children are such a gift; they are like ... immortality."

So this is what it took, Anastasia realized, to span the divide between her and this distant-by-nature man. Only a promise of immortality.

She lost the baby the following week. There was so much blood, and nothing seemed real. She didn't even know she wanted a child, not as Pavel did, but the loss was unbearable. A rejection unlike any other. She wouldn't leave the bed for weeks and then her room for months.

Pavel retreated into his writing, processing his grief through fiction. The keys of his typewriter seemed to shriek accusations at her, but she knew it was only her imagination.

It was still loud, though, too loud. Anastasia couldn't bear any noise. Nor could she bear to witness the happiness of the world that went on carelessly around her, and so she shuttered her windows against the bright Parisian summer and hid inside. Even Diego seemed to sense her sadness—he was quieter now, and there was a mournful tone to his trills. She drifted through her space as silently and desultorily as dust motes, relinquishing memories she never got to make, trying to come to terms with what had happened.

It would be a while before she would decide that she had had enough of her own company and her own thoughts.

Pavel was glad to see her up and about. She came to his writing studio, and he proceeded to tell her about his latest reading obsession—some American with Love in his surname who seemed to produce distinctly unlovely stories.

"He's good," raved Pavel. "It's like he's tapping directly into the secrets of the universe. Or better yet, the hidden truths of it. He has inspired me to incorporate more of my studies into my stories."

"That's nice, dear," Anastasia said with as much enthusiasm as she could muster. "Why don't we go out tonight?"

"Really?" He looked up at her with a hopeful smile.

"Really. It's been too long."

That night, she tried absinthe for the first time. Her husband had been introduced to it by Ernest somebody and found it to be charming but no match for vodka. For Anastasia, though, it was a revelation. The elation it sent spreading through her veins was the purest somatic delight she had experienced in a long time.

"They call it The Green Fairy," Pavel said, bemused by her reaction.

"And I am indeed off with the fairies for drinking it," she replied and asked him to order her another. The absinthe made everything easier by making it less real. It was magic, Anastasia found, pure distilled magic. It lubricated all the rusty social gears and cogs within her.

She didn't become the life of a party overnight, but she was happier now in the company of others. Slowly learning to appreciate the people she met, making the effort to find likable qualities in them.

Anastasia still didn't care for the French, but some of the Americans were lovely. F. Scott and Zelda, for instance, were an absolute delight. They were mad, and mad for each other, burning with a passion that wouldn't—*couldn't*—last, that much was obvious to everyone but them, but what beautiful flames they made. She almost became friends with Zelda, but the woman was simply too brittle for this world. Her breakdown and overdose came as a surprise to no one.

It was a good reminder not to get too close to anyone, Anastasia noted to herself. All that impermanence.

There were other things to try at the parties they went to, though she always went back to her beloved green fairy.

In time, Pavel and Anastasia resumed their marital relations, and if there was a hint of sadness there now, they both chose to ignore it. They never spoke of the baby they lost. He never said out loud how much he wanted another, but she knew. *She knew.* And secretly dreaded it. Fortunately, there was always something quick and bright within an easy reach to smother the dread.

"LOOK AT THIS," Pavel said one day, unpacking his latest acquisition.

It was a stack of magazines with bright and lurid covers.

"*Weird Tales,*" Anastasia sounded out slowly, picking one up. Her spoken English had been coming along swimmingly, thanks to all the Americans she was hobnobbing with, but reading and writing were another story.

"Perhaps we should get you a tutor," her husband suggested.

"So I can learn to read all these wonderful stories?" she joked, gesturing to his magazines

"So you can read some of the greatest modern literature in its original language," he countered. "You've yet to read *The Great Gatsby,* and you *like* the Fitzgeralds."

"*Liked,*" Anastasia corrected. "There's just something so careless about them."

"Well, it's a great novel at any rate, *ma chérie,* so brash, so American."

"I'll consider a tutor," she acquiesced. "Now what are these?"

"These, my dear, are only the latest and greatest craze in fantasy fiction. An entire magazine dedicated solely to genre fiction. Americans have been publishing it since 1923, and I have only now become aware of it. An unbelievable oversight. I've ordered every back issue, naturally."

"Naturally."

Anastasia picked up one of the magazines and flipped through its pages. Graphic, startling, hideous images. It looked cheap. It felt cheap. She didn't know how such a publication could ever hope to make any money.

"They publish all the greats. Lovecraft, Smith," Pavel said, misinterpreting her interest. "One day, me, perhaps."

Her husband had yet to find the literary success he'd been hoping for, but so far, the rejection had only spurred him on. There was no bitterness about it yet. The magazines gave him ideas, it seemed. While Anastasia spent time with her new English tutor, and her absinthe, and her casual acquaintances, her husband threw himself into his writing with renewed vigor. Until one day ...

"I'm getting published, *ma chérie*," Pavel exclaimed. It was perhaps the happiest Anastasia had seen him since she announced her second pregnancy a month ago.

"That's wonderful, dear."

"They'll publish three of my stories and, if the reviews are good, they might do an entire book in the future. A collection."

"I'm so happy for you," she said, wrapping her arms around him. "You deserve it. You've worked so hard."

It was something of a tacitly contentious matter that she didn't read any of his stories, but whenever she tried, she found them invariably too disturbing and impossible to finish. Eventually, Anastasia gave up, saying she wouldn't be a good judge of them since they upset her so much.

It was all easy for Zelda, of course, F. Scott wrote such *nice* stories.

WHEN HER HUSBAND showed her his first published story, Anastasia saw that it was done under another name. He had chosen a pseudonym.

"Paul Koshmaroff?" she teased playfully. "Isn't that a tad too obvious?"

"I didn't want to do it under my real name. I conduct all my other businesses as Pavel Rostov. I thought I'd try something different. This seemed to fit. Paul is just Pavel, anglicized for some international flavor, and Koshmaroff, well ..." He grinned charmingly. "I want to give them nightmares."

"That you will, dear," Anastasia said, kissing him on the cheek and meaning every word.

"Nightmares," trilled Diego. It was his latest verbal acquisition.

Alas, it wasn't the right sort of nightmares her husband was conjuring, it seemed. Pavel continued publishing an occasional story here and there, but the acclaim never came, the book deals never arrived. It was as if the world at large had deemed that there were just some notes he wasn't hitting.

He raged, he stormed, he brooded.

"It's too real for them," he told her. "The things I write about, they are true, researched phenomena, authentic facts. At the very least, they offer intelligent speculation on the mysteries of the universe. I try to show people a strange and beautiful world, but they don't want to look. They are too afraid to believe in anything outside of their immediate surroundings. People do not care for such complex offerings. They want their frights comical, laughable, easily explainable, and vanquishable. They don't want the real thing, and I don't know how to lie to their liking."

He shook his head.

"Lovecraft does it somehow. And they are eating it up. But I can't."

Anastasia didn't know what to say to him then, for she too had struggled with the darkness of his stories. They seemed to reach places within her that preferred to remain untouched. Perhaps it was a testament to how good he was as a writer. Perhaps it said more about her, the reader.

It didn't matter now. Pavel was in distress. To comfort him, she reached for his hand and placed it on her stomach, and that seemed to do the trick.

SHE LOST THE baby well into her second trimester. It was a horrifying ordeal, even worse than the first time. Perhaps her body was just older. Perhaps her body was simply outraged that she would put it through such trauma again. It was recommended to them that they should not try again, for her sake.

A month later they celebrated Pavel's fiftieth birthday.

"I'm getting too old for Paris, *ma chérie*," he told her. "Why don't we try somewhere else? A fresh start? What do you say?"

Anastasia tried searching her thoughts and found that she simply didn't care. La Ville-Lumière, this City of Light, didn't shine brightly for all. It had killed two of her unborn children and her husband's writing dreams. Maybe it was time to move on.

"Where are you thinking?" she asked.

"I hear good things about Berlin," he said.

CHAPTER 6

AFTER

THE EGG

WIMP WASN'T THE worst thing they called David at school, but it stung the most. Until his father sat him down and told him that in physics WIMPs stood for Weakly Interacting Massive Particles.

"Weakly?"

"Yeah, but don't focus on that, kiddo. Weakly is something of a pun. They are actually not at all weak. And also, it was coined after they came up with MACHO."

"MACHO?" the boy asked, his sulkiness already half forgotten.

"Massive Astrophysical Compact Halo Object," his father explained. "See, scientists know how to have fun."

David had more questions. His father had more answers. It was like venturing into a thrilling new world, while accompanied by a personal guide—the ever-patient and knowledgeable, bespectacled astrophysicist dad. The boy always felt calmer the more excited his mind got, and nothing excited his mind as much as science. The other school subjects never quite engaged his attention the same way. And he positively hated gym.

All that, combined with glasses and slight physique, had made him an easy target at his school, especially for the likes of Drew Mitchell. Drew, who seemed taller and more menacing every time David saw him. Drew, who was blessed with athletic genetics and wealthy, indifferent parents. Drew, who was strong enough to do whatever he wanted and privileged enough to get away with it every single time. A privilege that, to a certain extent, extended to his friends.

And what Drew and his friends wanted to do was make David's life miserable. The name-calling was the least of it, but still, no matter how many times his mom would tell him about sticks and stones, their words always felt more cutting than harmless.

And Dad ... Dad was mostly busy, but when he did spend time with David, when they talked, the world became a place that made sense. It was reassuring to learn of all the forces, known and mysterious, that made up the universe and to understand how small people were in a grand scheme of things. It was also a lot to process.

And so, David's world spun on its axis, alternating between helpless anger and intellectual bewilderment. Until one fateful day in October.

DAVID KNEW ALL about peer pressure but still found himself saying yes. So much of boyhood, it seemed, was just about accepting the gauntlets that had been thrown down before you. So stupid in retrospect, so irresistible at the time.

But what were the alternatives? More teasing? More name-calling? More humiliating jabs? This was easy by comparison. All he had to do was walk up some steps and ring the doorbell. Yes, the steps and the doorbell belonged to the creepiest house in the entire town, but otherwise it was a simple talk. And then, Drew and his friends would leave him alone. There'd be a relief, and who knows, maybe even tentative acceptance.

It was strange to do this now. At twelve, David considered himself almost aged out of trick-or-treating, even if skipping a grade had made him the youngest and smallest kid in his class. Sure, the free candy held a timeless appeal, but he probably wouldn't have even gone out this year if not for Drew's endless egging on.

Now here he was, clad in his old skeleton costume which still mostly fit, standing at the top of the creakiest looking steps he'd ever set foot on. He chewed his lip, working up the courage to ring the doorbell. He could feel the eyes on his back, unwanted attention crawling down his skin like fat spiders. It's probably why it took him so long to realize that the front door of the house had no bell, just an old-fashioned metal knocker, shaped like a claw.

A memory of being lifted up and thrown into the large garbage bin outside the schoolyard, clothes, books, and all, flashed in David's mind as vividly as a movie scene. *Never again,* he thought. He took a deep breath and banged the metal claw against its plate.

The knocker felt warmer than it ought to have on a blustery October night and sounded louder than expected. Time stopped, and the wind howled, portending something out of the King's horror novels that David was so fond of. He waited, shifting from foot to foot. There was no answer. Did he really expect one?

Of course, he knew the old lady Koshmaroff. Everyone did. "The witch," they'd whisper behind her back, though never to her stern, wizened face. She made a rare appearance in town now and again, but not so much lately.

What if she died? David wondered. *Maybe she died and is lying there, decomposing, and no one knows.* The thought creeped him out and all but moved his feet to leave. But then he heard steps from within and the rattling of the locks.

Open sesame, he whispered to himself as the door swung open creakily. And there she was, Mrs. Koshmaroff, looking even older somehow than he remembered. Ancient. David didn't know how someone could be this old and still alive. From the perspective of being twelve, even his parents seemed old to him. Mrs. Koshmaroff reminded him of the mummies he had seen once in a museum on a family trip to New York City.

"Yes?" she said in her old-lady voice that sent shivers down his spine. His imagination, fed by a steady diet of horror stories, likened the grating sound of it to a tomb being pried open. But there was something else there, a sibilance, like a winter wind through the old trees. He was overthinking things, as always.

"Yes?" the old woman repeated in a tone that suggested she wouldn't ask again.

"Trick or treat," the words rushed out of David, the conditioned, October-perfect response.

"And is it a trick or a treat you want, boy?" She seemed bemused, but how could you tell? That accent made every word out of her mouth sound like a freshly sharpened axe.

"Um ... some candy?" he mumbled.

"So a treat, then. Pity, I had such a trick in mind for you." And with that, she reached somewhere out of his sightline and brought out an old wood bowl. In it lay writhing an assortment of bloody fingers and tongues.

David's mind blanked for a moment, unable to process the sudden terror in front of him, and then several things occurred simultaneously: he dropped the pumpkin-shaped bucket he was holding for the occasion, screamed an embarrassingly high-pitched scream, and felt his bladder warmly release itself down the leg of his skeleton costume. Then David turned around and ran out of there, moving faster than he ever knew he could.

By the time Drew and his buddies caught up to him and saw the damage, he was shaking like a leaf and their jeering barely mattered. But from that day on, he became known as *pissboy*, which was so, so much worse than *wimp*.

THINGS DID NOT improve for David since that Halloween. Just the opposite. Nothing ever got forgotten back then, as if the school years preserved and amplified everything bad. The abuse got worse, the kids got even more cruel and creative with it, and the rage David had learned to suppress so well would burn brighter and brighter inside him. At night, it shone like daylight, keeping him awake. During the day, it was like a fire slowly consuming him.

And he knew, he *knew*, it was all *her* fault. The old lady, she had done something to him. She didn't just scare him with what, in retrospect, must have been some cheap gag tricks; she had planted something within him, an evil seed. That was the thing that made him so angry, so frightened. The thing that gave him nightmares night after night. The reason he had to learn to do his own wash, shamefully sneaking urine-soaked sheets to the laundry machine first thing in the morning.

David hated her. He wanted revenge. It seemed like a complicated concept, something out of a book. He did recently finish *The Count of Monte Cristo*, a story as dark as anything King could have written. Edmond Dantès' revenge took years of careful planning and execution. But maybe David's didn't need to be so elaborate. Maybe it could be even something as simple as ...

Okay, it did seem like madness to go back to that place, but this time he had a plan. A very simple plan: find an open or unlocked window, sneak in, steal something of value, book it.

A simple plan, for sure, made simpler still by the fact that the second window he checked gave way as if it had been expecting him. Now a year older and slightly taller and stronger, David was easily able to boost himself up to the windowsill and quietly ease through. Once inside, sneakered feet planted on the ancient-looking carpet, he looked around and listened carefully.

No one was there. The place stood silent. But then, David knew that, having scoped out the place prior to this trespassing stint, carefully peering in, doing his best spy impression. The room had a thick ambiance of abandonment; it didn't seem like anyone ever went in there at all. Dust motes danced around a bunch of neglected-looking antiques. What could be of value here?

Most things seemed too heavy and cumbersome to even consider. It took a moment, but then he found it. The egg. Or something that looked like a really fancy egg, elaborately decorated in what ... art? Was it art? David didn't know, but it looked like something someone might miss and was small enough to fit into the front pocket of his hooded sweatshirt, so it was good enough for him. He picked up the egg and felt something like a splinter in his thumbpad, sharp enough to draw blood, but only a small drop.

There was a slight rustling of the curtains in the corner. For an unsettling moment, David thought he saw old Mrs. Koshmaroff looking at him with something like restrained yet sinister glee. Then the moment passed, and he realized it was nothing but the wind from the window he had left open, sculpting nightmares out of dust and shadows. Still, there was a deafening drumming in his chest as he hurried out the same way he came in, carefully closing the window behind him, and sped away on his bike, his prize heavy in his pocket.

LIFE WAS NO book, and David was no Edmond Dantès. And so, nothing really changed after his act of revenge, not outwardly, and he continued to be teased mercilessly in school. But inwardly, there was a slight but perceptible shift, an acknowledgment of his own audacity, a small pride in asserting his agency. It was almost enough to help endure the endless pissboy gags ... until Drew came up with his latest ingenious torture idea.

He must have finally watched *Carrie*—Drew would have never read the King's classic or any other book for that matter—and from then on it was only a matter of procuring a bucket of piss and soaking David with it during a school dance. The act was so brazenly aggressive that it earned Drew a suspension, despite the school's traditional leniency towards him and their appreciation of his parents' wealth. The damage was done, though. This one was difficult to come back from, even for a seasoned punching bag of a boy.

David didn't think he'd ever be able to return to school; he certainly didn't want to. He couldn't imagine ever facing Drew again. But then as fate would have it, he didn't have to. Two days into his suspension, Drew, with suddenly too much time on his hands and his parents away on some ski trip or other, had generously indulged in his family's much-lauded wine cellar, and then went for a swim in the Mitchell's legendary pool. No one was sure what exactly happened, but by the time the family maid fished him out, his brain had spent too long without oxygen. Drew survived, if only on life support, but probably wished he didn't. For once, his family fortune was powerless to help. The Mitchells' pride and joy, their prince and scion, had slipped into a vegetative coma from which he would never come out. For the first time in years, David was free of his tormentor. Drew's friends, having lost the violent sun they had orbited for so long, drifted aimlessly in separate directions, collectively forgetting their former pursuits. David's newfound freedom tasted like lemonade on a summer day.

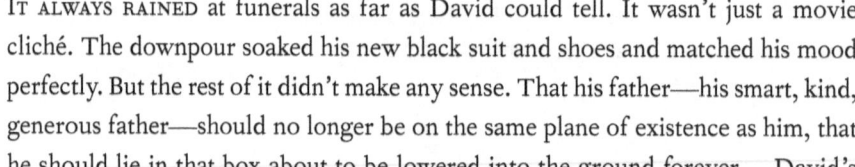

IT ALWAYS RAINED at funerals as far as David could tell. It wasn't just a movie cliché. The downpour soaked his new black suit and shoes and matched his mood perfectly. But the rest of it didn't make any sense. That his father—his smart, kind, generous father—should no longer be on the same plane of existence as him, that he should lie in that box about to be lowered into the ground forever ... David's mind refused to process this information. His heart couldn't cope much either. It was a nightmare; one he couldn't wake up from. It was all so sudden.

The last time they talked, they had a fight. It was all David's fault. A tree branch had crashed through his bedroom window during a storm. While his father was taking care of the damage, he discovered the stolen Koshmaroff egg. David had all but forgotten about it. At first, it was neat, the way you had to twist it just so to open it—and boy, did that take a while to work out, the way it played a strange and charming melody once it opened and, most of all, what owning it represented.

But in time, the thrill diminished in potency. David outgrew the charm of the music box and got tired of always pricking his fingers on its intricate designer shell. He put the egg away and let it become a distant but satisfying memory until the tree branch decided to rudely barge in and introduce itself.

When his father found it, he wasn't amused. David lied quickly enough on his feet, coming up with a story of finding the egg at a thrift shop, the one he liked to browse for old horror paperbacks with lurid covers, but his father didn't buy it, claiming the object was too valuable for a donation. Eventually, the truth came out, made all the worse by the initial lie, and his father made him promise he'd go and return the egg.

David didn't think he'd ever forget that fight. It was the first time his father told David he was disappointed in him. And, as it turned out, the only time. One fatal swerve from an oversized SUV on the hilly roads his father favored biking on, was all it took. They said the road was wet from the rain the night before and the bike brakes failed to engage. They said the death was instant. They said a lot of things, but in the darkest of the night, David believed that his father had lived for a while after being hit, that he had lain alone by the side of the road, tangled up in his destroyed trusty ten-speed, bleeding out, thinking about his thieving, lying disappointment of a son. These thoughts kept David awake, the way nightmares and bedwetting used to years ago.

TIME HEALS NO wounds, not all the way, but scabs make us tough. And the young heal the quickest.

In the two years that passed, David grew taller and stronger, becoming the man of the house as his mother quietly retreated into the hazy world of antidepressants and cocktails. Grief had changed them both but in opposite trajectories. David spent less and less time at home and more and more time at the library, true to his inner nerd. It was there he met Alice, the girl he thought was too wild and pretty to talk to until she talked to him first. They read the same books, laughed at the same things; her hair smelled like sunshine, and David thought it must be love, it must be what it was like in real life, all those things he'd always read about in books. This was it.

Alice made him emerge fully out of his grief in a way he hadn't imagined possible. David, no longer obsessed over that fateful fight with his father, made a choice to remember the happier times instead. And there were so many of those to choose from. David became a frequent guest at Alice's house with full approval and minimal monitoring of her parents. He shared meals and spent holidays with them. When Alice's family went on a vacation, they took David with them. His mother granted permission easily and even offered some walking around money.

"You look so much like him," she said, her palm lingering on his cheek. She looked frail; her breath smelled like alcohol.

She always said things like that, and it made David uncomfortable, but not enough to stop her. Instead, he kissed her pale cheek and left her to her gin and tonic-soaked reminiscences.

Maybe if he'd ever lost Alice, he'd be like that too. Unmoored. Worse yet, lost.

But Alice wasn't going anywhere. They'd been together for almost two years and were making college plans together. Recently she really got into Russian literature, proclaimed it to be the best in the world, and decided to study it. David wasn't sure what he'd study yet. Right now, his main concern was covering the tuition. He'd figure it out, somehow. There was time. They had all the time in the world.

And then one day Alice found the egg while helping David clean out his closet. He watched her eyes grow large with disbelief.

"Do you know what this is?" she asked in a voice full of awe and disbelief. "Why do you have it?"

"It's a long story," he said, trying to skirt her questions, but she wouldn't relent.

"David, this is a Fabergé. At least, it looks like a Fabergé egg. They are very rare and very precious. Fifty of them were made for the Russian imperial family, but only forty-three are known to have survived. This might be one of the missing ones. Seriously, why do you have it?"

While he scrambled to answer, Alice took a book out of her backpack, one of the many tomes on Russian history she was always toting around. In its pages, David recognized the familiar design.

What he had was a proper treasure.

"Estimated worth is millions." He exhaled sharply. "Wow."

"This is it," said Alice, finally pacified by his explanation of the egg being a family heirloom handed down from his grandparents. "This is how you pay for college. This is how you start a new life."

And she was right, of course. All of their dreams could be bought and sold for the cost of the object he held.

"It's pokey," Alice observed, drawing back her fingers, one of them sparkling with a blood ruby. She sucked the wound thoughtfully. "This is like a dream. Like those people on *Antique Road Show* or something you read about and think, *That only happens to other people.*"

They made a plan to have the egg appraised and researched the best places to do it. They were young and excited, and life seemed like such a promising adventure. They kissed like the sky was on fire, and David knew he'd remember that night forever.

OF COURSE, HE joined the search party. The first night and the night after that and every night that followed. Girls like Alice didn't just disappear. Someone had to have taken her. Someone evil. David shuddered to think about it. Instead, he bundled up, grabbed his thermos and flashlight, jammed his pockets with energy bars, and went into the woods. He stopped sleeping altogether in those days, it seemed. Walking, moving with purpose, was what kept him alive, what led him through the endless hours and fought off the invasive tendrils of despair.

There was no sign of her. She wouldn't have left on her own accord, and happy young women with promising futures didn't just vanish into thin air. David was interviewed by the police time and again, but had nothing new to tell them, and eventually, his plainly obvious devastation overrode their suspicions of guilt. He didn't know what to say to anyone anymore. It didn't seem to matter. His mother was no comfort, though she knew more than most of the brutal swiftness with which a loved one could be taken away.

Alice's body was found two weeks later buried in the woods, in the small clearing he was sure he'd searched before. David thought it was important to see the body. Something about closure. But there was nothing of Alice left in the decomposing remains. Her index finger, the one she had pricked on the egg, was black and oozed nightmarish ichor, like something out of a scary movie. David couldn't stop staring at it. Once the body was released, there was a funeral. He went. It rained.

He KNEW HE had to return the egg. It was a certainty felt deep in his bones. A conviction that would not be denied. It made no sense. In fact, it was downright irrational, given the recently acquired knowledge of the object's worth, but it had to be done. Urgently. In his mind, it had become a matter of life and death.

It pricked his finger when he picked it up. "Oh, come on," he whispered. "Don't be like that. I'm taking you home." He placed it into his pocket carefully. Then he went back to the Koshmaroff estate to right the wrong that, as far as he knew, had never even been reported as such. An oddity, given the object's likely value.

Once again through the window, into the world of shadows and dust; egg replaced, and he was gone. It was as if the theft had never occurred at all. For all he knew, it had gone unnoticed even by its owner.

If this simple action of restoring the egg to its rightful place had the power to undo the tragedies and deaths of the intervening years as if by some strange magic, it didn't seem inclined to do so. But David did feel lighter. And that would have to be enough.

A GREAT MANY experiences in life didn't turn out the way you thought they would or the way they were depicted in movies, but college was a rare exception to the rule. College was exactly how David imagined it, a place just far enough, just different enough, just wild enough to afford a complete personal reinvention.

Without the Fabergé egg's fortune, there would be debt for years to come, but just then it all seemed worth it. He had come a long way from a small town pissboy to a reasonably popular college guy. A long way indeed.

David tried not to think about the past, doing his best to erase it from his mind entirely. He never went back to his hometown. There was nothing for him to return to. His mother, who was by then too far gone to act as one, required a part-time attendant just to get by. He occasionally phoned to check in, but there was never anything to say between them, and the silences were never comfortable. It was a tether to the past that he didn't need or want. David had put in a lot of work into remaking himself as someone he could live with—a happy or happyish, well-adjusted person—and would do nothing to risk his transformation.

The reinvention stuck. After graduation, David moved to the biggest city that would have him and lost himself in its noise and busyness and distractions. He got a job, and then a better one. He made friends. Life was good. As good as he knew how to make it.

He might have never gone back home if not to bury his mother, who passed away quietly in her sleep, the grief and sorrow finally claiming her for their own. There was no shock, no surprise, in his reaction when he received the call from his mother's attendant; it was more like letting out a breath he had forgotten he'd been holding. David didn't believe in the afterlife but hoped his mother had found some peace, at last.

IT WAS THE first sunny funeral he'd ever been to. It didn't seem right at all, and David kept looking up at the sky as if questioning its choices. Afterward, he took a walk around town. These days, David looked different enough to not have to worry about being recognized. Nicer clothes, better posture, a good haircut, contacts instead of glasses—what wonders it could do.

The walk was idle curiosity. The town had changed in subtle ways but remained uncomfortably familiar. There were ghosts on every corner. Places he had been happy once. Places hiding the daggers of memories.

He didn't notice the flyers at first, but then the wind blew one into his chest and, once he read it, he recognized the address immediately. An estate sale. Turned out, Mrs. Koshmaroff wasn't immortal after all. Just a lonely old woman. Just as he was once a scared imaginative young boy. Just like he was once a thief and then a righteous man. Funny how time and distance change perspectives. He'd go to the sale, he decided. It would be a closure of sorts.

Once he got to the house, David had forgotten all his rationale, all his logic. There was a fear at work in his soul, a fear so primal, so atavistic in nature that no reason could touch it. He almost turned around on the still creaky stairs and left, but somehow found the strength — or was it weakness? — to move one foot in front of the other until he was inside.

Beyond a single room, he'd never seen the house. It was just as he had always imagined in appearance: a grand thing undone by age and neglect. The atmosphere inside was darker, thicker than he could describe, as if it had its own gravitational force. It made him think of his father's astrophysics lessons. Here, it seemed, was the great cosmic darkness to suck you in and never let you go. It warped time. It warped his mind.

David didn't consciously consider what he was doing or looking for, but it was only ever the one place, it was only ever the one thing. The room with the perpetually unlocked window, the swirling dervishes of dust motes, the eerily undulating curtains. The cabinet made of the darkest wood and inside it the brightest of objects. David closed his hand around the egg and felt a thousand tiny cuts. He felt his blood rush out to an object seemingly starved for it. With trembling fingers, he opened the egg and listened to its music. And with it, the memories came rushing in—shoving, cutting, killing—the bloody, brutal memories of things he couldn't have possibly done. Not in this life.

CHAPTER 7

BEFORE

BERLIN WAS A madhouse, as far as Anastasia was concerned. Paris without grace. The hedonistic decadence was everywhere. The moribund Weimar Republic seemed to have decided to live it up with the desperation of a dying harlot. It was the kind of delirious dance that ends with participants dropping dead from exhaustion. There was something hysterical about all of it.

Anastasia didn't like it, but she was intrigued.

Pavel, or Paul as he would often go by in those days, loved it unreservedly.

"There's magic here," he declared.

And sure enough, magic was everywhere; the city was mad for it. Spiritualism and the occult were some of the brightest burning fads of the moment. It seemed the dead spoke loudly in this place, though she couldn't imagine who'd want to hear what they had to say.

THE YEAR THEY arrived in Berlin, Anastasia received a long letter from Uncle Oleg, written in his increasingly shaky hand. Her parents had died. There was a small fire, nothing serious, just an electric shortage, but the smoke inhalation was enough to carry off two fragile elderly people. Oleg himself was able to get out in time, but she read between the lines that he wasn't long for this world either.

Anastasia felt curiously detached from the tragic news. By the time the letter had reached her, it was too late. Too late to attend the funeral or do anything, really. From their sporadic writing, she had gleaned that her parents felt old, spent, and tired of life. Perhaps, in a way, death was a small mercy, a release from the world they no longer found joy or comfort in. She had been away from her parents nearly as long as she'd been with them. Her life was so different now. Their happy days together seemed unimaginably long ago.

Anastasia was saddened by their passing but not devastated. She needed no closure. She did find a strange irony in the fact that they were ushered out of this life and into the next by a fire after all.

She wouldn't want to speak to them again, though. What a grotesque notion. To sit around the table and have someone, usually a strange woman, try to contact the spirits and convey messages from beyond.

Oh yes, she'd heard all about these séances. There were some in Paris, but nothing like here. In Paris, it was, like many things, a lark, an amusement, but in Berlin, it was serious business. One her husband had become hopelessly enchanted with.

He went out often and stayed out well into the night. Anastasia didn't think there were other women and didn't think she'd care either way. But Pavel's interests appeared to be increasingly less carnal and more spiritual.

Whatever the dead told him, he wanted to hear more.

"*Achtung*," thrilled Diego. She didn't know where he was picking up the new language. It had to be the maids.

Anastasia was often left alone to her own pursuits. She found the art scene quite compelling, if not entirely to her liking. She attended galleries and cinema. She saw Fritz Lang's *Metropolis* three times and still couldn't tell if she liked it. What she did like was the Bauhaus movement, becoming absolutely enchanted with its strange symmetries. Her favorite was Kandinsky, their compatriot. When Pavel asked what she wanted for her next birthday, Anastasia didn't hesitate a moment. Thus began her art collecting. It ebbed and flowed over the years, but she had never forgotten her first—a symphony of colors and shapes that she felt spoke directly and exclusively to her.

As she became older, her interest in politics increased. Or maybe the politics simply became impossible to ignore. Anastasia heard the rumblings of a radical new party, the Nazis, and it scared her. They reminded her of the Bolsheviks in their willingness to spill blood to bring about a radical change.

Of course, Berlin needed a change; it couldn't possibly go on as it was, sustaining that high a note. She knew there was poverty and privation, echoes of the Great War, things that her husband's money had always shielded them from. But she didn't think the Nazis were the answer, and she certainly didn't think the Communists were, and that didn't leave too many options.

"Would you look at that?" said Pavel, passing her the newspaper over the dining table at breakfast. "The great American Wall Street, as it turns out, is not invulnerable after all."

Anastasia scanned the article. Pavel made sure they received French and English newspapers. She didn't think she could ever master the language here; the harshness of it was entirely too foreign to her ears.

The American financial markets had collapsed. The article foretold a bleak future.

"Will this affect us?" she asked, stirring her tea.

"Not so much as you'd notice, *ma chérie*." Her husband seemed bemused by her newly found seriousness, her questions. At times, he appeared delighted to find her no longer a naïve youth or an absent gone-with-the-fairies gossamer of a person. She was becoming more substantial to him, someone to converse with as an equal. Anastasia felt it too, this new power.

"What do you think will happen in America?"

"Oh, you know, they'll starve for a while and then sort it out." He dabbed his lips with a linen serviette. "They are scrappy if nothing else."

Whether Pavel was downplaying the situation to avoid worrying her unduly or simply being uncharacteristically unprescient, she couldn't say, but the following year proved him wrong.

The echoes of the American crisis resonated around the world, swiftly reaching Europe. It changed the tone of local politics, and in the next election the Nazis had gained a staggering number of Reichstag seats. The Communists were making strides too, but nowhere near enough to matter. None of the Weimar political parties did. It was the end of the Republic and the beginning of something new and infinitely darker.

Anastasia tried sharing her concerns with Pavel, but he was too preoccupied by his other, more esoteric, interests. He was meeting new people. He told her he was expanding his worldview. Or maybe it was *worlds* that he said.

She didn't remember the first time he mentioned Crowley, but soon, the man was all Pavel would talk about, in increasingly reverent tones.

"I'll introduce you, *ma chérie*. You must meet him. There's no one like him in the entire world."

And sure enough, he had Crowley over to their house. This was unusual. They seldom hosted, so she knew this was a special occasion. The cooks were given instructions. Her party dress and jewels were set out. Pavel looked so handsome in his wool gabardine dark grey suit.

The years had been kind to her husband. She never knew him as a young man and couldn't imagine him as one, but he never really looked old either. There was no middle-age softness to his stomach, no stoop in his shoulders. Pavel was lean as a blade, tall as a tree, and his tailored suits cut clean lines. To her, his form conveyed a spare functionality of a Bauhaus chair.

That evening, he paced, awaiting his guest's arrival, so eager, like a schoolboy waiting to perform for his favorite teacher. Unseemly for a man his age, but charming all the same.

She felt anxious about having over this strange man she had heard so much about, but nothing prepared her for meeting him in person.

Aleister Crowley wasn't all that tall, and certainly not when compared to her giant oak of a husband, but he was the most imposing man Anastasia had ever met. It was as if he sucked the air right out of the room and inflated himself with it. Heavyset, balding, with a jowly face and the most piercing set of eyes, Crowley dominated their gathering, their conversation, their very house.

He was perfectly polite, as most Englishmen were, but he said the most extraordinarily far-fetched things and did so in a way that made them seem like empirical facts and not mere strange speculations. Her husband, she observed, was eating it up. Anastasia even found her own mind beginning to bend to Crowley's imposing will.

He spoke of Thelema, the religious commune he had founded in Cefalù, Sicily over a decade ago and his subsequent eviction by the Italian government only a few short years later.

"They didn't understand me," Crowley complained. "Didn't approve of my ways." He waited a pregnant pause, before adding, "Oh, but for a time, it was paradise." The longing in his voice was palpable.

Crowley expounded on his involvement with various occult groups. O.T.O., M.M.M., A∴A∴. So many acronyms, it made her head spin.

Eventually, their conversation turned to art, for he too was a fan and had dabbled in it himself. He browsed Anastasia's growing collection with considerable interest. She had been venturing into Russian Futurism by then, an art movement destroyed by the Revolution, much as her own childhood had been. There was a wildness there that spoke to her. The impossible symmetries and striking palettes and just a hint of anger beneath it all.

They discussed Cubism. Anastasia hated it—and Picasso, especially. There was an ugliness to the art and the ugliness to the man. Surrealism, on the other hand, intrigued her. She was thinking about acquiring a Dalí.

She tried to steer the conversation toward art time and again, largely due to the general discomfort with the other directions Crowley insisted upon taking it

No, she did not attend séances. No, she did not wish to contact her dead parents. No, she did not want to align herself with her True Will through magick. And no, she did not think "Do what thou wilt" was a good motto to live by.

Anastasia had said as much, but as politely as she could, fully aware of how much this man's good graces meant to her husband.

It was an uncomfortable evening. By the end of it, Anastasia felt her rings cutting into her fingers and invisible daggers stabbing at her tensed-up shoulders. Crowley's direct and seemingly unblinking gaze had made her skin crawl. She took a long bath as soon as the evening was over.

Later, when her husband asked what she thought of their guest, Anastasia had politely intimated that she would prefer not to partake in his company in the future. So seldom did she make such requests that Pavel, albeit disappointed, acquiesced willingly.

"You didn't like him at all then?" he asked. "Didn't find him interesting?"

"To be fair, his reputation precedes him. They call him The Great Beast. The wickedest man in the world."

"Anastasia, darling." He sighed. "People say things. People—" he stressed the word as if it were a derogatory term "—historically speaking, have never found a man of new ideas they didn't want to tie to a tree and set on fire."

"Do you believe these things?" she asked him. "These things that he believes?"

"I'm interested in them," Pavel prevaricated. "It's intriguing, no? That there should be more to life than just this." He gestured around vaguely.

"What is so wrong with just this?" she countered. "Don't we have a nice life?"

"Of course we do, ma chérie, but what I am talking about—what Aleister is talking about—is how restricting the modern society is, how narrow its morality is. How we can be so much more, physically and spiritually."

"Are you talking about reincarnation?"

He appeared to be pleasantly surprised by his wife's knowledge of the subject.

"Well, yes. That and more. Our life together is wonderful." He kissed her hand. "Why would I want it to ever end?"

"It seems wrong." She found herself charmed but not swayed. "Things end. Lives end. It's only natural. It makes them all the more precious while they last."

"Well, maybe I shall learn the right kind of magic, and we'll continue in perpetuity, happy together," he said lightheartedly, with a smile. She wasn't sure if it was meant as a joke but didn't press.

ANASTASIA KNEW HER husband continued seeing Crowley after that evening, but true to his word, he never brought the man to their house again. There were so many people Pavel was meeting, it seemed, including a great deal of writers. The names drifted through her mind, Aldous something. Christopher someone.

He told her stories about them, and she told him about the art she saw and the artists she met.

She told herself that it was perfectly normal to maintain separate interests. Of course, they'd be passionate about different things. After all, they were two very different people.

The alcohol that free-flowed at the galleries she attended, the beautiful people who created beautiful things, who found *her* beautiful—it was all too intoxicating.

Anastasia found herself finally coming into her own in those days, a belated sort of blossoming. She had always been comely, but at last, the vagaries of life—and her husband's fortune; she had to be honest, the money always helped—had shaped the planes of her pleasant, if unremarkable, face into something akin to striking. It was all angles" sharp cheekbones, pointy chin, high brow; plus, the always immaculate hair and clothes. And her eyes. Somehow no longer just mere blue, they were described as ice blue by those who met her. Ice had permeated her appearance entirely and stilled her features into a forbidding kind of beauty.

"You are a Russian winter come to life," Anastasia was told by a famous artist once. It was the best compliment she'd ever received.

She was finally beginning to get noticed for her looks. Artists she hobnobbed with wanted her to model for them. She turned them down, for now—an acquaintance of hers had her portrait done by Klee once. and it came out positively caricatural and garish, making its subject look like a decorated child's balloon.

To be drawn was tempting, of course. It was the only time she understood and related to Pavel's talk about the dangers of fleeting years. She too could see the appeal of arresting a perfect moment and making it last. Her newfound attention seemed too good to merely be permitted to vanish into the tides of time.

It was easy to lose herself in the scene to avoid thinking about politics, thinking about her husband's strange drift into the realm of the supernatural.

When Pavel told her he joined a society, Anastasia didn't think much of it at first. It had to be simply one of those social things that people of a certain status and wealth did. He had been traveling to England lately, to see that terrible Crowley man, she suspected. And so, what if there was a society where they sat around, puffed on their cigars, and exchanged their insane ideas? It seemed civilized enough.

The more her husband talked about it, the more Anastasia understood it wasn't that kind of a society at all. Well, not entirely.

The Hermetic Order of The Golden Dawn, he told her, was a magickal order dedicated to the study and practice of metaphysics, paranormal, and the occult.

The word *practice* in the description gave her pause.

She asked for more information, and Pavel was all too happy to talk about it. There was an enthusiasm of the newly converted about him. Much to her surprise, Crowley wasn't a part of it. He had been once but left a long time ago after an argument with a poet. Anastasia wondered if perhaps Crowley's brand of magick was, after all, a cry too far even for her open-minded husband.

The overall system, Pavel explained, was based on initiation and hierarchy. There were three orders to it. Golden Dawn, the first, was based on Hermetic Qabalah and intended to further personal development through the study of classical elements in addition to things like astrology, divination, and geomancy. The second one, The Inner Order, specialized in teaching its disciples magick, including alchemy, astral travel, and scrying. The third order was that of Secret Chiefs, skilled magicians who guided, directed, and oversaw the entire operation.

There were, alarmingly, too many words in that description that she would need to look up later. She didn't like that. And after finding out their meaning, she liked it even less.

The magic, without or without the "k" in the end, was all a bit much. Too far from the world she knew, the one they both lived in.

Anastasia didn't relish the idea of her husband becoming the dotty gullible old man in a ridiculous ornamental ceremonial robe—that was how she always imagined him there—playing at magick. But what could she do?

"They are very egalitarian, you know," he told her. "They allow women in, welcome them even. There are many women who are members."

She would never consider such a thing, though she didn't say it aloud.

"So many authors too," Pavel went on." Machen, Doyle, Stoker."

Maybe that's his main interest in this silly business, she thought. *Maybe he still dreams of being a successful author.*

Pavel's stories were getting published here and there from time to time but it was nothing worth raving about. He'd been working on a novel lately, she knew, though he wouldn't talk about it outside of promising her it would be the best thing he'd ever written.

"Is there anyone I've read in this society of yours?"

"Well." Pavel inclined his head, considering the question. "There's Yeats. You like him. 'Now that my ladder's gone ...' and so on," he quoted just to demonstrate that he had the right man.

Indeed, she did like the melancholy Irishman's poetry. Her English was nearly flawless now, and she had been reading more and more in it. She'd even revisited some Austen. Pavel was right—things were supposed to be read in their native tongue.

Anastasia had more questions—she was curious which order of the three Pavel belonged to and what exactly that entailed—but at the same time, she didn't want to know, unwilling to learn something about her husband that she could not unlearn.

Instead, she occupied herself by finally sitting down for a portrait. It took ages, with the artist obsessing over every detail. Anastasia found a strange peace in sitting still for hours on end, her mind entering a perfect state of calm. She came to love it and the portrait too, once it was finally finished. She had seen herself in mirrors and photos, but none had been able to present her true face to her the way this did.

Tracing the lines of oils on the canvas felt just like tracing her own face with her fingers. *This*, she thought with a smile, *this is me*. Anastasia overpaid for the portrait lavishly. Had she known the artist would soon be dead, she would have commissioned another.

Pavel loved the portrait too. He had a tough time appreciating her less conventional art choices, but this was something they could both agree on. It was given a prominent place in their living parlor, where it couldn't be ignored.

"I'll stay young and beautiful in it while I get old and ugly out here in the real world," she jested wistfully.

"Yes, Dorian," Pavel joked along. "Behold your picture."

He put an arm around her, pulling her closer.

"But just so you know, *ma chérie*," he added, "you'll always be young and beautiful to me."

"Only because you are so very old, I'm sure."

They shared an amused laughter, enjoying a lovely moment of togetherness—a testament to how comfortable they'd become with each other over the years.

"Don't worry, we'll never put this one in the attic. It'll always be on display for all to see."

"In that case—" Anastasia punctuated her repartee with a smile "—I should mind how much I sin."

Sins were easy to mind, and easy to overlook, when considered against the background of the unfolding national politics. They continued to ignore it all as much as they could, but it was becoming increasingly difficult to do so. Impossible, even.

"This country's going straight to hell, while you're off gallivanting with your friends in England," she'd complain to Pavel. "That horrible man …"

Anastasia never said the name out loud in the house and forbade the servants to; she didn't want Diego starting to shout *Heil Hitler* at random.

The country was indeed becoming virtually unrecognizable from the manically wild place they had found upon their arrival years ago.

"The things they are doing to the Jews," she'd say, horrified.

"They did these things back in Mother Russia too, *ma chérie*. Lest we forget the pogroms. The Jews are the ready-made victims of Europe. It is terrible, but don't fret, it won't affect us at all, all this nonsense," Pavel tried reassuring her.

Anastasia wanted to believe him and to be reassured, but simply couldn't, not in good conscience.

And then the politics hit her beloved art scene with all the unwelcome subtlety of a sledgehammer.

Entartete Kunst. Degenerate art. Goebbels' Ministry of Propaganda, armed with their latest insane mission, proceeded to confiscate thousands of artworks from the nation's museums.

"It's an outrage," she told Pavel. "An outrage."

But it did make for a terrific exhibition. After a series of smaller schandaussellungen exhibits all across the Reich, there was one grand one at last. They had traveled to Munich for it especially. As it turned out, degenerate art was the only art worth seeing.

"What will they do with it all?" her husband mused aloud.

"They'll probably burn it the way they burned the books back in thirty-three. Those terrible savages."

There was a talk of selling some of the art off to raise funds for the Nazis. It was appalling to even consider.

There'd be nothing left; nothing worth loving and admiring. The place purged of beauty was a place purged of its soul. The art compatible with national values was nothing compared to the stunning pieces that were banned.

"They said this art was an attack on their values." She sneered. "They said it was an affront to them, a sign of cultural decline. How can culture decline further than burning books and banning art?"

Pavel agreed with her, Anastasia knew, but his heart wasn't in it. It simply didn't mean as much to him. By now, he was putting the finishing touches on his novel and had just started a new collection. "His mystical objects," as he referred to them. Things imbued or intended to be imbued with magick.

He'd show his latest acquisitions proudly, eager to explain the meaning and purpose behind them. They seemed to be mainly ordinary household items. Although one object caught her eye.

"Is that a Fabergé?" she asked, picking up the lavishly ornamental egg. The legendary beautiful toy of the royal family now in her home. Anastasia knew they were wealthy, but she had no idea they were *that* wealthy.

"Ah, not quite." Her husband smiled. "It's a perfect facsimile made by an Italian artisan. Isn't it marvelous?"

"And what's its special power?" She smiled back. "Looking just like the real thing and fooling the beholder?"

"Not quite," Pavel said. "Not quite."

PAUL KOSHMAROFF'S NOVEL titled *Nothing but the Night* was published in England without much fanfare. Originally, he tried shopping it around in Berlin and Munich, but it was dangerously close to what could be considered degenerate art and thus, wasn't worth the effort or the risk.

"Who's going to touch it here?" he lamented bitterly. "Not Eher-Verlag, those Nazi lapdogs. I wouldn't want my book to share the same print blocks as *Mein Kampf* in any case."

He was getting political, after all, Anastasia observed, not without pleasure.

And so, *Nothing but the Night* became an English book. Pavel did his own translation. The publication was widely celebrated within the Golden Dawn, especially since the novel espoused so many ideas shared by its members. It seemed every one of them bought a copy. It also seemed that those were the only copies sold. The few reviews received were lukewarm at best. At worst, they panned the book for being a competently but flatly written propaganda for the author's esoteric ideas.

Pavel didn't hide his disappointment. And disappointment didn't become him. Anastasia missed her husband's steady resolve, his unflappable demeanor, his reassuring calm. She drank more in those days and taught Diego obscure words in different languages, words she'd forget the next day, until the bird reminded her. Over and over and over again. He had a memory of an elephant, and an appetite of one too.

"You're getting fat, Diego, darling," she told him affectionately, petting his soft green feathers with her finger.

"*Au contraire, ma chérie,*" he countered. He tipped his head to the side jauntily. "*Ya krasivy.*"

"Yes." She smiled. "You are very beautiful, my love."

"I MET THE most interesting man," announced Pavel at breakfast one morning.

"Not another Crowley, I trust?" Anastasia asked with mock panic.

"On ho, there's only one of him. But this guy, his name is Otto, he's a writer too, a medievalist. You'd like him, I think. Would you object to us having him over some day?"

"Pavel, you don't need a special dispensation from me to invite people over," she chided.

"Well, no, of course, but I don't want to make you feel uncomfortable either."

There was a toast crumb in his newly grown beard. Anastasia didn't know if she cared for the look. It seemed like he was trying to look the part of a serious author. The beard came in almost white, while the hair on his head maintained youthful darkness almost entirely free of grey. She reached over and brushed the crumb off.

"Invite this Otto," she said. "It'll be nice to have company."

In retrospect, nice wasn't exactly the word one would apply to Otto Rahn. He was an anxious-looking man of approximately her age with the slight, harried mannerisms of someone not entirely comfortable in their own skin. His long face was pale and clean-shaven, with dark eyes and the most strikingly expressive eyebrows.

They talked of his research, which, she had to admit was far-fetched but fascinating—the man was looking for the Holy Grail, of all things. He was convinced the Cathars had the answers. His second book had just been published recently.

Pavel wanted to know all about it, especially the Cathars.

Anastasia was more interested in Otto's SS service. He didn't seem at all like the type. In fact, if she read the clues correctly and, after years in the art scene, she believed that she had, the man was a homosexual. She knew how the Nazis felt about that. But it was a thing she couldn't possibly ask.

It had entered the conversation anyway, after Pavel inquired what it was like to have Himmler as a fan and patron.

"It is a nightmare," Otto said, his voice shot through with sadness. "I wanted patronage, but never like this. The man terrifies me. He made me an Obersturmführer, and now he has posted me to Dachau as a guard. He knows what I am like, and he punishes me for it, but he won't let me go."

Otto Rahn struck Anastasia as a sympathetic but tragic figure. They talked about him often afterward, though he never came back to their house. She knew her husband still saw him from time to time.

"Aren't you afraid to be associated with a man like that in this political climate?" she worried. "What will people say?"

"That man is a treasure trove of ideas. I refuse to let such petty concerns enter the equation," Pavel protested empathically and, in Anastasia's option, naïvely.

"He should move, though, don't you think? Go somewhere more tolerant?"

"There's nowhere for him to go. He'd be just as persecuted in England. Here, at least, he has some protection. Plus, Himmler would never let him leave," Pavel finished grimly. "No one leaves the SS."

To his credit, Otto tried. He resigned from the Nazi Party in 1939. Soon after, he was discovered frozen to death on an Austrian mountainside. He never found his Holy Grail. The official verdict was suicide. Pavel didn't believe it for a second. Neither did Anastasia.

The event turned out to be the latest drop of blood in the overflowing bucket of unignorable atrocities. They knew they could no longer stay in Berlin. In the country. Change, once again, was upon them.

"Where will we go?" Anastasia asked Pavel, experiencing an uneasy déjà vu.

"The continent is no longer safe, and I have plenty of contacts in England," he pointed out, reasonably.

Anastasia groaned inwardly. She knew he meant Aleister—the old goat was somehow still alive despite all his debauchery—but she hoped her husband was only speaking of his Golden Dawn associates. She was convinced the latter were the proverbial lesser evil. Whatever madness Crowley was conjuring up with his acronym societies, she wanted Pavel to have no part in.

So then, London. A new place their peripatetic life's compass was pointing to. Anastasia didn't know if she'd like it. After all, it was still Europe, though away from the mainland. But what choice did they have? London it was.

CHAPTER 8

AFTER

THE CUP

Y OU NEVER FORGET your first kiss. So they say. I certainly remember mine.

I remember Tony Giotto shoving me against the gym lockers after a school basketball practice, remember the metal eating into my back, remember the kiss itself, aggressive but melting into something almost tender. I remember the whiplash of the aftermath, when Tony pushed me away. The look in his eyes was a mixture of disgust, anger, and something remarkably like desire. Tony put his finger to his lips and shook his head. No words were needed.

Things changed that day, and I didn't even know it. Didn't know I went from an easily ignored butt of a joke to a full-on punching bag. The difference was startling. From wearing my lunch on my shirt to wearing my blood. From damaged books to damaged ribs. Tony clearly intended to make me pay for that kiss, and through it all, throughout all the torment that he and his friends dished out over those last two years of high school, he never once met my eye. It was a strangely distant kind of abuse, with the fist refusing to acknowledge the flesh it mauled. Refusing to know.

High school couldn't be over soon enough. I took the first scholarship that got me out of that place, determined to never come back. By then, I knew enough about myself to know that a small town would never be the right place for me. I just didn't know how wrong the big city would turn out to be.

IT WAS GLAMOROUS at first, albeit in a sordid kind of way. The dirt, the crime, there was an edge to it. When you're young, walking that edge can seem exciting; when you get older, you realize you're just getting your feet cut up. My first apartment was a fifth-floor walk-up studio the size of a walk-in closet. In it, I was the king of the most finite of kingdoms. My bed was a beat-up, thirdhand mattress, but I could sleep with whoever I wanted on it. The freedom of it was thrilling. Consuming. It distracted me from my studies and made me feel alive in all the ways I had only ever dreamed of back home.

The music was always too loud, the clothes and hair too garish. The skinny strutting wannabe rockstar boys that sent my heart racing were a dime a dozen. My romances then were like the ubiquitous New York pizza slices: quick, cheap, and easy. And just about as satisfying.

There was a certain delicious impermanence to all of it—you skimmed the life's cream and left the dregs behind, not merely forgotten but unthought of in the first place. I'm not sure how I managed to get my degree, but I did. The degree got me a job in a restaurant frequented by Broadway stars and their hangers-on. By then, I had an almost addiction to coke; enough to eat into my budget, but not enough to make me dare to try new, more dangerous things.

I didn't know danger was already there, walking the city streets with my name in its books. To this day I'm not sure how I managed to survive the eighties. Looking back, it seems surreal to have beaten the odds like that. I should have played the lottery then; could've struck gold and changed my destiny forever. I didn't, though. I didn't do much of anything. Life became a series of parties and funerals with varying ratios. Sometimes the funerals were done up as parties. Sometimes the parties had a funereal atmosphere to them. Lovers, friends, acquaintances ...

I gave up sleeping around. I distinctly remember waking up one morning, hungover from yet another funeral party, and making a decision to walk away from it all. It wasn't a far walk; I stayed in the city. To stay busy and sane, I threw myself into my work with the coked-up energy of the permanently bereaved and afraid. I climbed the ladder, ending up with my own catering business. Work, work, work. In those days, I was too busy to notice being lonely.

The city evolved around me, while I stagnated. Things got more expensive, but I wasn't making more money. People around me got younger and hipper as I got older and more sedate. My catering company became one of what seemed like a million similar businesses with nothing to wildly distinguish it from the rest. I was getting by on my connections, but there were only so many of those.

Eventually, I just got tired. It wasn't any one big thing but many little ones. The death by a thousand cuts. I did the thing I swore I'd never do, telling myself it was a sign of maturity and not of giving up—I moved back upstate.

I HAD VISITED intermittently throughout the years, though never stayed long. There was only so much time one could spend with a well-meaning but clueless family, only so much self-editing one could put up with. My parents both knew the truth about me, of course, they just didn't know what to say to me about it. I know we were both relieved that I never brought anyone home with me for my infrequent visits. Honestly, there was never anyone worth it. I think secretly my parents had always hoped I was merely going through some elaborate phase. It wasn't a hope strong enough for them to try setting me up with one of their friends' daughters or nieces, but rather a smaller, quieter kind.

What did I know? I never had a kid and never wanted to. I'd seen too much death to want to bring life into this world. Maybe I just wasn't equipped to understand my parents' well-intentioned concern.

Or maybe I was overthinking it, and it was simply that they didn't want me to die alone, whereas I was just glad to be alive at all.

The thing about a small town is how easy it is to be big in it. Small pond theory all the way. I went from being one of the many, many caterers in the city to the owner and proprietor of one of the only two companies in town. My competition was Trisha

Longwood, a girl I remembered from high school as the cheerleader least likely to succeed. Turned out I was both right and wrong. Her cheerleading days were well and truly over. Since high school, Trisha had eaten her once svelte figure into Mrs. Santa proportions, and no, she never did find herself a quarterback to marry. But she did own a successful business and a small, lovely cottage on a nice street, where she lived with her well-fed accountant husband and their two equally well-fed teens, while I was alone, stuck in yet another rental apartment—albeit considerably larger than a closet and for a lot less money—and trying to get established.

My parents gave me a single goldfish in a small aquarium as a move-in gift. I named him Sam, after a long-ago lover who, I swear, made the same facial expressions. Both Sams weren't big on conversation. Both were low maintenance. I appreciated that.

The reason for all this backstory is to make it clear that Tony Giotto had a choice when it came to hiring someone to cater his wedding to my cousin Sylvie. It didn't have to be me. Trisha would have done a perfectly adequate job, I'm sure. The reason he chose me was because people don't change all that much over the years. They say they do, but those changes are superficial. Beneath the latest fashions and stylish accessories and trendy outlooks is the same old poison. One look at Tony, and I knew it for a fact.

Smug cunt. At least he meets my eyes now. The years have been kind to Tony, but he's right on the verge of overstaying that kindness. His flesh is straining his Brooks Brothers finest; his hair is beginning to threaten retreat; his cheekbones are just about to give up the fight with impending jowls; his skin has a purplish-reddish tint to it, warning of a man who turns beet red when enraged and gets enraged more often than one ought to. In short, he is slowly morphing into his father, Tony Giotto Sr., an irascible, corpulent, combed-over, wardrobe-shaped man, who has been, allegedly, the best contractor in town for as long as I can remember. There have been mafia rumors for as long as I can remember too, but organized crime seems like too exciting of a concept for a town as unexciting as ours.

It's no wonder Tony is getting married. Daddy had probably laid down the law. Giotto Sr. wants the business to stay in the family and wants a family for the business to stay in. Tony still looks and acts the ladies' man, with all that stupid swagger. But I remember the desire in his eyes after that poisoned kiss, tearing him up, twisting his guts. I know what Tony is really like.

I don't even question why he chose Sylvie. It makes perfect sense. She goes through life with just the right kind of obliviousness that'll make this marriage perfect, in its own way. Sylvie is the kind of woman who doesn't ask questions she doesn't want the answers to. Her desires are limited to real and practical things. And her features are plain enough underneath all that makeup to make Tony seem like the greatest of catches.

Sylvie would have been the happiest decades ago as a perfect fifties or sixties housewife. Her hair and her spine both have that telltale stiffness of a woman who desires stability above all else. The only fragility is in her smile. No sense of humor, poor thing. And like many inherently unfunny people, Sylvie worries about being the butt of a joke. It's almost ironic in a way, though I'll never be the one to mention it to her. We are not close and never have been.

If Tony and Sylvie want to build a marriage on the foundation of lies, who am I to stop them? Whatever idealism I may have harbored once has been beaten out of me long ago. By life. By Tony himself.

I don't believe in true love. That's for fairy tales—the marriage, the happily ever after. Even if it wasn't, it's not like that institution is open to everyone. The government has very strong ideas about whose love is worth protecting by law and rewarding by tax breaks. So much for romance. It's all business, one way or another. So, if two self-serving adults want to enter into a symbiotic union that will give them both what they want and need, they should go for it. Fuck them. Seriously.

I just really don't want to be the one to feed them and their guests on their wedding day

The thing is, I can't say no. I'm snowed under with bills. My rent is due. There are only so many catering opportunities in a small town, and most people tend to go with the better known and established local gal than some wayward prodigal son. There are rumors flying around about me, I'm sure, but nothing to substantiate them. I don't telegraph my sexuality. I flaunt nothing, outside of dressing well. It's no one's business but my own. But still, it doesn't help.

And this wedding is a huge occasion for the town. Anybody who's anybody will be there; plenty of opportunities to drum up future business. It's too good to pass up.

We can be adults about it, I tell myself. We *are* all adults. High school ended decades ago. I treat it as any other gig, say all the right things and think all the right thoughts, until I see that look in Tony's eyes and wonder if anything ever really ends.

FOR AN EVENT this size I have to hire some temps. They are cute and young, but I know better. For all the company Sam provides, I have been lonely since coming back. But I don't dare to do a thing about it within the confines of the town's limits. Every so often I drive to the city to "visit old friends" and indulge in long stolen weekends here and there. I haven't gone in a while, though. Something about those visits just leaves too sad an aftertaste.

Other than that, it's just me and my memories and my imagination and some mail-ordered magazines. If it wasn't mostly by choice, it would be pitiful. Sure, I look. How can I not? There's a cute assistant manager at a local store where I find myself shopping with unreasonable frequency. His name is Dave. Nice kid. Too young, though. And too straight, I'm sure. Like the rest of them.

I've read Kinsey, and I don't for a second believe this town is the one to defy the man's statistics. Everyone here is either really straight or a really good liar. I know which one I am.

There are many conversations to be had and arrangements to be made when it comes to weddings. It's the most elaborate of all the events one can cater because, despite the ever-increasing divorce rates, people have managed to successfully convince themselves it is the most important party of their lives.

Sylvie is surprisingly unfussy, but Tony is another story. I make sure any meeting I have with the happy couple is attended by both of them. I don't want to be alone with Tony. I'm not a coward, just a big fan of avoiding social discomfort whenever possible. Our latest in a series of meetings regarding desserts is supposed to be attended by Sylvie and Sandra, the local baker I'm working with, but it seems like it's just Tony and me.

"Sylvie got tied up at the dressmakers," he offers with chagrin I don't buy.

"We'll just wait for Sandra then," I say.

"I met Sandra earlier. She dropped off some samples at my office, said she had some kind of family thing to attend. She sends her apologies."

It seems perfectly plausible, but I don't believe him for a second. The walls get closer. I take a steadying breath.

"Why don't we sample what we have and then we can let Sandra know what's best?" he suggests, a picture of innocence. "Sylvie says she trusts me implicitly."

I just bet she does. Poor stupid Sylvie who has never met a principle she wouldn't compromise for a two-story colonial with a garage and 2.4 kids.

"Sure," I say out loud with what I hope is amicability. "Sounds good."

Tony takes out a large sample box. It all looks and smells terrific. Sandra is a clear and present danger to one's waistline. She even looks like butter in person, all blonde and soft and slightly shiny.

We sample some cakes. It feels weird, strangely intimate. Sylvie really shouldn't have skipped this one, I don't care how concerned she is about fitting into her wedding dress.

"What do you think of the tiramisu?" asks Tony, licking his lips. I don't want to think it's anything, but it looks suggestive.

"Delicious," I reply noncommittally. "But all of Sandra's creations are delicious. It's really just down to your personal preferences."

"If this was your wedding, what would you choose?"

I look up at him, suddenly desperate to answer truthfully that there are no weddings in my future. Then I push down the urge.

"I'm not sure."

"Not the cake type or not the wedding type?" Tony presses.

You know, you know, you know, you know, you fuck. I concentrate on wiping the chocolate off my fingers with a napkin and say nothing.

"I remember you." Tony's voice is quiet, almost wistful. "From high school. Do you remember me?"

Of course, I remember you. You beat me. Teased me. Pushed me. Bruised my ribs. Tore my clothes. You kissed me.

"Yes, I remember you," I say evenly.

"I was kind of a brute to you then, wasn't I?"

I look up at him again. He seems sincere. It's disarming.

"It was a long time ago," I prevaricate.

"But I was," he insists.

"But you were," I agree.

"I'm sorry about that," Tony says simply.

There's nothing simple about this to me. It's an apology I have never expected. An apology I don't believe in. An apology I don't know what to do with.

"It was a long time ago," I repeat, quietly stunned.

"I was such a stupid kid then." Tony shakes his head. "So angry. Had troubles with my father and took it out on everyone around me."

Oh Tony, you walking, talking cliché of daddy issues. I don't want this now. It's too late. It doesn't matter. Can we just choose a fucking cake?

"And are you still?" I ask instead.

"What? Angry? Stupid?" He smiles. "Yeah, probably, but you know, less so."

"Good."

We both pause for a beat, pretending to consider the remaining cake options.

"So how have you been? How was the big city?"

We are not doing this. We are not catching up like a couple of old friends. We are not ...

"It was good. Different. Busy."

"And now you're back?"

"And now I'm back."

"To build a catering empire in the great middle of nowhere?"

Is that sarcasm, Tony? I can't even tell. I'm so thrown off balance by this conversation.

"Something like that."

"But seriously though?"

"Yes?"

"Why are you back?"

"Financial reasons," I tell him, steadily, making eye contact, expressing confidence that simply isn't there. "The city just got too expensive."

"Not personal?"

"Not personal."

"Never found anyone in the city worth staying for?"

I let that one go unanswered. Fuck Tony and his rhetorical questions.

"I've been to the city numerous times over the years," he goes on, unfazed. "Maybe we've passed by each other and didn't notice."

"Maybe."

"Maybe we've gone to the same bars."

There's an unignorable implication there, and I must make a conscious effort to ignore it. Tony doesn't get to have that much of me. Not for a catering job. Not ever.

He isn't discouraged by my silence. Men like Tony are used to getting their way.

"I've thought a lot about things over the years." He seems so serious, so sincere. "I know I will live and die in this town. I know the kind of man I ought to be for to make that life an easy one. I know there are other lives to be had out there, outside of this place, but I know how much courage that would take, and I'm not sure I have it in me. But you—" he appears to be sizing me up, and my heart skips beneath the weight of his regard "— you do. Or did." He shakes his head again.

"Why did you come back here, Artie, when you got away clean?"

Artie. He fucking calls me Artie. No one calls me Artie. I've been Arthur for so long now. King to my close friends. Art to a couple of lovers. Never Artie. Artie was a school kid whose head got pushed in the toilet bowls. Artie was skinny, all knobby knees and stuck-out ears and ugly jeans. Arthur is 5'11" with arms strengthened by carrying endless platters of food, gym-toned; modestly but nicely dressed, and with ears smartly obscured by fashionably longish hair.

"Don't call me that."

"What? Artie?"

"Don't call me that. My name is Arthur."

"See how much you've changed. I'm still here and still Tony." He spreads his arms and smiles mock ruefully.

This conversation needs to be over. This conversation needs to be over *now*.

"Why don't we try another cake?" I suggest, struggling to return our meeting to its professional purpose.

"Why don't we?" Tony grins as he reaches into the elaborate pink box, picks up a sample-size cake slice, leans over, and smashes it into my mouth.

Or maybe *smashes* isn't the right word. It's rougher than merely pressing but doesn't feel like violence. Or maybe I just can't tell with Tony, because he is suddenly so close. Maybe I never could.

The next thing I know, he is kissing the cake off me with a hunger that leaves me stunned. And though I know it's wrong, and I know I shouldn't, I find myself kissing him back. It feels familiar because, as they say, you never forget your first.

AND SO, IT begins. Our toxic affair. From a kiss to a fuck to a myriad of lies to arrange the next time we can do it all over again. The lying isn't on me—I'm beholden to no one but Sam's disapproving gaze. I can only imagine what tangled web Tony weaves to come up with excuses to see me. He never tells me and, frankly, I don't want to know. When I see Sylvie, I feel no guilt. Mostly what I feel is shame. Shame and a sort of nauseating desire. It's possible I've been underestimating my loneliness while overestimating my self-sufficiency. Had it been anyone, anyone else at all, I would have found a way to rationalize this. But it's Tony, and I can't.

He's still the brute I remember him to be, but amid his brutality, there are glimpses of devastating tenderness, and it slays me. Suddenly, I'm a cliché, something from a sordid paperback romance. He makes me into someone I barely recognize, someone so fucking weak.

I tell myself it's temporary, it's only the last of his wild oats being sown, it's just until the wedding, but I know, *I know*, these are lies.

We are liars. We have become or have always been liars. Each of us is a two-faced Janus, with one face turned toward the world and one toward each other.

Tony bruises my skin when we're together, and I love it and hate myself for loving it. When he leaves, those bruises are my souvenirs. Am I regressing to a school-aged kid in awe of the popular guy? Am I turning into a masochist?

My romances never used to have this amount of retrospection. I don't want to analyze what is happening between us—I want to end it and can't bring myself to do it. I am poisoned, he has poisoned me with shame, and it left me weak-kneed and spellbound with it.

I should have stayed in the city and taken my chances. Or, maybe, I should have found somewhere in between. A compromise. Just not this town. A place with a community might have been nice, a place where I can be myself. It occurs to me that as things are, the only person I can be myself with is Tony, and even then, only some of the time.

Tony, curiously enough, seems to be himself all the time. He just has different selves and puts them on as the occasion demands. I want that too. I want to know his secret, to learn to be that comfortable inside a lie.

We rarely talk. When we do, he asks me questions about my life in the city. While listening to my answers, he gazes into the distance wistfully, as if imagining a road not taken. Or a bullet dodged.

When I ask him questions, he seldom answers. He knows all the right ways to shut me up.

THE DAY OF the wedding approaches slowly, then time speeds up, and suddenly, it's here. It is a perfectly catered affair. I am not just a wizard behind the curtain, I'm on the floor, working the event, carrying the trays. Smiling. Smiling.

Once you serve someone a drink or an hors d'oeuvre, in their mind you become a waiter. It doesn't matter that you own the catering company, the action always wins over the notion. It rubs me the wrong way; no, more than that, it abrades me, angers me, but alas, there's nothing to be done. This is still exposure, an advertisement, best foot must be put forward, and all that.

Tony looks great, his tailored tux compliments his frame while obscuring its flaws. Sylvie is the perfect blushing bride/ The perfect fool. I don't kid myself; it isn't me that's made a joke out of her, a cuckquean. A woman who's been cheated on. Nine months of dating a linguist years ago, and I still remember all the abstruse words he's introduced me to, though the man himself is but a faded memory.

Poor Sylvie. If not for me, it would have been someone else. Tony isn't the faithful type, and she isn't the woman to inspire unflagging allegiance. Still, I don't meet her eye unless I have to.

And Tony ... Tony won't even look at me. In his perfectly bicameral mind, I'm once again nothing more than the hired help. But I look at him. I see him—a prince poised to become a king at last. A poisoned shard of desire courses through my veins. If only it would stab my treacherous heart and release me of this man.

He comes to me when I'm packing up the tablecloths in the back. He locks the door and takes me rough and ready. It's over in minutes, and he walks away from me to go be with his new wife, to start his honeymoon, his new life. I'm left alone with a pile of soiled linen. It feels tragically appropriate.

THEIR HONEYMOON LASTS three weeks. Three long weeks that give me the breathing space to try to gain some clarity, some resolve. I get two new contracts out of the wedding, a sweet sixteen party and a retirement bash. The alpha and omega of life. I contemplate the way people bookend their lives with food and celebrations., briefly enjoying the reverie. And then I get to it, losing myself in all the work that needs to be done. The busyness does the trick—I swear there are now days, okay, maybe not days, but hours when Tony doesn't haunt my mind. It feels like some kind of freedom.

And then he comes back. I see him in town, He doesn't notice me or pretends not to, but it doesn't matter. He's back, and all my stupid desires come flooding back to me, obliterating the tentatively erected dams in my mind, in my heart, in the stupid hungry center of me that still wants him, that always wants him.

Tony doesn't come to see me for a full week after. Seven days of nothing. I tell myself it's over, well and truly over, and wait to feel happy about it.

And then he's there again, on my threshold, with that shit-eating grin and a newly acquired tan. And I let him in, of course, I fucking let him in.

"How was the honeymoon?" I ask.

He grabs me, pulls me close to him, all conversation attempts abandoned.

Afterward, I count my bruises in the shower, pressing down on them to relive their infliction. Tony was rough this time, there was blood. But now, there's nothing but shame. I give into it.

There were more bruises this time than usual, though. Some of them, I can't recall the origin of. I don't think about it and don't think about ... until it becomes impossible not to.

"YOU KNEW?"

"Calm down, Artie," Tony says, consolatory, raising his arms. "I don't know what you're talking about."

"YOU KNEW!" I scream at him.

"Keep your voice down," he hisses at me. "This is my place of business. I work here."

It's the first time I'm in his office. The protocol has been breached. I'm in his space now, in his life— almost real. This conversation couldn't wait. Now that I'm here, I will have my say. And I won't calm down.

"What are you even talking about?" says Tony. He's being reasonable. I've thrown him off his game, and he's trying to regain his equilibrium.

I toss the paperwork at him. The pages flap their wings like the ugliest, most graceless of all birds. He catches it and looks it over. There's a sudden pall in the space. It's all different now; the few words on paper have changed everything.

"So, you're positive," he says, not a question, quietly as if to himself. "And you think it's my fault?"

"I *know* it is. There's been no one else."

"I don't believe you."

"I don't care."

We look at each other. This is a standoff. All that's missing is a clock tower and some pistols. Tony looks away first. It's as good as a confession.

I take a few steps and glance around. Everything is too normal; it doesn't match the storm raging inside me. I pick up the first thing off his desk, just to have something solid in my hands to anchor me. It's a plain drinking cup with HPB initialed into the glass.

"Who the fuck is HPB?" I say, conversationally. Like this is a social visit. Like no lives have been changed only moments ago.

He shrugs. "Oh, it's some stupid thing Sylvie picked up at an estate sale the other week. It's her grandmother's initials, so she liked it. Don't know why the fuck it's here."

I hurl the glass at him. Full force. I'm not sure if I mean to hit him. It happens so quickly. The cup sails right past his head and explodes against the wall. The flying shards catch the sunlight and dance. For a moment, it's almost beautiful.

"Fuck!" Tony screams, grab his face.

One of the larger shards has hit his temple in its ricochet trajectory There's more blood than there ought to be, but then again, head wounds tend to do that.

I stand there and watch his poisoned blood slip through his fingers, and I feel hatred so pure, so steely, that it obliterates all else. I cross the distance between us and push Tony. He falls over, suddenly not so imposingly substantial after all. And then I hit him and I hit him and I hit him again.

My fists sing through the air. There's nothing but blood and a beautiful crystal calm of the moment. By the time I come to feel people's hands on me, prying me away from Tony, I know it's over; he isn't breathing. I'm covered in blood. His, mine, it no longer matters. It's all the same now. I smile, because it's finally well and truly over. I'm finally free.

DETECTIVE FRANK COSTELLO finished taking down the confession and left the room. There was no air left in there. He'd heard some messed up things in his day and still *this* had disturbed him more than he would care to admit. *Some people*, he thought, as he stepped outside into a welcoming drizzle. He knew Tony well, saw his new wife at that estate sale Mina had dragged him not too long ago. What a mess this was, what a sorry bloody mess. And to what end?

CHAPTER 9

BEFORE

THEY GOT OUT just in time. A month later Hitler invaded Poland. Two days later, France and Britain declared war in retaliation. It had begun, once again. The chaos, the bloodshed, the madness. The war. Was it always inevitable?

The quote from her beloved Yeats came to her:

"Things fall apart; the centre cannot hold;
Mere anarchy is loosed upon the world."

"And to think, they said the last one was the war to end all wars," Anastasia remarked ruefully in the living room of their new London home.

"A natural state of the world, *ma chérie*." Pavel shook his head. "People cannot maintain peace for long."

"Will we be safe here?"

"I should hope so." He neatly refolded the newspaper he had been reading. "It seems the Führer shall have plenty to do on the continent without troubling this small island."

"Not so small, I'm afraid, as to avoid his deadly attention. Maybe we should have gone to Switzerland."

But they wouldn't have, of course. Pavel didn't like the Swiss very much. "Soulless people," he'd say. "Obsessed with money." Anastasia had always found them reasonable, polite, safety-minded. Their chocolate was absolutely heavenly.

"We'll manage, darling, you'll see." He kissed her hand and got up, and she knew the conversation was over, at least for now. In these precarious times, the future seemed impossible to predict, but they would face it together, and there was a comfort in that.

They were safe for a while, a year or so, though it was an eggshell sort of safety. There wasn't enough to distract one's mind from that kind of fragility. She found herself anxious, restless, missing her continental life and her fairy-fueled contentment.

Pavel was as busy as ever with social engagements, now that he was, at last, in the same country as his Golden Dawn society. Anastasia was almost tempted to attend some of their meetings, if only to give herself something to do. But by then, he had stopped inviting her, out of deference to years of her demonstrated lack of enthusiasm, and she wasn't quite sure how to bring it up.

Many women in London were joining the war effort. There was much to do, but she couldn't muster the inspiration. England didn't feel like her country; this didn't feel like her fight. Perhaps she simply wasn't a fighter.

For so many years Anastasia had been protected and insulated from the ugliness of the world, first by her family and then by her husband. Now that it was here, peering through her windows and edging towards her threshold, she wasn't quite sure how to process it. Ignoring it seemed much safer than letting it in. There were so many books, after all. London had the most delightful bookshops.

They weren't useless in this new country of theirs— Pavel was donating money to all the right causes. Who knew if it would prove to be enough? War was such an unpredictable beast.

"Well, you mustn't worry about safety anymore, *ma chérie*. Gerald and his friends are up seeing to it," he declared one day, interrupting her reading.

Anastasia looked up from her book. Pavel appeared to be positively bemused. She recognized the name he mentioned. Gerald Gardner, the man and his witches.

"And how exactly are they seeing to it?"

"Why, Operation Cone of Power, of course."

"Do tell," she urged, placing the bookmark between the pages of her book. She sensed a potentially more entertaining story ahead.

"Gerald and his witches gathered in the forest and projected all their energies towards a raised cone with the intention of conveying the message directly to Hitler's mind that he must not come here, must not set foot on English soil."

"How pagan of them. Were they nude and dancing in the moonlight while they did it?"

He laughed. "I wouldn't put it past them."

"And they believe it'll work?"

"They certainly do."

"And you?"

"Only time will tell, *ma chérie*," Pavel answered diplomatically. Over the years, he had proven himself to be profoundly unflappable when it came to her expressed cynicism. It was as if he had so much faith, so much confidence in his pursuits, that he didn't require outside approval or even agreement. She marveled at such strength of conviction.

THE BOMBINGS BEGAN soon after. The Blitz. Such a small word to describe death raining down from the skies. Hiding in the cellar made Anastasia feel claustrophobic, echoing some forgotten memories, perhaps some childhood trauma. She couldn't cope with it, and Anderson shelter didn't offer enough safety for her peace of mind. Pavel understood. He moved them to a quaint small village far enough from London to convince oneself the war was a thing too distant to matter.

Their temporary house was small, a cottage, really. All dark stone on the outside and dark wood on the inside. The ceiling beams were so low that Pavel constantly hit his head on them until he learned to duck at just the right moments or to traverse with a stoop. The walls barely offered enough space to display any art.

"To think," he said dreamily, "this place has been here for hundreds of years, housing family after family, and now we're here. These walls are a living history book, a testament to perseverance."

"These walls could do with some wallpaper," she joked back. "Most days, I think they intend to close in on us, like a living tomb. Something out of your beloved Mr. Poe."

Anastasia was reading darker books in these darker times, and the dour American Poe's works fit the bill perfectly. She was, at last, beginning to approach an understanding of the genre's appeal, though it wasn't anywhere near the level of her husband's passion for it.

Pavel still wrote, she knew. She thought of asking to read his next book. She felt well prepared for it. Reading nightmares had the ability to refine one's appreciation for the macabre. And there was a certain allure in being able to leave it all behind, ink on pages, and close the book, trapping the horror between its covers. Real life offered no such neat solutions.

ANASTASIA CHRISTENED THEIR new abode Dove Cottage, after the home of William and Dorothy Wordsworth, who spent years in a place she imagined to be very much like it, dedicated to "plain living, but high thinking."

The name amused Pavel.

"How English of you, darling," he said and from then on would only refer to the cottage as *golubyatnya*, using their native Russian's word for dovecote. It was a perfect fit for the mishmash of languages they spoke to each other.

In a way, their time in the cottage was one of the most intimate they had ever shared as a couple. There had simply never been such undistracted, focused togetherness before. Just the two of them, hiding away from the world. They came to genuinely enjoy each other's company—there were card games, book discussions, long walks in the countryside, pleasantly meandering conversations.

Funny thing, but she felt like she was finally getting to know her husband. After all these years.

They weren't strangers before, of course. They knew each other's quirks, foibles, and passions. But now, there was a more profound understanding forming between them. The whys beneath the surface were getting answered.

He was an apple to her before, and now he had become an onion—a fascinatingly multilayered soul.

She wondered what it was like for him. Was it the same? Was he discovering her complexity too? But how did one ask a thing like that? How did one measure how well they were known?

Occasionally, Pavel went to Golden Dawn meetings, now fewer and farther in between. He'd tell her of them, but only on an anecdotal level.

He did invite her along to visit Crowley at Torquay.

"You'll love it there, darling," he said, and she did.

Crowley still made her skin crawl, and his antipathy towards Yeats, now dead, and resentment of his old cohorts still reigned supreme. So much so that

Pavel, she noticed, carefully avoided mentioning The Golden Dawn altogether. The Great Beast knew how to hold a grudge, it seemed. He was visibly older and more worn out, embattled by the vicissitudes of life, infuriated by the continued financial strain, embittered by his offer of services being declined by the Naval Intelligence Division. The man raged on and on like a tired storm.

On the other hand, the seaside town of Torquay was bathed in peaceful quaintness. They stayed a week there, drinking in the sunshine. Anastasia thought she finally understood the appeal of small towns and told her husband so.

"I'll remember that," he promised, "for when we are old and tired."

"But darling, we are old and tired now," she jested.

"Speak for yourself," Pavel bantered back gamely, "I have the vigor of a man in his twenties." With that, he picked her up and twirled her like a bride on a cover of a romance novel. She rested her head against his broad chest to hear his strong heartbeat confirm his boasts. She felt so safe. It was impossible to think there was a war being waged somewhere not so far away.

We are living outside of real time, she thought. It was pure magic. If only it could last.

EVENTUALLY, THE BLITZ ended, and they left the Dove and returned to London. The city had been left in ruins. It was devastating to behold. Anastasia wouldn't even go outside; the damage was too visceral a reminder of the brutality ravaging the world at large.

Pavel was glad to be back. The real-life nightmares permeating the city fueled the nightmares his imagination spun and unleashed upon page after page of his future book. But for the sake of his wife and their screeching, traumatized parrot who had to have been a pacifist all along, given how much the war had unsettled him, Pavel took his family somewhere safe.

CHAPTER 10

AFTER

THE TYPEWRITER

SHE TOOK IT well at first, or so she thought. Too well. Uncharacteristically so. Displaying good graces that didn't come to her naturally or sometimes at all.

There was indeed something charming about the notion. If he were to become a writer now, if that was how he chose to embody the proverbial midlife crisis, well, she could live with it. She'd take it over the other clichés like sports cars and mistresses. She'd be supportive.

She gamely helped him set up the office, now referred to as the writing studio, and even tried to hear the musicality in the castaneting of the typewriter keys. She told her friends over cocktails about the next Great American Novel being conceived right under her very own roof.

And then the thrill began to ebb, as thrills are wont to do. The novelty wore off as time marched on, producing nothing to show by way of progress. The increasingly unkempt man occasionally making appearances in the kitchen for provisions, offering no updates, no attention, barely a conversation, became more and more difficult to think of as a writer and easier and easier to think of as a neglectful spouse. When she talked about him to her friends now, she couldn't keep the bitterness and sarcasm out of her tone and, though she tried to cover it up in jocularity, it never quite took. The next Great American Mediocrity, if ever it should be finished, was nowhere near as appealing to contemplate.

The dirty, haphazardly stacked dishes in the kitchen displayed evidence of his steadily declining diet. Sometimes he smelled, and she didn't know how to bring it up, not to the man who had won her over all those years ago partially due to his ever-present deliciously woodsy aroma. My lumberjack, she'd jokingly call him, though he had never felled a tree and would sooner hug it. Now, her husband had taken to wearing robes. One in particular, a dingy dark thing, oddly reminiscent of an orthodox monk's robe. The word phelonion popped into her mind, the years of being a dedicated cruciverbalist randomly paying off.

She had come to hate the sound of typing. It dragged nails across the chalkboard of her mind. It found ways to creep through her newly acquired protections of earplugs and earbuds. It haunted her waking days and uneasily lullabied her to sleep. The only thing worse than that was silence, for it was fraught with the weight of her husband's failure that the typing staved off. She hated knowing and hated not knowing and hated not being able to ask.

Most of all, she hated that typewriter. What a pretentious piece of junk. An outdated anachronism that provided the metronomic beat to their days. One stupid whimsical estate sale purchase and now this, an eternity of *this*. It didn't seem fair. Pushing the boundaries of appropriate daytime drinking ever south, she wished to rewind the time and undo it all. Undo seeing the estate sale notice, undo thinking it would be a nice couples thing to do—a fun way to spend a Saturday afternoon, undo ever walking into that creepy old place.

The state of the estate, she remembered joking as she looked around, just look at the state of the estate. It was lamentable indeed, the brutality of time made blatant in brick as if it were flesh. She could barely recall seeing the old lady who owned the place out and about. When she searched her memory, a small, stooped figure dressed in black came to mind. No one she'd ever recognize as the attractive, formidable woman in the portrait on the wall. The room it was in must have once been a great library, and the art was so lifelike that the woman's steely gaze seemingly followed her as she browsed.

Ultimately, she found the entire thing too morbid to enjoy—estate sales were nothing more than raking through the possessions of the dead—and wished for nothing to remember the experience by. But he was already in love with the dreaded machine, the future bane of her existence.

Admittedly, the typewriter had a nice look to it, seemingly exuding the same forbidding allure as its former owners. It was too large and heavy to be practical, with strange Cyrillic writing on the side, but perfectly user-friendly English alphabet on the keys. In the end, it proved too cheap and conveniently operational to offer a good reason not to buy and thus a purchase was made.

As far as she knew, her husband didn't even harbor any writing ambitions until then. Or maybe he always did, but he had the decency to indulge them quietly and clandestinely on his computer. At any rate, it was too late now. Even if he hadn't taken to locking the office—no, of course, the writing studio, the typewriter was simply too cumbersome for her to grab and lug away during one of his infrequent outings. She knew because she had tried.

There was nothing to do but wait. Wait out this whimsy. Wait for things to get back to normal. Wait for the machine to realize it was way past its working prime and quit. And so, she waited, with the rat-tat-tat of the keys punctuating her time like the ticking of the clock.

And then one day, there was a pause and a scream, too loud to ignore and too anguished for something minor like a stubbed toe. She rushed in, finding the door surprisingly unlocked.

"Look," he said, holding up his arm. Blood coursed down the length of it, a red ribbon spiraling the pale, hairy flesh and disappearing into the dark robe sleeve.

"I've cut myself."

"Yes, I can see that, but how?"

"On the typewriter somehow. One of the keys popped up, and there was something sharp. Not quite sure exactly what happened, but look how much blood."

She did look, and there was indeed so much of it, even on the typewriter itself. Making no attempt to clean it, he seemed oddly mesmerized by it—the act of something that belonged inside suddenly making such a striking appearance on the outside.

She led him to the bathroom, sat him down on the closed toilet lid, and took down their first aid kit. She cleaned and bandaged the wound, which turned out to be fairly small once it was plainly visible. She found herself enjoying this temporary interlude, not so much her brief return to the role of the caretaker, but the small genuine joy of being needed. They shared a short-lived amusement over the fizziness of the sanitizing agent. And then he thanked her and went back to his room. Soon after, the typing resumed.

She was enjoying her second "it was five o'clock somewhere" cocktail when he startled her by coming into the kitchen.

"It won't stop bleeding," he told her. "Look."

She looked. The bandages she had applied so carefully were soaked straight through, as was the robe's sleeve. The redness of it made her dizzy for a moment.

"I might need stitches," he said.

She reluctantly agreed, feeling the alcohol-infused mellowness slowly leave her veins. Since he didn't want to change, they left immediately.

The ER was busy. They waited. And then she waited by herself. She wrote information on the forms. There was more waiting. She tried watching TV, but everything on the news was too bleak and matched her mood too perfectly so she had to look away. She tried to think about what it all meant. All that blood.

Eventually, a kind and harried looking professional appeared, ending her wait. Her husband was all sewn up and recovering, she was informed. She went to see him—he was barely recognizable, as pallid as a vampire and small looking.

"Two blood transfusions," he said with something like a wistful disbelief. "They said they never seen nothing like it."

"You'll be all right now," she said, trying for a reassuring tone, inwardly cringing at his mangled grammar. Some writer he would make. She banished the unkind thought with another reassurance. "You'll be all right."

She was told he was to remain under observation for the night and then would be free to go. The beds were at a premium for people who were still bleeding. There wasn't much left of the night, and she opted to stay, settling into the tall, reasonably comfortable chair beside his bed and watching him ease into sedated slumber.

She must have dozed off, because she was awakened rudely by a shrill beeping. Somehow, his wound had reopened, and the bleeding had started again. They came rushing in, a swarm of white. She was ushered out. Shaky with adrenaline and exhaustion, she paced the corridors outside.

Eventually they came to her; their faces tired, bewildered, sorry. "Sorry," they said. "We couldn't save him. We did all we could. It was just one of those freak things."

"What was?" she asked feebly.

"It was like his blood was determined to leave his body," one of them said reluctantly, momentarily abandoning professional reserve. "There was no way to stop it; there was just no way."

AND JUST LIKE THAT, SHE was a widow. The official cause of death was exsanguination. There were more forms to sign. So many more forms. It seemed to her as if she had entered a strange twilight dimension where things were recognizable but different from her real life. She wasn't this person; she didn't wear black or plan funerals or accept condolences.

In all this time, she had avoided going into the office, though occasionally she thought she heard the typewriter rattle its bones in her direction. Sometimes plaintively, sometimes menacingly. Too tired for another sorry, too steeped in her own sorrow, she had disconnected her phone. In the ensuing quietude, the typing had increasingly become like a siren song, strange and irresistible. Until one day there was nothing to do but go to it.

The space was just as they left it. There was a trail of blood drops on the floor, all the way toward the desk. Presiding over the desk sat the dreaded machine. The blood on the keys seemed obscenely fresh. The eyes beneath it glowed with something like measured rage and mild amusement.

"You've kept us waiting," it said in a voice that sounded like sanity leaving.

She took a step forward. "I'm sorry," she said. "I'm sorry. I didn't think it would be like that. It was too ... I didn't mean it. Just wanted him to stop, just wanted ..."

"A deal is a deal," the voice cut in." We made a deal. You should have minded the wording. Somehow no one ever does. Do you know what that's like for a typewriter to endure such disrespect of words and their meanings? And you think yourself a grammarian," it added with something like a sneer or maybe a laugh. It was impossible to tell.

She swayed with fear, then steadied herself. There was nothing to be done now, a deal was indeed a deal.

"Sit down," the voice said, peremptory and terrible, and she found herself drifting, seemingly boneless, to the chair in front of the desk and lowering herself into it. "Now, let me tell you a story. I have so many."

She sighed and placed her fingers on the keys. The typing began.

CHAPTER 11

BEFORE

ICELAND WAS OFFICIALLY neutral during the war. It was also infinitely easier to get to than Switzerland, even if Pavel was willing to put up with the Swiss. The British were already occupying Reykjavik; the rest was only a matter of greasing the right palms.

It was a place unlike any other they had been to. So small, so isolated, so icebound. Being there felt like they had traveled back in time.

"I'm expecting the Vikings to pop up at any moment and raid us," Anastasia told Pavel.

"But we will be safe here, *ma chérie*," he said. "And it's only temporary."

The Icelanders were hostile to the British, but the Rostovs didn't really rate any local ire, only curiosity. They rented a cottage not dissimilar to the Dove in size, but very different in style, with plain clean lines and tall ceilings.

"At last, my head will be safe," Pavel remarked with delight.

"I would have gotten you a Viking helmet otherwise," Anastasia said, for her husband was as tall and solidly built as any Norse warrior and better than most.

"Viking, Viking," piped in Diego, always a quick learner.

She quickly learned of Pavel's ulterior motives. There was simply not enough space in their new home to successfully keep secrets. Besides, by then, they didn't hide much from each other anyway.

"Seiður, that's the magic they practiced locally during Viking times," he explained. "There were amazing powers concentrated here in those days. The sagas tell of the practitioners of Seiður entering altered states of consciousness and traveling to different dimensions. They believed their power was given to them by Gods themselves."

She found it curious; it was difficult to tell if they were following magic or it was following them. Perhaps it was simply everywhere, if you knew how to find it.

PAVEL'S STUDIES MOVED along slowly. A lifelong polyglot, he was unaccustomed to being encumbered by a language. It took a while to find a friendly translator, but eventually, one was located—a real bear of a man named, appropriately enough, Bjorn.

The friendly giant, once he made sure they were indeed not British, had introduced them to his entire family. By then, any company was a welcome thing, though Anastasia could never get used to the food. Later in life, she'd realize that their time in Iceland had permanently put her off seafood.

Appearance-wise, the Rostovs fit right in. Pavel with his size and his huge bushy beard and her with her ice-blue eyes. The local language proved nearly impossible to pick up. Even the prodigiously-talented Diego gave up, despite Bjorn's numerous failed attempts.

"Viking," Diego hurled at him in every language but Icelandic. "Bear." It amused everyone greatly. They had never seen a beautiful creature like him before and had certainly never met any bird of his conversational gifts. The feathered beast lapped up the attention.

"YOU'LL NEVER BELIEVE what I was able to find," Pavel said one day, brandishing something all but obscured in his giant hand.

Anastasia turned away from watching the evening snowstorm outside through the frosted window and looked closer at the object he was holding. "Ah, a drinking glass. Is it that time of the day? I *could* use some vodka to warm up."

"Oh, but it's no ordinary glass." He smiled in that clandestinely proud way of his.

She took the glass from him to examine it. It was plain as plain could be, but a closer examination revealed a small monogram on one side.

"HPB?" she asked.

"Indeed. Madame Blavatsky herself. She loved to monogram her things. And this was allegedly the very glass she used in her séances."

"To trick people, you mean?"

Pavel steepled his long fingers. "According to select individuals, maybe. But some of what she was able to do was genuinely difficult to explain. There have been mediums that passed the scrutiny of scientists and skeptics throughout history."

"But this woman, from what you've told me of her, she was ..." Anastasia made a vague gesture to imply a less-than-sound mind.

"Oh, she was a character, certainly. But what an interesting character at that. A walking study in contradictions. She had all these ideas, you know."

"Tell me," said Anastasia. The early darkness outside left her craving a good story. Books had been hard to come by lately, and she found herself rereading the ones she brought with her and tiring of always knowing the outcome.

"Well, it might have been that she had spent so much time in the East. It conflicted with her Orthodox Christian views too radically and created a strange and contrary system of beliefs."

"Such as?"

"Well, in her theosophy, for one thing, Blavatsky urged for egalitarianism and equality, but in real life, she espoused some vilely racist and antisemitic ideology."

"Ah." Anastasia curled her lip in distaste.

"But darling, you mustn't judge our compatriot too harshly. She was fun in her own way the few times we met. Not to everyone's taste, mind you—a rather coarse woman, very vulgar in her language, but you never knew what she'd come up with next. She had this one theory about the Atlanteans ..."

"The people of Atlantis?"

"The very same. It was just like something out of the pages of *Weird Stories*."

"And did you believe her? These things she said?"

Pavel shrugged noncommittally. "I appreciated her, her knowledge, her passion. She was absolutely obsessed with the Orient; it informed so much of her teachings and writings. And she had this strong monastic way about her. Another giant contradiction for this great, corpulent woman of many appetites who had never married, had a child, or even expressed interest in such things. Blavatsky was an indulgent ascetic, if you will. Just look at this cup—so plain and yet monogrammed."

Anastasia smiled. She didn't fail to notice that Pavel avoided answering her question. All along, she had been trying to gauge his system of beliefs, to learn how far apart their respective understandings of the world around them were. But her husband had been too clever, too diplomatic, too noncommittal in his answers to pin down, and she loathed to pry aggressively. Some things, after all, were best left to speculation.

"So where did you get this glass?" she asked instead.

"A follower of hers, a Finn, ended up here and found himself low on funds and eager to sell. A fortuitous situation for all involved."

"You meet the strangest people, darling."

"Oh, this guy is very strange indeed. He's convinced he's an Atlantean, a descendant. Claims he has found a way to access his repressed memories of Atlantis and will talk about it to anyone who'll listen."

"Of course, he is." She all but rolled her eyes. "You know, that sort of thing is only going to encourage the locals' distaste for foreigners."

"They just don't want to dilute their pure Viking blood." Pavel smiled. "Or so says Bjorn."

"Bjorn told me that his sister is pregnant with an English soldier's baby. He is worried that once the war ends, she'll leave with her soldier and never return."

"Ah, that'll do it. But doesn't he have several sisters?"

Anastasia laughed. "Yes, but that one is, allegedly, his favorite."

"Oh, the exigencies of war." Pavel sighed. "Poor Bjorn."

"Bear," chimed in Diego, with incongruously inappropriate cheer. "Viking. Viking bear."

"How are your studies progressing?" Anastasia asked Pavel one morning over Skyr, a concoction that took a long time to get used to and never quite satisfied her more traditional cravings.

"The more I learn, the more there is to learn," he said, setting aside the book he was reading. "I can't wait to share it all with the society once we get back to England."

"Is that where we're off to next?" Anastasia asked. It was the first time her husband had mentioned it. England made sense, of course, she simply wasn't thinking about it. She had been trying to live in the moment, in all the icebound moments of relative tranquility found in this strange land.

"Do you not wish to go back there?" Pavel asked, concerned. "Should I not have presumed?"

"Presume away, darling." She smiled. "Another year of this, and I'll swim there myself for a decent meal and some art."

"Icelanders must be proud," he joked. "It's no small task to make English food seem desirable by comparison."

They both used to make fun of British cuisine until the rationing put a cork in it. The food here had Russian or even German heaviness to it, but lacked the appropriate heartiness and flavor and, of course, there was no comparing it to French cuisine at all. The two were not only not on the same page, they weren't in the same book.

"I would murder for some chocolate," Anastasia said, wistfully.

"Ah. If only Führer's armies could be fought by people on a promise of good chocolate, the war would be over by now."

"You're getting funnier with age, dear husband." She smiled and blew him a kiss.

"There simply isn't enough competition these days," he countered with fake modesty.

"Chocolate," trilled Diego, never one to forgo a chance at the last word.

CHAPTER 12

BEFORE

A T LAST, THE war was over. The collective breath they'd been holding for years could be released at last. The world didn't end, after all. Like a boxer, bruised but unbroken, Europe was getting back up to its feet. And then, there it stood, a bit unsteady but proud, throwing a victorious fist into the air, poised for a new beginning.

The Rostovs sailed back to England as soon as they were able to, saying a heartfelt goodbye to Bjorn and his family and the island itself.

"One day, it'll be a wonderful little country all of its own, now that it has shed the shackles of Denmark," Pavel predicted.

"Funny, I thought all the best things about it were Dutch."

"You're such an imperialist," he teased. "The Icelanders have a terrific wealth of history and customs of their own to draw upon. You shall see, time will prove me right."

"Well, I trust you. After all, you did just spend all that time learning everything there was to know about them."

"If I could share it with you, *ma chérie*. If only you knew what can be made possible."

"All to what end?"

"I'm sorry, I ..."

"What is the ultimate goal for you, I wonder." Anastasia had never asked her husband this before, such a pragmatic question to such an esoteric quest.

He considered his answer carefully.

"I suppose I'm thinking about a form of immortality. Something more than this world. Something *beyond* this world."

"It sounds so ... tiring," she tried joking.

"Not to me," Pavel countered with certainty. "I'll never tire of this. I wish to see what's next and next and next. All the endless tomorrows."

"Well, I'm sure I'll be too tired of it all to join you on your journey of endless tomorrows."

"Oh no, darling. You say this now, but I'll change your mind," Pavel said with the great confidence that was so uniquely his. "We're too good together."

Anastasia smiled at her husband and reached over to take his hand. Of all his whims she indulged over the years, surely the romantic ones were the easiest.

LONDON WAS IN ruins. Still. Of course. Anastasia didn't know what she had expected and was devastated by what she found. Everywhere she looked, there were visceral signs of the ugliness of the recent years that she had, once again, largely managed to avoid.

A curious thought occurred to her—despite everything that had happened, Hitler never did set foot on the island.

"Your Mr. Gardner and his witches protected England, after all, it seems," she noted to Pavel.

"Indeed they did." He drummed his fingers on his desk in delight. "Somehow, I had forgotten all about that. But yes, all hail the Cone of Power. Gerald will be positively insufferable now. Probably going to start a religion or something."

Pavel was thrilled to be back, to have the opportunity to share his newly acquired knowledge and newly found objects with his fellow members of The Golden Dawn.

However unusual or odd his pursuits were, there was always a purpose to them. But what would she do now?

Art was unimaginable at a time like this. She was glad enough to have her collection survive this madness. Pavel might have disliked the Swiss, but he trusted them well enough to take care of their valuables. The most beautiful things Anastasia owned were kept safe in Switzerland this entire time. She hadn't seen them in years, though she dreamt about them sometimes. The splendidly mad colors of Kandinsky lent themselves especially well to dreaming it seemed. Anastasia couldn't wait to be reunited with her art. She wondered if her beloved portrait still held true to her visage.

But then, it was the other way around, wasn't it? She was the one who would eventually be left behind.

In London, time felt heavier somehow. Anastasia was in her thirties, and it seemed like a weighted-down decade, though physically, after years of disagreeable cuisine, she was lighter than ever.

She craved the mainland but feared the return. If London was in such shambles, what must the cities directly marred by the war on the ground—Berlin or Paris or Petrograd—be like? Leningrad, Anastasia knew it was Leningrad now and had been for years; she just couldn't bring herself to call it that.

It would be wise to give the continent time to rebuild. After all, what difference would a few short years make?

THE YEARS TURNED out to be long—these things were seldom predictable. The Londoners were indeed rebuilding, proudly. Anastasia was profoundly impressed by their indomitable spirit.

"It must be all the tea," she quipped, but the sentiment was sincere. She never thought of herself as someone tough and resilient but recognized and admired those qualities in others.

It wasn't clear if Pavel had any plans for leaving England at all. From the few things of his studies that they did discuss, she gleaned that he had been working steadily alongside others at The Golden Dawn on the astral projections and the next plane transfers.

She also gathered that her husband's loyalties remained split, and he continued to stay in touch with Crowley.

"Aleister isn't long for this world, and he's getting desperate," Pavel shared with her one night.

"He too wants immortality?"

"It's more complicated than that. He believes in reincarnation but wants to assure a swift transfer to an elevated soul."

It all sounded impossibly wooly.

"And why does he believe in this reincarnation?" she asked. "Does he have any proof?"

"Nastya, darling." Pavel sighed. "He is an old man. He's broke, tired, and reviled. He must believe he'll have his second chance."

Ah, *that* was easy enough to understand. Desperation fueled make-believe. Anastasia wondered if her husband's sympathy was of a deeply personal nature.

"Well, then, I hope Crowley makes it into an athletic body with a genius mind," she told Pavel. Privately she wasn't sure the old goat should have any more chances, considering the way he spent this one, but it just wasn't a thing to say.

ONE EVENING SOON after, Pavel came home looking pale and shaken.

"We're going to the continent, *ma chérie*. I've booked us on a lovely ship," he announced.

It felt sudden, but too thrilling to question. There was packing to do and plans to make and so much to look forward to. Anastasia wondered how many of her old acquaintances were still around. She knew with a heart-wrenching sorrow to rule out most, if not all, of the Jewish ones and the homosexual ones. So many bright lights had been extinguished, while a few lucky ones were able to flee to lands far away. She doubted any of them would ever come back.

Were they too foolhardy, Pavel and she, to imagine a fresh start might be possible for them in a place they had once left behind? How did one say no to the irresistible appeal of second chances, at any rate?

Only once they were aboard a ship, as lovely as Pavel had promised, did Anastasia finally ask about the abruptness of their departure.

Her husband chewed his lip before answering, uncharacteristically reticent.

"Something went wrong at Crowley's," he finally said.

"What happened?"

"He's dead, I'm afraid."

"Oh, darling." She enveloped him in his arms. "I'm so sorry. I know how much he meant to you."

Pavel rubbed his forehead. "It wasn't that he died. It was how he died. The transfer did not exactly go as planned, and, to a nonbeliever, his death might seem like something that had occurred under rather suspicious circumstances."

It reminded her of the plots of the mystery novels he used to read, before switching largely to horror. In fact, the situation mixed the two genres quite cleverly. What was it that Oscar Wilde said about life imitating art?

"It's probably nothing, but I thought some distance right now, in the interest of prudence, would be best."

Ah, prudence. Pavel and his prudence.

"I'm sure you're right," Anastasia said, kissing his cheek. So, she had Crowley to thank for finally getting them to leave London. Funny how things worked out sometimes. Either way, this was the right direction, she knew. She hoped.

CHAPTER 13

AFTER

THE MAGNIFYING GLASS

HAPPY WIFE, HAPPY life was Frank's personal motto. It was the thing that usually got him through the tedium of marriage, the unexpected and always slightly too-long visits from his mother-in-law, the occasional themed and—*somebody shoot him*—costumed parties, and these things, her passion, the endless estate sales.

Frank's wife perused the local estate sales with a piratical abandon in vain hopes of unearthing some treasure, but usually walked away with just more junk. Frank drew the line at one of those damn shopping excursions every month, and they both agreed on a spending budget. Once the parameters were established, he felt obligated to stick with them—he was just that kind of a guy.

Yet today, he was reconsidering his guiding aphorism, thinking how much happier he'd actually be right now in his favorite recliner, feet up, beer in hand,

ESPN or History Channel on TV than this ... this pointless trudging through a place too large for someone to comfortably live in. Judging by the state of things, it was obviously too large for someone to even maintain up to code. There were signs of neglect and years of relentless deterioration everywhere he looked: peeling wallpaper, curtains and carpets worn too thin, and dust. So much dust. In fact, the dust was the liveliest thing in this place, swirling all around in the rare beams of light reluctantly permitted inside by the dirty windows.

"Look at these curtains, aren't they lovely?" cooed his wife Mina. "Real brocade, I believe."

Frank looked. It was fabric. Some sort of fabric with what looked like a gold thread woven through. Was it brocade? He didn't know. It could have been something special back in the day. Now, like everything else in that house, it appeared to have surrendered whatever glamor and gloss it had once possessed to age. The curtains just hung there, looking sad and saggy, like the face of an old-time movie star who hadn't aged well. It reminded him of a documentary he once saw on that actress, what was her name? The gorgeous and really smart one, the one that had invented something to do with communication.

"Frank? Fraaaank. You're doing that thing again."

Mind-drift, he liked to call it. Checking out, was how Mina described it. Either way, not okay. Not what a happy wife needed.

"It's nice, honey," Frank said as noncommittally as possible. He didn't want these curtains in his house; didn't want any part of this house in his house. It was all decidedly creepy, like raking someone's grave. Wasn't that what they were doing here?

The old lady Koshmaroff had finally checked out for good. He knew of her casually, everyone in town did, the way all the villagers were once aware of their local witches. *The Cryptkeeper* was how he and some of the other guys on the force had jokingly referred to her, until the chief's "show some respect" put paid to that. No fun to be the boss, but the authority must be nice.

Frank's mind slowly drifted into another pleasant reverie of power and respectability, career advancements, and so on. He'd been a plainclothes detective for years now, his career plateauing after one single not-quite-by-the-books investigation. Internal Affairs didn't have enough to make a thing about but left a mark on his record all the same. He'd been paying for it ever since.

Frank's wife had drifted too, into another of the seemingly endless procession of rooms, each with their own dedicated purpose. How people lived back in the day, she marveled. No office-cum-guest room, den-cum-craft room multipurpose nonsense. Just awesome expenses of space for whatever you might want to do with it. Mina thought this house was a treasure. A real treasure. She couldn't believe the old woman had lived here by herself for so many years. There must have been no way for her to keep all of this up, and she didn't—one could tell from the general condition of the place. But beneath that patina of dust and neglect, Mina saw, plain as day, the original beauty and glamour. It was like something that belonged in her beloved old movies. Every girl dreamt of being a princess, of having a palace worthy of her royal stature. This house felt like a continuation of that childhood dream. Frank never understood this, but he was a good sport for coming anyway, and Mina knew he would grumblingly carry back home whatever treasure she uncovered here. Within their agreed budget, of course.

And yet, for all her dreamy fascination with this house, nothing quite stood out in that take-me-home way. Frank would never go for the curtains, she knew. It would have to be something small, maybe.

She looked around once more. The latest of the rooms she found herself in had to have been an office. The solid wood desk was nearly the size of their entire office/guest room at home and appeared to be sturdy enough to withstand an apocalyptic event. An old man she recognized as a fellow estate sale aficionado had walked out of here earlier with what looked like a fancy quill. Mina approached the desk, perused its contents, and immediately noticed the most remarkable of objects. Small and delicate, with a delightfully ornate handle, it was just what she was looking for. She checked the tag; it fit within her budget perfectly.

Frank was relieved when his wife finally said they could go home. Whatever she bought or didn't buy was apparently no larger than her purse could carry, and he was already dreaming of his trusty recliner.

"HAPPY BIRTHDAY TO you,
　　Happy Birthday to you,
　　Happy Birthday, dear Fraaank,
　　Happy Birthday to you."

Yep, all four lines. Like he was a kid. Ridiculous. But he could tell his wife went all out with the cake, and she had, thankfully, respected his wishes for a quiet, party-free, celebration this year, so Frank just smiled and blew out the candles.

"Thanks, honey, this is great."

"Wait till you taste it."

It tasted great too. Carrot cake had always been his favorite. Frank didn't have the sophisticated palate of a gourmand, and his wife knew that and obliged happily. The woman liked to cook, and Frank had to put in some serious time at the gym to fight against the plentiful, delicious calories, the middle-age spread, and the ever-slowing metabolism. Plus, the workouts helped his moods. A fair trade, all in all.

"I got you a present," Mina said, smiling at his enjoyment of the cake, and handed him a small, ornately wrapped flat box.

"Oh, hon, you didn't have to," Frank protested casually, but he knew his wife would never let a gift- giving opportunity waltz by. So, he courteously accepted this object she chose to mark his official descent into middle age, unwrapped it, and ...

"It's a magnifying glass," Mina chirped, as if to set a tone for the appropriate amount of enthusiasm.

"A magnifying glass," he repeated, thoughtfully.

"You'll be just all the TV detectives, finding clues, solving crimes. Like Sherlock."

Yeah, Sherlockian deducting powers would be just about the only thing to put Frank on a path to a promotion after all these years. As for the magnifying glass, there was no purpose to it in Frank's mind. He had his reading glasses for details— perfectly modern-looking and convenient. This thing looked like it belonged to a different age, when people actually took the time to craft something authentically. Before the mass seduction of the mass production. Where did she even ...

"I got it from that estate sale we went to last month," Mina said as if reading his mind. "Isn't it lovely? Look at all those tiny carvings. They just don't make things like that anymore."

Probably because they don't need things like that anymore, thought Frank. But remembering *happy wife, happy life*, he put on his most gracious expression, doused it with gratitude, and thanked his wife as sincerely as he could. The real gift came later, in the bedroom, in the form of new lingerie Mina wore to bed and, while it didn't bring with it any new moves, Frank, a huge fan of consistency in all things, fell asleep thoroughly satisfied.

THE CASE FRANK was working on was driving him crazy. And yet, he was convinced this was the one. The one that would get him out of this purgatorial career rut. The one that would finally pay off whatever imaginary debts he may have accrued with IA and leave him in the clear. The one that would give him his well-deserved promotion and a long-overdue raise.

The facts were as follows: the local man named Sidney Shaw, age forty-seven, was arrested for driving erratically and failing a breathalyzer test. It would have been an absolute nonentity even on a slow day except for the blood found in his backseat. And the fact that the blood was a perfect match for his missing wife, a forty-four-year-old Paula Shaw. Sidney claimed the blood must have gotten there when Paula had injured herself on a recent hike, and he had to rush her to the ER. This was supported by records. Sure, okay, good. But there was still no Paula. Sidney maintained that she had left him, that she had done it before and always came back. This was also his rationale for not reporting her missing sooner. A grown woman taking off like that wasn't an unheard-of thing. Except that something didn't quite add up.

And Frank was on to it. Sidney Shaw was too self-satisfied, too slick, a car salesman through and through. The man's expensively coiffed mane was suspiciously lacking grey. He sported a year-round tan. There was a certain oleaginous quality about him. Talking to him could feel like wrestling a particularly smug eel. But for all that, unlike a lot of scumbags Frank had arrested over the years, this one could afford a good lawyer. Unless some new evidence turned up, Sidney Shaw was set to walk.

"It's always the husband," said Marla, the station's front-desk maven, who alternatively terrorized and baked her way into the hearts of everyone working there. Marla was a thriller aficionado, and her opinions were based on extensive, albeit fictional, research.

"That's exactly the kind of prejudicial thinking this department needs to rid itself of," the chief stated, after grabbing one of Marla's gingerbread men. The cookies were decorated, made to look like they were wearing tiny blue police uniforms. You had to love it.

FRANK KNEW THERE had to be something else. Some overlooked clue or a tiny omission that would blow the case right up. Sidney was slick but not that smart, certainly not as smart as he thought himself to be. He had to have made a mistake.

Sidney was your typical local boy made good—with daddy's help. Sure, he went away to get himself a proper, fancy East Coast education, but he crawled right back here when Sidney Shaw Sr. told him to and took over his daddy's car lot empire. Shaw Sr. was now golfing himself to death somewhere in Florida, while Sidney prospered over his undeserved gains. He married the prettiest girl in town. Frank would know, he had dated Paula in high school, before she realized she wanted more; before he decided to try being all that he could be and gave his youth over to Uncle Sam.

By the time Frank came back, Paula was Mrs. Shaw and that was that. They saw each other around town, but there was nothing there. No smoldering glances. No telegraphing regret at each other with longing looks. They both had well and truly moved on. When he married Mina, that was it for him—a decision made for life.

Paula and Sidney had a set of twins, obnoxious college-bound teens well on their way to a comfortable life that their daddy's money would buy them. The Shaw cycle continued.

This wasn't personal. Frank was sure of it. Not after all these years. It could have been anyone other than Paula, and he would feel the same about the case. This was about justice. And so, he took the evidence folder with him, to study in his tiny makeshift office, in hopes that something in the photos of Shaw's house would yield a clue.

IT BECAME A ritual. Frank would sneak out after supper to his desk to study the photos until Mina came and dragged him away to watch whatever TV show they could agree on. He told himself he was just being thorough. It wasn't really an obsession.

One evening, Frank found himself digesting Mina's delicious meatloaf, while studying the images of Shaw's living room. The intense concentration was making his shoulders tense up. He leaned back in his chair, resting his head on his interlaced fingers, exhaled noisily, stretched, then returned to the photos. His right elbow brushed something, an object he barely palmed in time to prevent it from crashing onto the floor.

It was that magnifying glass Mina had gotten him for his birthday. Frank had all but forgotten about it. *Well, I can use all the help I can get*, he figured, picking up the magnifying glass and training it over the image from the opulently furnished Shaw house.

He felt a momentary sharpness; and then there was a drop of blood on his palm. *Mean little fucker*, thought Frank, wiping the blood on an old Post-it note.

The small magnifier was surprisingly potent, that much was clear from the start. Frank was immediately able to notice a number of minute details. None of them were incriminating though; unless garish taste could be considered a law violation. But wait, what was that? In a small-by-Shaw's-standards room designated as the library, Frank spied with his magnified eye something that didn't belong. Specifically, a trace of something sticking out from under the floor rug. How did it go unnoticed all this time?

Frank looked and looked at the triangle abutting a curved line, trying to make it out, until the word pentagram blinked into existence in his mind. He looked up pentagrams in the illustrated dictionary Mina had, and sure enough, the image fit. But then again, it might have been a great many things. He needed a closer look. Now.

"That magnifying glass you got me cut me to blood," he said to Mina in the kitchen.

"Aww, you're using it," she said, smiling, "I knew you'd like it."

That's what she heard out of what I said, Frank marveled.

"You don't care that your birthday gift has violently attacked your dearly beloved husband?"

She cocked her eyebrow at him. "Any mortal wounds?"

"Just my pride."

"Well, there you are then," she said, planting a kiss on his forehead. "Now go set the table."

AFTER TWO TOURS on foreign soil and two decades on the force, breaking and entering was no challenge at all. It was practically like walking in. People were much too trusting in a small town, even with all the home safety town hall lectures he'd had to do as part of the local police community outreach. Even rich people. Even people with something to hide.

The only thing Frank had to do was make sure Shaw was out of the house. There wasn't enough to justify another search warrant. Frank knew that, but he couldn't very well leave the only new trace of promising evidence he found alone.

He located the library quickly enough and took a look around. There were freshly dusted, uncreased spines of imposing volumes he'd bet his bottom dollar Sidney had never even read and a lavishly framed world map. Two leather chesterfields sat opposite each other, bookended by dark wood side tables with solid-looking reading lamps. The desk had been strategically placed by the window to get the best light. Nice. Very nice. Not so garish in person. No old futons doubling as guest beds in this office. *Fuck you, Sidney.*

The carpet featured an elaborate design Frank didn't quite know what to make of. It looked fancy, like something he'd seen at all the estate sales Mina had dragged him to over the years. He didn't notice the outline he'd espied in the photos, but those images were taken a while back. Sidney, recently released, entitled, and threatening to sue, would have had plenty of time to clean it up.

Frank had to move the chesterfields, which proved as heavy as they looked, to free the carpet. Only then did he roll it back to reveal the expanse of high-end wood floors. Clean. But was it, really? Frank reached into his pocket and got out his new trusty friend, the magnifying glass.

On hands and knees, he studied the floor for traces of something, anything ... And there it was, minute but definitely there. Chalk. Or some kind of powdery substance. Frank followed its curves and contours up close but realized he had to back up to take in the entire picture. He stood up, knees cracking, and from his new and improved perspective was able to finally see the grand design. It was, indeed, a pentagram. In fact, it was coming clear into focus now, and Frank was surprised he hadn't noticed it straight away.

He didn't recognize the images surrounding the outer circles. Nor the words. The alphabet appeared to be Cyrillic. Maybe. He reached for his phone to take pictures but found it unresponsive. Dead battery. Well, hell. But okay. Frank would have to make do. He never left the house without his notebook for this very reason. There was a pen tucked into the spiral binding of it.

Frank sat down and meticulously copied down the images. Satisfied, he put the notebook away and set to restore the place to its original condition. He exited the premises as stealthily as he had entered them. A quiet ghost on a mission.

"WHAT DO YOU mean you can't read this?" said Frank. "Ivan, what the fuck?"

He had been so sure his colleague would be able to help him out.

"I mean, I can't read this. I can't read Cyrillic alphabet. I'm from Finland. It's a completely different language. And fuck you for assuming any guy with an accent and a Slavic name is going to be your free translator."

"But your name ..." Frank felt like a fool and didn't like it.

"I was named after a Russian soldier who saved my grandparents during WWII, if you must know. And now, while I appreciate your sudden interest in my life's story, I have work to get back to."

Well, fuck a duck, thought Frank. It would have to be dictionaries from here on out, preferably ones with pictures. Unless he could look things up online. He resented the way Ivan had spoken to him but couldn't really blame the guy. The Shaw case was a wash, everyone had moved on, everyone but him, anyway.

FRANK WAS NEVER what one would call an early adapter of new technology. The internet was an interesting concept, but to him, there was still no better place for research than a good old-fashioned library.

It took an inordinately long time to translate the words and get some reference for the symbols. He spiraled all the way into research from Siberian shamanism to Russian cosmism. Rasputin, Blavatsky, Fyodorov. It was too much and not enough at the same time. But eventually, the thread did emerge—Frank was, after all, a good detective no matter what anyone thought. This case seemed to be about life everlasting, eternal life, fountains of youth, and all that nonsense. The promise of forever for the right sacrifice.

Is that what Shaw was after? Is that what he learned in his fancy ivy league school back East? It sounded like some secret society bullshit that only a vain man with too much money and time on his hands would pursue.

Frank had to find out. He was *determined* to find out. It wasn't the sort of thing he could bring up at work. Not unless he wanted to be laughed out of his job. Or committed. Much like in the army, much like in life, there were things you had to do as part of a team and then there were things you had to do alone.

BREAKING AND ENTERING the second time around was as easy as before, but now there was the added component of waiting. Frank was good at waiting. It was all about mind over matter and separating yourself from the constraints of time. He had gotten good at it during his first tour, when a buddy of his had taught him some tricks to steady and quiet his mind during the long recon missions.

This wasn't a dusty desert full of hostiles, either. This was pure luxury. Frank waited.

He had tried talking to Shaw on the up and up first, did everything by the book: showed up, flashed the badge, requested a follow-up interview. But by then, Shaw was too irate and too lawyered up to get through to. All that came out of the attempt was a brutal chastisement by the chief. Frank didn't need that on his record. He'd already been put on notice for some office politics bullshit. Ivan must have said something. Fucking Ivan.

Frank decided it was best to do things his way. Clean and simple. Just him and the guilty party.

By the time he heard the key turn in the lock, Frank's resolve was galvanized. His speed was dialed up to predatorial. Shaw and his gym muscles didn't stand a chance against the man who regularly beat punching bags into shreds in his local gym. Not a chance.

SIDNEY CAME TOO, blinking water out of his eyes.

"Welcome back, princess."

"What the ..."

Sidney didn't finish, but as he took notice of his duct-taped-to-the-chair situation and a gag hanging just below his chin, his expression rapidly shifted from confused to alarmed. The goose egg on his head sang nauseating lullabies. He stared at the man who had inflicted this injury upon him. Rage began to make its way to the surface, pushing through the fake tan.

"What the fuck is this, Frank?" he snarled. "I'll have your badge for this. I'll destroy your life for this."

"I don't want to have to gag you, Sidney," said Frank amiably. "It'll make the conversation one-sided, and I have questions to ask you. Just wanted to make sure you were in a position to realize the importance of this inquiry and answer me with the utmost sincerity."

Sidney made a sound of a restrained growl. And then started screaming, really loudly. Frank sighed and put the gag in, rougher than strictly necessary.

"Okay, that's disappointing, Sid, but hear me out. See, I think I'm onto you. I think I've discovered your dirty little secret. This is the case of a man who had it all but wanted one more thing—and figured out how to get it. You think I don't know you, but you forget, we were in school together. You were ahead of me by a couple of years, but I remember you—an arrogant prick, then and now. I remember the parties at your daddy's house. I remember the cops who'd show up for noise complaints and walk away bought off with your daddy's cash. I remember that stupid sports car you drove. I even remember the date rape allegation that Daddy Shaw made disappear. You always did have an eye for younger girls, didn't you? Seedy Sidney, I remember that. *You* remember that? Not a nice nickname, was it? I checked with Yale's records. Looks like you were a naughty boy there too. But your secret boy band society took care of that for you, didn't they? Skull and Bones— nice name. Real nice. Is that where you got your ideas from? A lot of Russians there same year as you, right? The sons of oligarchs getting their decorative diplomas, before taking over daddies' empires. Like you did, Sidney. Just like you did."

Frank paused and studied the man's face. There was mainly anger there as if Shaw was already planning his revenge for this violent intrusion into his cushy, orderly existence.

"I found the pentagram, Sid. You didn't erase it as good as you thought you did. There were traces of chalk. Traces of blood I bet too, somewhere there. Wasn't your life good enough? Did you need it to go on forever too? What'd you do, Sidney? What'd you do with her? Where's Paula? Was she so worthless? Your wife, mother of your children?"

At this, Sidney started making some noises. Frank removed his gag and stared expectantly.

"Is that what you think, you crazy fuck?" gasped Sidney. "You think I murdered my own wife in some ritual for what? Immortality? Are you this far gone, man? It's pure crazy sauce."

He paused for breath and went on, picking up steam, giving voice to his rage. "Can you hear yourself, Frank? Sure, yeah, I partied when I was younger, there were some girls. So fucking what? Who hasn't done that? It meant nothing then, and it means even less now. They were never that young. It would have been legal in England. Some of them just wanted my father's money. Everyone does. You do, don't you? Is that what this is all about? You've just been jealous all these years? Jealous that I got all this, and you got nothing? Jealous of me marrying Paula? Shit, she told me about you, man. Gotta hand it to her, my girl knew a loser when she saw one. A loser, Frank, that's what you are. Always have been. Always will be. How long have you been riding that desk at work? Or that shitty car of yours? You love your mailbox of a house? Your small stupid life? You think you're going to put this on me and finally be someone? Think again, man. Your ship has sailed. You were never even on it. After this is all over, I'll ruin what's left of your life. I promise you that."

At some point during Shaw's tirade, Frank started seeing red. Literally. Large red splotches overtook his vision, and Sidney had all but vanished behind them. Frank didn't even feel himself throwing the first punch. It was a roundhouse, with decades of pent-up frustration packed into his fist like a roll of quarters. Sidney's chair tipped backward, taking him with it; his head making a terrible thud as it hit the floor.

After that, there was more of the same. Frank had righted the chair for the optimal angle and let his fists do what his words could not—get the confession out of a suspect. It worked in the desert, why wouldn't it work now? People were the same everywhere. Liars. Liars all.

Frank didn't notice when Shaw stopped talking. And he didn't notice when Shaw stopped breathing. He only noticed when it became dark outside, and he realized that he suddenly felt so very tired.

There was a small tattoo that became visible on Shaw's chest as his shirt's buttons came undone during the beating. Frank cleaned the blood off it, then wiped his bloodied hands on his pants, got out his trusty magnifying glass, and studied the inked letters. It said *Live Forever*. To Frank, it was as good as a confession.

Sure, he still didn't know what Sidney did with his wife's body, but it had to have been somewhere around here. Maybe under the pentagram?

PAULA SHAW FOUND Frank ripping up the floorboards in her library. He was covered in blood and looked absolutely crazed. It was only afterward that she noticed her husband's body, duct-taped to the chair in the corner. She knew he was dead right away; no one could have taken that kind of a beating and lived. It didn't seem real, and she closed her eyes.

Paula meant to leave home, but she never meant to stay away for that long. She had done it before and came back within a fortnight, but it was different this time. The world had been weighing too heavily on her lately, making her need to disconnect stronger and stronger. And so, she hid away in the old off-grid cabin inherited from her grandfather for almost two months. No phones, no news, no calendars. The life she left behind was too smooth-running a machine to hit any glitches while operating without her, and she knew Sidney could take care of himself.

If anything, she reasoned that the separation would give him time to resolve the affair with his latest conquest. They were getting too old for lies and sneaking around. Paula didn't mind her husband's dalliances; she had become accustomed to them the way one did to any other spousal quirk. She knew, in all the ways that mattered, Sidney belonged to her. And she got him, his stupid jokes and his unresolved daddy issues and his insecurities masked by vanity and his ridiculous obsession with the band Oasis, right down to his one and only tattoo. He cried afterward, coming to her, looking for pity. "Try giving birth," she said, and that shut right up. Then he grinned and started singing the "Live Forever" song. Her fool. Her overgrown foolish boy. There was love there, between them, despite it all. Always.

And now he was dead, and her high school boyfriend was ripping up the floor of her house with her husband's blood on his hands. Frank didn't seem to notice her. He was talking to himself or maybe to the antique-looking magnifying glass he was holding in his hand. It was all strange mutterings. What little she could discern of it made no sense.

Paula slowly backed away and went to call the police. There was nothing more to be done.

CHAPTER 14

BEFORE

PAVEL, AS IT turned out, had nothing to worry about. One of Aleister's many associates with all the right connections had performed something of a magic act, albeit of a purely bureaucratic variety, and Crowley's death was ruled to have resulted from natural causes. No one cared enough to investigate further. The case was closed.

The Europe the Rostovs found upon their return was a scar tissue of a land. The ravages of war were everywhere, terrible and unignorable. Some rebuilding had commenced, but two short years were nowhere near long enough for any significant progress to show.

They didn't even try Berlin. They had seen the photos and the newsreels—the city had been all but obliterated. It wasn't a place to go. And it wasn't the place she missed the most, either.

Paris was in ruins too. That broke her heart. Anastasia remembered all her petty complaints about the city back in the day: the pretension, the music—she never quite learned to appreciate jazz—but now what she wouldn't give to have it all back, to magically erase the intervening years, reset the clock, and be surrounded by all that beauty once again.

They spent some time in Paris anyway, but it was much too depressing.

"Is it like this everywhere?" she whispered to Pavel one night. "Is there nowhere to go?"

It felt that way, but it wasn't true. The following week Pavel took them to Prague, the city that had defied the odds and remained proudly intact amid the ruins of Europe. Prague, a place that embodied the golden standard of a proper European city so perfectly that even Hitler had spared it. He had plans for it and had established The Protectorate of Bohemia and Moravia to ensure the city stayed safe.

The City of a Hundred Spires didn't come through the war completely unscathed. There was the Allied bombing, the occupation, the lean years of struggle. Still, compared to the rest of Europe, it was like the miraculously alive sole survivor of a plane crash, emerging from the wreckage with nary a scratch.

The Rostovs enjoyed their time in Prague, at last reunited with their Swiss-saved possessions. Pavel did some traveling and found a few more objects for his collection. The art market in postwar Europe had an insane, free-for-all, manic energy. It scared Anastasia but excited her husband.

"Look," he said, showing her his latest treasure.

"It's a magnifying glass."

"Oh, but not just any magnifying glass, ma chérie. This one is rumored to have been made with a very special lens. It belonged to Caravaggio himself, given to him by a wealthy patron of his, Francesco Del Monte. It is said Caravaggio used it to create the most magnificent minute details in his work."

Anastasia had always thought Caravaggio to be a dangerous madman. All that violence. All those severed heads. Her opinion of the artist had colored her view of his art, although it was, she'd admit if pressed, technically spectacular.

"Well, good for you." She smiled. "Now all the magnificent minute details are yours to see."

She felt like her husband needed his collecting more than ever. He had finally finished his book, but the idea of publishing a horror novel in postwar Europe seemed to be in bad taste. Now, there was a certain restlessness about him. His mysterious objects gave him something to focus on.

Anastasia found Prague magnificent, though her husband was convinced it was bound to fall to the Soviets at any moment. So much of their conversations revolved around politics now. It was unavoidable.

"They'll take over all these places, I'm afraid," he told her, his voice weighted down by the certainty of the struggles ahead. "Stalin will strongarm them all into submission. To the victor go the spoils. They'll be all too eager to split the spoils with the Americans and still take the lion's share."

"Stalin," Diego repeated.

"No, Diego, not that word," they said in unison, but alas, it was much too late.

"Great." Pavel laughed. "We've politicized the parrot. There will be no going back to Mother Russia now."

"Did you want to?" she asked. She, herself, had never entertained the idea seriously.

"No, *ma chérie*. It seems to me that our journey should take us forward not backward," he replied thoughtfully. "We've experienced Europe at its best and, now that the dance is over and the floor has collapsed, it's time to leave the party for good."

"So, then ..." Anastasia knew what was coming but wanted to hear him say it.

"On to The Brave New World," Pavel supplied obligingly, quoting Aldous' book title. What a spectacularly strange and frightening book that was. Perhaps not the most auspicious way to describe their new destination. He changed it.

"America," he said, simply.

CHAPTER 15

AFTER

THE CLOCK

M Y NAME IS *Adam McGregor. I am thirty-four years old. I work in accounting. Through a quirk of persistent genetics, I look exactly as Scottish as my name suggests, with reddish hair and a ruddy complexion, despite being barely on speaking terms with the sun and having never set foot in Scotland.*

I've never set foot anywhere really, never traveled, and now I won't even set foot outside my house. I have agoraphobia. It's an anxiety disorder, specifically—and here I quote, "fear of places and situations that might cause panic, helplessness, or embarrassment."

Actually, no, scratch that. I don't like that definition. It's too vague and impersonal, and the goal of me writing all this is to get up close and personal, as it were, so let's see ... OK, to me, agoraphobia is a fear of losing or surrendering control. Because that's what happens when you find yourself in an unfamiliar place or situation. And that's terrifying to me; that uncertainty is terrifying to me.

So, I avoid it. I stay where I'm comfortable, which is inside my home. Small and rather shabby, it may not be the nicest of homes. But for me, it's only the inside that matters, and on the inside, my place is pretty cozy and full of my favorite things: books, music, comics, movies, and my computer. The latter is crucial because otherwise you'd never know about me at all. But ever since I got online, I've been thinking about telling my story, and once I found out about LiveJournal ... Well, it was only a matter of time until I sat down to write it all out. This is my first post; I am officially a blogger now.

The reason for this blog is because I think I'm losing my mind, and I wanted to chronicle it, so that there would be a record of it. It all started ...

DELETE> DELETE>DELETE

What was I thinking? That's a terrible first post. Too personal. Too melodramatic. Not even that well written. No one's going to read that. To be honest, I don't know what I expect from all of this, don't know who reads these blogs people are creating. When I first came across LiveJournal, I was just so intrigued by the concept. It stuck in my mind like a nagging splinter, urging participation. To think that whatever I write can potentially be read by anyone in the world, that I can reach people I never would have otherwise, that my words can travel further than I ever have ...

But it's a strange exercise, isn't it? Almost like talking to myself, which I do anyway, because I spend so much time on my own.

I set up a page months ago, but what was I going to talk about then? There was nothing exciting about my life at that time, nothing out of the ordinary, nothing worth sharing. It is only the last couple of months that have been ... different. Alarmingly different.

I don't have anyone to tell in real life. In so much as my life is real, anyway. It often doesn't feel that way.

I wasn't always like this. Maybe that's how I should start the blog ...

I WASN'T ALWAYS like this. I was just *like you, like anyone out there. I left the house daily, went to work, to grocery stores, to movies. I had friends. They weren't close friends, the retrospect has demonstrated that amply, but still, they were someone to socialize with. There were other people in my life too: my parents and my brother. They lived close enough to visit, though seldom took advantage of it. The year I bought my house I decided to change that and invited everyone over for Thanksgiving. I even tried to cook. Well, I contemplated cooking before giving up the idea for dead and grabbing a catered meal. It went well, that celebration. Everyone seemed comfortable and happy and all that. No ugly bygones were dragged out into the light. My new house was a hit; the food was a hit.*

On the way back, my family had the world's worst jackpot of sharing the road with an overtired semi driver who was desperately trying to get home for the holidays. He wasn't even drunk, just exhausted and jumpy on caffeine supplements. There was a crash. And there were no survivors.

Afterward, I went through all the motions: signed papers, met with lawyers, made funeral arrangements. I was in a fog, but I was functional.

One week later, I had my first panic attack. I thought I was dying. I was told I wasn't, reassured by the experts and given mild sedatives.

The second panic attack came a week later. The one following that didn't even wait that long. The snowballs turned into an avalanche quickly enough. There didn't seem to be enough chemicals out there to help me cope with it all. I tried and tried. Some made me tired, some made me stupid, some made me sad.

Eventually, I recognized modern science's failure to help me manage my condition and proceeded to help myself through trigger elimination. Which is how I got to now.

I'm at peace within these walls, and I haven't set foot outside them in years. I believe that if I were to do so, I would probably die. Melodramatic? Maybe. But I am not willing to take the chance to find out.

Or rather, I haven't been willing to until recently. Now, it seems that staying inside might be just as dangerous. I think something in here may be trying to kill me.

I READ AND reread what I've just written. That's more like it. More dynamic. Someone out there is bound to read that. And if someone knows my secret then I won't be alone. I hit POST.

The wait descends like a heavy, smothering blanket.

IT's BEEN TWENTY-FOUR hours, and I haven't looked at my blog once since uploading my post. I'm having regrets. I'm thinking I've misused the platform. It's probably meant to be for angsty teens and not mentally disintegrating adults. I've been sitting here with curtains drawn and earplugs in, self-flagellating for what, in retrospect, seems like a stupid indulgence.

TODAY IS A good day. Tina's coming. If I was given to poetic reveries, I'd compare her to a beam of sunlight upon my gloomy soul or some such nonsense. If I were given to romantic notions and Tina was into guys, I suppose I'd be in love with her. But this is real life, and there are parameters and boundaries, and we must tread accordingly.

Technically, Tina is my carer. I prefer that term over caregiver, which makes me seem distinctly helpless. Once the state determined that my disability is indeed crippling, they've assigned me Tina. It is quite possibly the best thing the state has ever done for me. I don't qualify for financial disability assistance because I am still employed, albeit on a very part-time basis, working from home. My job is to help out with the overflow of accounting from Giotto's construction company, the place that has employed me pretty much right out of college and kept me on ever since. Whatever else the Giottos may be into, and yes, I've heard the rumors, they are loyal to their employees.

I also have the money from my parents' and brother's death, morbid as that sounds. So, I'm okay in that respect—my house is paid for, and my bills get taken care of.

Honestly, I didn't think I needed a carer until Tina showed up. Now I can't imagine my life without her. No, that isn't quite accurate. I can, but it's too bleak and sad, and I try not to think about it.

Tina is a sparkplug of a person, both in stature and temperament. Not bubbly, mind you, that would annoy the crap out of me. Just very ... dynamic. It's like there's a magnetic charge coming off her, and it draws you in and makes you want to partake in it, split those atoms, siphon that energy. Maybe I'm not explaining it right. I don't know. t's all a bit too ephemeral for me. My mind is more fact-based. Data and numbers, that's me.

Facts are as follows. Tina knows all my favorite movies and most of my favorite books. She can match me toe to toe in sarcasm. She sings along, terribly, to pop music, but her heart belongs to grunge, and she assures me it isn't merely due to her love of flannel. She bakes the best oatmeal raisin cookies. The. Best. She is the only person I've ever met who can kick my ass in *Jeopardy*.

Also, she is as lonely as I am. She doesn't have to say this—I know. Our small town is as restrictive to her as my house is to me. Both of our lives are circumscribed by limitations, self-imposed and otherwise. I think Tina and I are friends. I don't care if she is technically paid to be here.

"How's MY FAVORITE recluse today?" she says, cheerfully.

"Oh, you know, mostly same." I go to help her with the groceries, though, of course, by now she knows exactly where everything goes in my kitchen.

"Mostly?" She arches her right eyebrow. She's very good at it; I can't do it. My eyebrows are static lines that go up and down in tandem only.

"I ..." Should I tell her? Yeah, might as well. "I started a blog."

"Like online?"

"Like online."

"For everyone to read and comment?"

"I don't know if anyone is going to read and comment on mine."

"Oh, whassamatta, Adam? You don't think you've got what it takes to boggle the minds of strangers?"

"Your mockery wounds me. Is that any way for a caring carer to be?"

"If I didn't care, would I have brought you these?"

"I take it back." I reach for the cling-wrapped plate of cookies. They smell terrific. "You obviously do love me very much."

"Indeed, I do." She smiles. "It is only your flawed anatomy that prevents me from expressing my love in any form other than baked goods."

"And your faulty wiring."

"And *your* faulty wiring."

This is an ongoing joke with us, though not a happy one. On this, we agree. Our wirings are faulty. Not innately. There's nothing wrong with Tina being into women or me being ... well, me. It's merely wrong within the context of our surroundings. It just doesn't work here, in this town isn't big enough for diversity and is too fond of bland uniformity to appreciate anything else.

It's easier for me, I'd have the same or similar life in many other places. But Tina, I imagine, could really blossom away from here. I can picture her happy, amid the hustle and bustle of a large city, surrounded by all kinds of different, interesting people.

Small places breed small minds or maybe small minds breed small places, but in any case, Tina needs to go live somewhere that isn't so restrictively small in so many ways. We talk about it a lot, but in the end, this town, for all its shortcomings, is her comfort zone, and far be it from me, of all people, to push someone out of their comfort zone.

We sit at the kitchen table and eat cookies in companionable silence. I'm glad she brought milk. I've been out for days and craving it.

"So, tell me about this blog of yours," she prompts eventually.

"Oh, it's no big deal. Just some thoughts," Now that she's here, and it's broad daylight, and I'm having an actual conversation with an actual person, my blog does seem like nothing more than that. Just some stupid, irrelevant thoughts.

It's the strangest thing, this distance between then-me and now-me. Much like the way the morning sun dispels nightmares, my fears have been assuaged by good company, and I loath to bring them back.

"Just some thoughts," Tina repeats, thoughtfully. She narrows her eyes and taps her finger to her chin. "I don't think I believe you, Adam McGregor. You're one of those proverbial still waters."

If only she knew.

I try to change the subject. For a while, we talk about the latest batch of rental movies she has brought me. Then our conversation turns to books.

Tina's friend works for a major publishing house in the city, meaning Tina gets her hands on the best advanced copies, meaning I get the hand-me-downs. Currently, she is raving about *The Amazing Adventures of Kavalier and Clay*, saying that it may be one of the best books she's ever read.

"Will I like it?"

"Only if you have good taste."

She laughs and assures me I will love it. Says it'll play right into my love of comic books. I trust her taste implicitly. Well, almost implicitly. I still can't get into Don DeLillo. And I have tried and tried.

Eventually, Tina leaves. I know she always stays longer than she is paid to, and I appreciate it. But this is still her job, and jobs come with schedules.

Now, I'm all alone again. Fortified by company and cookies, I feel sane, comfortable, with maybe even a hint of confidence. I turn on my computer and log into my LiveJournal account. Maybe I'll just delete the stupid post and forget all about it.

Oh, crap. People have been reading it. There are comments too.

Mommasays   "Is this real or fiction?"

Tommygun   "Either way I'll read more."

JerryK5   "It reads like a desperate cry for attention unimaginatively ripped off from a cheap horror paperback."

ConnieWr   "Shame on you for making fun of a serious condition. My sister has agoraphobia, and it has ruined her life. And no, she doesn't blog about it for all the world to see. I bet this is just some stupid kid, trying to get a rise out of people."

KramerRulez   "Yur not wrong there, pal. Yu ARE losing yer sh*t."

Tommygun   "Get a life, KramerRulez. Or at least a working knowledge of English grammar and spelling."

Mommasays   "How has agoraphobia ruined your sister's life, ConnieWr?"

KramerRulez   "Fuck you, Tommygun. See, I can spel dat just fine."

Sylviel1   "I don't know about y'all, but I'm intrigued. Post again, FirstMan."

FirstMan   "Thanks for the comments, everyone. I have no way of assuring you of the veracity of my account, but I appreciate you taking the time to read it."

I am bewildered by the attention. Almost intimidated by it. I think about all these people. Are they real? They seem real, but you can never tell. Where are they? Who are they? Would they really believe me if I told them the entire thing?

Should I say more? Less? Delete the entire thing and try to forget about it? I want to. I would, but the sun is already setting, and I know enough of the night I'm in for to tremble in fear.

My fingers drum against my desk before settling on the computer keyboard.

SOMETIME INTO MY seclusion, I became obsessed with time. The concept of time. Especially the fleeting aspect of it. They say we are the only animals aware of our own mortality, but I think what they mean is that we are the only animals aware of time. After all, what is mortality but terrible awareness of the limitations of one's time, of the terminal trajectory of one's lifetime. You'd think it wouldn't matter so much to someone like me, someone who doesn't have a lot to live for or look forward to, and yet it does. It matters greatly.

    I think about all the things I haven't done, by choice or circumstance. All the things this stupid disorder has robbed me of. And I worry about not knowing how much time there is left to do them. How much time do I have left? How much time do you have left? Because you never know. One day you can be sitting down to eat with your family, and the next thing you know, you're burying them. My parents, and certainly my brother, were much too young to die. When they woke up that fateful Thanksgiving Day, they didn't know their lives were nearly at an end. That afternoon, at my house, they had no idea the meal they ate would be their last. I think about the weight of all the nevers: neverdones, neverbeens, nevertrieds—and it's crippling.

    The only thing that can lessen the heaviness is more time, but there's never enough of it to be found. Time keeps getting away from us. it's slipping through our fingers like sand through an hourglass. It is ticktocking away from us, every clockface a mocking scowl.

The life that supposedly flashes before our eyes during our last moments ... is it all regrets?

I want more time. I do. Selfishly. In hopes of having more to show for it someday. In hopes of minimizing regrets. In hopes of lightening the crushing bulk of the looming end. Am I alone in this?

There. A nice, noncommittal post. Personal but not beholden to the main plot's themes of spiraling madness. Let's see what my new internet readers will say about that.

JerryK5	"Oh, come on. What is this juvenile blather? FirstMan, you're not the first or the last on this amateurish soul-searching navel-gazing quest. You should outgrow it around the same time you start thinking of yourself as an adult."
Mommasays	"I found your words to be moving, FirstMan. Write more."
KramerRulez	"F*ck dis twat for weistin time bitchin about time."
TommyGun	"I see someone hasn't managed to get a dictionary yet."
KramerRulez	"I got a DICKtionary rite here for yu man."
TommyGun	"That's just sad."
Sylvie11	"Is this what's driving you crazy, FirstMan? I was kinda hoping for ... more."
NerdWord3	"Wait, Is this a suicide note?"
Mommasays	"Oh my, I hope not. You never know, though, these days."

MrSpocket   "Nut up and spill, FirstMan. Don't be scared."

I wish I wasn't, MrSpocket, whoever you are. I wish I *was* making this up. Everything would be so much easier.

For supper, I eat more cookies. I can almost hear Tina berating my poor diet, so I supplement my meal with an apple. It's a Red Delicious that lives up to its name perfectly. If only life worked like that.

It's full dark outside now. I wish I could see the stars. If only my place had a skylight. I turn on the lamp in my bedroom and try to settle in with my latest Tina-recommended book. It's good, but my attention wavers. My guts are coiled tighter than a contortionist inside a suitcase. I know it's about to begin, and—tick tock, tick tock—there it is. The maddening sound is coming loud and clear straight through my earplugs.

I dig the foam orange puffs out of my ears. Useless. Tick tock. Tick tock. It won't stop, gearing up to ring out, tearing clear across the already fragile fabric of my psyche.

I'm haunted by a clock.

And there, I have the opening sentence of my next post.

I'm haunted by a clock. But let me hit reverse and go into the backstory for you.

Two months ago, on my birthday, my friend Tina gave me a clock. It was a small, old-looking thing. She told me she got it at the estate sale she went to. Said she saw it and it made her think of me. Presumably because of my obsession with time. I didn't like it but thanked her anyway for the thoughtful gift and put it on my desk in a manner that resembled a display of gratitude. Because that's what you do, right? It's the polite thing to do. After that, I gave it no second thought. It became just another addition to all the debris one inevitably accumulated in life.

The surprising thing about it was that the clock actually worked. Kind of. It maintained accurate time but only occasionally. Every so often, I'd glance at it, and it would either be right on the money or wildly off. It ticked loudly, sure, but not insanely so. It was tolerable. Ignorable, even.

I never tinkered with the clock. I didn't care enough. Until the day it woke me up.

Confused, I glanced over at my nightstand. "2:33 a.m.," read the bright neon display of the digital clock there—the one I trusted, the properly-working one. At first, I didn't realize what the sound was, but eventually I traced it to the culprit—my weird birthday gift.

It didn't have the shrill quality of the typical alarm. Nothing as simple as that. Instead, there was a musicality to it, albeit a strangely atonal one. Either way, it wasn't something I wanted to hear at 2:33 a.m. Or ever, for that matter. Until then, I didn't even know the clock had an alarm feature. Now I had to find and disable it. Less than gracefully, with limbs heavy with sleep, I slapped at the clock, hoping to hit the snooze button. It must have worked, because the noise stopped. I went back to sleep. Case closed.

Or so I thought.

The noise returned the following night. I managed to shut it off again, but in the morning, I took the time to seriously inspect the auditory offender. Frustratingly, I couldn't find the power source. It had to be a battery-operated thing, but there was no place to put the batteries. The rear part of the clock was damaged as if by fire, and it was entirely possible that the battery flap had fused itself to the back panel.

It was plain, such a plain object. I didn't know the proper names for any of its parts, though oddly enough the word for a clock expert popped to mind: horologist. I like words that sound like they mean something else; in this instance, maybe a horror fan, like me.

There was a small winding knob sticking out of the side. The brand of the clock, featured under the twelfth numeral, was too faded to make out. Lost to time. It sounded like irony to me. There was writing on the body of the clock too, but it appeared to have also sustained fire damage, rendering it illegible.

All in all, it was a weird thing and certainly a weird gift to give someone. Last year, Tina gave me a cactus, a nice and normal sort of present. The year before, it was a paperweight replica of an antique gun.

If there's a rhyme and reason to her gift-giving, I am yet to discern it.

Anyway, two rude awakenings were about my threshold for

politeness. I took the clock to the spare bedroom and left it there, in a nightstand drawer. I'd love to say that was the end of it. That I forgot all about it and lived happily ever after. But then, of course, I wouldn't be here, telling you all this.

The comments don't take too long to show up this time.

JerryK5   "Oh oh, someone's afraid of the big scary clock. Boohoo. Pathetic, really. But at least the writing's improving. Though if you're going to go down that road, J.M. Barrie has already utilized the tick tock thing in fiction. Superiorly, I might add."

Sylvie11   "FirstMan, have you looked into the possibility of audio hallucinations? They can be brought on by lack of sleep, depression, a variety of mental disorders, really."

KramerRulez   "Yea, dis dude is Krazy for sho."

NerdWord3   "Well, if this was ever meant to be a suicide note, at least it's a creative one."

Mommasays   "I once stayed in the country with some friends for a month, and every morning I'd wake up to a deafening cock-a-doodle-doo. Later I found out there were never any roosters on the property."

KramerRulez   "I got a cock for yu rite here, momma."

TommyGun   "No way to ban this idiot, is there? I'm talking about KramerRulez, not the original poster."

MrSpocket   "I'm actually intrigued by where this story is going."

JerryK5   "Sure. Watching people mentally disintegrate is at least as compelling as a slow-motion train wreck. It stands to mention, though, how wildly derivative this is. From the aforementioned Barrie to Poe. Would some originality really be that much to ask for?"

Starkstork   "I don't know about you, guys, but I'm kinda into this. Though I'm sure it's all a total load of horseshit."

Sylvie11   "So what happened next?"

I'M BLOWING UP in popularity. Becoming a known entity for a few select strangers I'll never get to meet. What a strange world we live in. I'm contemplating this over toast and eggs, which is one of my four signature dishes. The other ones are beans and toast, mac and cheese, and tuna casserole. Tina's always on my case about improving my diet, so sometimes, to appease her, I throw in some vegetables at random, whatever's available. My culinary skills have no one to impress. I do take vitamins, though. Lots of them. It's my own personal stab at immortality.

It's been raining since I woke up, the kind of steady dreary downpour that makes you forget all colors but grey. Tina comes and complains about the weather, albeit halfheartedly. She's in too good of a mood to do it properly. Tonight, she and Amy are going to the movies. Nothing will come of it, of course, the same way nothing has ever come out of Tina's obsessive doting on Amy over the past few years, but who I am to question true love in whatever sad form it takes. Tina loves Amy. Amy loves Tina ... as a friend. There's a crucial difference there. I want more for Tina. Tina's great. Amy's kind of an idiot, from what I've heard, seen in photos, and put together from conversations. Amy dresses like it's the seventies and parties like it's the eighties. In a perfect world, she would have been swept up by some cult or a commune by now, and Tina would have found someone who can love her the right way.

We don't live in a perfect world.

"Do you miss the rain on your skin?" It's a game we play, amusing ourselves with Q&A.

"Nope. Never really liked the rain."

"Do you miss the sand between your toes?"

"I prefer shag carpet fibers."

"What do you miss the most?"

The answer to that for me is almost invariably, "The stars." The awe-inspiring celestial blanket of the night sky. Tina knows this, but neither of us minds repetition. After all, my repertoire is pretty limited.

"Would installing a skylight really cost that much?" she asks, but we both know the truth.

Yes. No. Enough, for sure. I can afford it, but I'm choosing not to. Something like that requires construction workers, plans, interactions. Too many variables. Too many unpredictable factors. Too much triggering potential.

We watch prerecorded *Jeopardy*. We talk books. We even talk Amy.

Amy's latest obsession is apparently ley lines. I read something about that in a horror book once. To me it's fiction, but to that anachronistic hippie, it's a real thing. According to her, our town lies at a very auspicious intersection of them.

"You don't really buy into that, do you?"

"I believe she believes it."

"That's an interesting equivocation, Tina."

"That's a very long word, Adam."

We can do this for hours.

"You can meet someone online, you know," I try. "There are all sorts of communities for that now. People are blogging and talking to each other."

"But Adam, they are not like ..."

"Not like what?"

"Not real."

"Of course, they are real, as real as you and me." I almost say how much I mean it and tell her about all the people who read and comment on my blog, but I don't. I don't think I should. I don't know if she'll get it. Tina doesn't care for internet socializing of any kind.

"They are just made-up personas and opinions. Nothing good can come out of that much anonymity. It's like granting people permission to be their worst selves."

I frown, mock-ruefully. "And here I was kind of thinking it's the way of the future."

"Well, I don't want any part of that future," she says adamantly. And then softens it by adding, "It just isn't right for me."

Meaning for others, like friendless weirdos who don't leave their house, it might be just the ticket.

Oh Tina, if you only knew how right you are.

I find myself wanting for her visit to end, so I can return online and tell more of my story and exorcise my demons through words. Then I kick myself inwardly for thinking that. Maybe Tina is right. Maybe the blog is messing with my perception of what's real and what isn't. Tina is real. She cares. She is literally a carer.

Besides, what will I do once it's over and my story is out there? Will any of these commenters be able to help me? No, I don't really expect that. I don't know what to expect. I just feel compelled to let it all out. I've been holding on to it for so long.

The moment I'm alone, I rush to my computer and turn it on.

THE BANISHMENT DIDN'T work. The alarm sound seemed to get louder and louder. I would lie awake in my bed, listening to it, thinking about how it sounded kind of like chanting. But then again, things do sound strange in the middle of the night—the perfect quiet distorts the sound.

I let it go for a week, strangely reluctant to take things further than simply shutting the sound off each time. But eventually one of us had to go. I chose the clock. I would just have to come up with a perfect lie if Tina ever asked about it.

I got the hammer out, spread a towel across my kitchen table, set the clock on it, and paused to take a deep breath. Then I hit it. The clock made a strange sound, not what you'd expect from metal meeting metal aggressively, more along the lines of a plaintive cry. And no, I'm not trying to deliberately anthropomorphize it. That's just what it sounded like.

I hit the clock again. This time I did manage to inflict some proper damage—a sharp shard of it came off and bit into my arm. I hit it again, angry now, in the way that seeing your own blood makes you angry, and got stabbed with another shard for my efforts.

Another hit, and then, I paused and looked. The damn thing wasn't impervious to my attacks. The clock was definitely showing the signs of inflicted damage, but it seemed to be assimilating into the general ruinous state of the thing, much like a boxer absorbing new blows.

I wasn't sure what to do. Burning the clock seemed like a natural solution, but I didn't have a fireplace and wasn't about to go outside to do *it. Besides, I was convinced the end result would be somewhat Dali-esque at best—melty but far from a total destruction.*

It occurred to me that I could somehow hide the clock in the trash and wait for Tina to take it out. But what if she somehow saw it? How would I explain it?

So, I did the only thing possible. I opened the window and lobbed the worst birthday present ever outside as hard as I could. The action proved only mildly triggering, and seemed like a good permanent solution. I paced to ease my panicked breathing until I noticed that the wounds inflicted by the clock shards were bleeding. Then the survival instinct took over, and I went to grab my first aid kit and tend to them. The clock saga was over. Or so I thought.

Starkstork   "OOOH, this is getting good."

JerryK5   "Still sounds trite as ever to me. FirstMan seems to have never met a cliché he didn't like."

Starkstock   "So whatcha reading this for then?"

JerryK5   "I actually don't have a rational explanation for you, Starkstork. There's some social psychology behind such attractions, but it doesn't seem worth it to rake my brain for the correct terminology."

KramerRulez   "Yu sound pretenchious as fuck, Jer."

JerryK5   "Will the wonders never cease? Just look at that, everyone. KramerRulez used a polysyllabic. Almost spelled it right too."

TommyGun   "Ha, I was just going to say the same thing, JerryK5. You beat me to it."

KramerRulez   "Ye, I bet yu beat each othe off, yu stupit fucks."

TommyGun   "And he's back to form."

Mommasays   "Can we talk about the blog some, y'all?"

NerdWord3   "I'm kinda waiting for the author to spring a *gotcha* on us all."

MrSpocket   "I'd be down for that. A good prank, if drawn out."

Sylvie11   "Sure, yeah. But like what if it's true?"

FirstMan   "Thank you for your comments. And for taking your time to read my posts. There isn't much more left to say."

JerryK5   "Ooh. Ominous."

NerdWord3   "Go on ..."

And thus, encouraged, I continue.

THE CLOCK WOKE me at 2:33 the next night. And the night after that. Always at the same time. Now that it was outside, I had no way of silencing it. I thought I had thrown it far enough away, but it sounded so close. And closer still each time. It wasn't possible. But then again, nothing about this should have been possible.

I thought one of my neighbors would hear it too. And upon hearing it, come out, find its source, and destroy it. But no. Nothing. Nada. It was as if the clock played its haunted serenade for my ears only.

The person who eventually found it was Tina. She brought it back inside. There was a puzzled look on her face.

"If you didn't like my present," she said, "you could have said something."

But of course, I couldn't have. Not to my only friend. Not while I was trying to be, or at least trying to pass for, a reasonably sane person and not a clock-out-the-window-lobbing lunatic. This was exactly what I was trying to avoid. Now, it seemed, I should have gone with the hiding-it-in-the-trash option.

"Adam," Tina prompted.

"It kept ringing," I blurted out. "Waking me up in the middle of the night. And I couldn't figure out a way to shut it off."

She looked at the offending object, turning it over in her hands. In the light of day, it appeared perfectly innocent. Innocuous. And abused.

"I don't even think it has an alarm feature," Tina said, studying the back panel.

I just shook my head. What could I say?

"Adam, how long has this been going on?"

Aha, I was afraid of that too—the professional concern notes creeping into her voice. Friend or not, Tina was a pro through and through and could section me if she decided it was the best course of action.

"You know what?" I pivoted. "It's nothing, really. It's for this story I'm working on. A writing project."

"Oh?"

Hearing the skepticism in her voice, I doubled down.

"It's this thing I'm doing. The blog. I mean, I'm posting it online like a real blog, but it's meant to be hyperrealism. With horror elements. Think Blair Witch Project."

That movie seriously freaked me out. Tina insisted I watch the rental after dark, and she was right. The nightmares alone ...

I couldn't tell if she's buying it or not. So, I took her to my computer and showed her. I was so freaking glad right then that I hadn't written much about her in my blog posts. Nothing personal, anyway.

Tina took her time reading them. She read the comments too. I couldn't tell what she's thinking; her body language was all wrong. Finally, she turned to me.

"So you threw the clock outside for verisimilitude?"

"Yep."

She pursed her lips and studied me. "I don't know what to think," she said after a while.

"I know, I know, it's pretty weird," I rushed in with reassurances.

"But I just wanted to do something creative, and I really do believe this to be the medium of the future, and it just seemed like such an interesting opportunity ..."

"All those people" Tina shook her head. "They are all thinking it's real."

"It doesn't matter, though," I interjected quickly. "You said so yourself. They are not real. None of this is real. It's all one wild existential experiment."

(Apologies to all of you, readers, but needs must and all that.)

"So, just so we're clear here, you are not actually hearing chant-like sounds coming out of this clock every night at 2:33 a.m.?"

"Absolutely categorically not," I lied bald-facedly. I wasn't even that ashamed—I was too relieved to feel ashamed. One Tina-shaped bullet dodged. Whew.

"So then you don't mind having this clock back in your bedroom?" she asked.

"I do, I do, I mind very much," I was screaming on the inside, but what could I say to her then but, "Of course, not."

And thus, the nightmare clock returned to my nightstand.

JerryK5	"I must say, this is turning meta in the most interesting way. Kudos to the author. Continue, please."
Mommasays	"I don't know what to think right now."
Starkstork	"Me too. But I'm intrigued, for sure."
KramerRulez	"Dis dude be fuckin wich y'all and y'all ar eating it up."
TommyGun	"An interesting, if lamentably expressed, thought from KramerRulez, for once."
KramerRulez	"Eat my shorts, Tommy. How's dat for yu? N ineresting thouht?"
TommyGun	"Oh boy."

Sylvie11   "It kind of does have that Blair Witch thing going for it."

KramerRulez "Dat movie was da bom."

NerdWord3   "I don't know about everyone, but I'm waiting for another twist."

One last time, I oblige my audience. The typing sounds almost soothing.

THE CLOCK HAS rung every night since. The sound pierces straight through earplugs and headphones. It refuses to be absorbed or even dampened by piles of dirty laundry and couch cushions and can be heard loudly and clearly from every place in the house: kitchen, bathroom, closets, drawers. It has rung after being placed into a pot full of boiling water and after being immersed in a bucket of ice. It has rung from the attic and the basement. Every night. At exactly 2:33 a.m.

Are you familiar with the deleterious effects of sleep deprivation? I have become an expert on the subject. My naturally ruddy complexion makes me appear more awake and robust than I feel, but I've been consistently worried that Tina might catch on. Consequently, I have become an Oscar-worthy actor, performing the part of Normal Adam every time she showed up.

And now, I am exhausted. Above all, I am just so very exhausted.

I know what the clock wants. It wants to be buried. Laid to rest properly. I don't know how I know this; I just do. And for that, I must go outside.

I have been trying. My goal has been to inch further and further out each day until I can get into my backyard. But it's been hard. So hard. Almost every attempt finds me curled into a ball, hyperventilating.

I've been reading up on exposure therapy, which is technically what I'm doing. But reading about it is one thing—in practice, it's brutal.

Tonight is the night, though. I'm going to do it. Whatever it takes. I will bury it as it rings. At 2:33 a.m. Even if it kills me.

I HIT POST, close out of LiveJournal, and shut down my computer. I don't want to know what the comments will say. I don't care. I'm tired and scared, but above all, determined. I have the shovel; I have the clock. All that's left is to open the door and walk through it.

My feet feel like they weigh a ton each. Lifting them and taking small steps takes a monumental amount of effort. My heart is pounding like an ancient ritual drum. I can hear my own blood swooshing in my ears, obscuring the sounds of the night.

For the first time in so long, I'm outside, but there isn't enough air. I can't get enough air in me. I'm suffocating. I'm weightless and I'm about to float away. I'm as heavy as a boulder, unable to move another inch. I am eternal, a faulty accumulation of star matter on a journey through space. I am mortal, an insignificant speck of dust blowing on the indifferent winds. I am nothing, and I must walk. And so, I force myself, though it feels like my mind and my body are shutting down on me. One step after another, until I'm standing in my backyard in a location that feels right,

Setting the clock on the ground, I begin to shovel. I can't feel my hands. I can't feel my arms. My synapses are misfiring. Electric connections are fizzling out. But I don't stop.

The clock rings. Chants. It sings its terrible song one last time as I put it into earth and shovel dirt over it. And then, at last, I am gifted with a beautiful silence

I collapse on the ground. I'm done. I did it. And there, above me, is my reward. The stars. There are seemingly billions of them, not just the several thousand one can see with a naked eye. Billions of stars have been weaved into the night sky tapestry for me to behold. At last, I can see them again.

That's how Tina finds me. I guess she must have read my blog, after all, and decided I'm not that good of a liar. Tina is angry and relieved; she's laughing and crying and calling me an idiot. She can't believe I'm outside. She's worried I might have had a minor cardiac event. It doesn't matter, though. Not now that it's quiet. I lie there in her arms. And I never take my eyes off the stars.

JerryK5   "I'm guessing this was all FirstMan had to say. No twist, after all, looks like."

NerdWord3   "Yeah, a major disappointment."

KramerRulez "Fuk dis guy, yo."

TommyGun   "I agree, this didn't really go anywhere."

Starkstork   "Maybe it's meant to be left unfinished so that we can imagine our own ending?"

Mommasays   "I hope FirstMan is okay."

JerryK5   "OK and laughing at our expense, I'm sure."

NerdWord3   "We the Gullible."

MrSpocket   "Actually, I think I hear a clock alarm going off."

KramerRulez "For realz?"

TommyGun   "Very funny."

Sylvie11   "But pretty unsettling, overall, don't you think?
             This entire story. I don't know where this guy is from, but
             there was an estate sale here not too long ago with some
             pretty creepy old objects."

NerdWord3   "Hope you didn't buy any, Sylvie."

MrSpocket   "Sylvie ... ?"

CHAPTER 16

BEFORE

THE JOURNEY FELT long, the waters rough. Anastasia couldn't sleep.

"Tell me a story," she asked her husband. It was midnight or thereabout. They were the only people on the deck, the only people in the world it seemed. The waves softly moved below, and the stars glittered above. It was the kind of night that made people believe in magic.

Pavel thought about it for a moment, stroking his beard. She was almost used to the damn thing by now.

"One time, when I was a child, my father took me to see the Thurston and Kellar show. It was the most incredible thing. The first time I encountered magic. Of course, I later learned that it was all trickery, smoke and mirrors, but at the time I was mesmerized. They had this trick where a woman appeared to be floating mid-air with no visible means of support. "The Levitation of Princess Karnac." I've seen it since, I've watched Carter the Great, another magician, perform it. But it's never the same as that first time when you behold it as a child. When your imagination knows no earthly bounds. It made me feel ..."

He paused, and Anastasia didn't want to rush him. It was thrilling just to hear him speak of it, for he almost never talked about his childhood. Over the years, she had gathered bits and pieces of information. Her husband's family had seen more than its share of tragedy, with death as their steadfast companion. First, Pavel's father, who never even got to see his sons reach adulthood. Then, Pavel's beloved younger brother, who had followed some strangely potent patriotic instinct and was shot down in France during the First World War. His mother died soon after of a broken heart. Pavel was the only one left.

Anastasia knew that technically her husband was a count, but he never seemed to use his title. When they first met, Russia was full of princes and counts. The political climate of the time had made the titles first unpopular and then downright dangerous. Thus, like lavish estates and caste labor systems, most were abandoned to the past.

Pavel reached out and took her hand, bringing her closer.

"It made me feel like anything was possible," he continued his story wistfully. "Like there were extraordinary forces in this world that could do anything once mastered. Thurston and Kellar, they made objects disappear and reappear seemingly at will: lamps, coins, cards. And being only a child, I thought that the objects themselves were magic. For many years now, I've had this notion of magic objects and all the things they could do, if only one could find them and figure out how to work them."

"And now you've … mastered it?" she pried ever so lightly.

"And now I try," he replied modestly.

"And what if you're wrong?"

"Ah, *ma chérie*," Pavel countered with a smile. "But the real question is what if I'm right?"

THE NEXT DAY the sky was red.

"Not a good sign," Pavel observed grimly.

It was obviously a cause for concern, although here in first class, the crew of the ship had made every effort not to worry their passengers unduly.

The storm came on suddenly. The sky turned black, stealing away the daylight, and the waves grew giant, crashing all around them with a menacing roar. In all their travels, Anastasia had never seen anything like it—this grand display of an indifferent and deadly power. It made one feel devastatingly small. Fear pierced her heart like an icepick and tore straight down to the pit of her stomach.

The waves pushed in closer, like curious and hungry predators. The panic overtook the passengers, and there were no reassurances now. Everyone was simply too busy. Too tired. Too scared.

She clung to her husband. "Pavel, I don't want to die. I am not ready."

He seemed preternaturally calm, as if considering some obscure notion.

"Do something. Anything," Anastasia pleaded with him. "Use your magick. It cannot end this way. *We* cannot end this way."

She thought about their bodies decomposing into the ocean floor. She thought about her art collection disappearing beneath the waves. She thought about all their charmed years. Had it all been on borrowed time?

"It'll be all right, *ma chérie*," Pavel promised her solemnly. "I shall take care of it."

Anastasia didn't know what he meant and understood not to ask. All she could do was hide in their cabin, clinging to a life preserver, thinking of how insufficient such a protection would be in the open water. She knew as a woman and a first-class passenger, she'd have a guaranteed seat on the rescue boats, should the ship go down. But in a storm of this viciousness, it hardly seemed to matter.

There were a great many noises all around her, noises she learned to discern and categorize. The rumbling of an angry sky, the pleading of a battered ship. And then there was something she couldn't quite work out.

"What was that?" Anastasia asked, peering outside their cabin.

"The aft mast has collapsed," someone screamed.

That didn't sound good. That sounded downright terrifying. She wanted to go find Pavel but was too scared to leave their cabin, so she drew back and closed the door. Diego was her only company, and the bird seemed even more frightened than she was. He screamed gibberish, which was completely unlike him.

Eventually, even the flood of adrenaline wasn't enough to keep her awake. Her mind simply shut down, and the body soon followed suit. She slept heavily and dreamt of being trapped in a small space.

When Anastasia woke up, her first thought was that the dream had followed her out—she was indeed trapped in a small space. But she soon got her bearings, remembering that she was in her first-class cabin, aboard an ocean liner bound for America. She stood up and stretched. The sun was streaming through the window. Outside, the bright blue cloudless sky stretched as far as the eye could see. It all felt impossibly peaceful.

She looked over at Diego's cage. He was awake and looking right back at her. "Good morning, Diego."

"*Bon matin*," he trilled.

AND THEN SHE remembered. The previous night's terror came back to Anastasia with disorienting speed, so potently that she stumbled and nearly fell, catching herself on the bed. She tried listening, but there was no screaming, no rushing around. All she heard were the sounds of repairs mixing in with the murmur of the sea. She steadied herself, straightened her clothes as much as possible after sleeping in them, and went outside to find her husband.

The ship was abuzz with activity. The mast, she quickly found out, had indeed fallen last night, crashing onto the deck and taking several lives along with it. The force of its collapse had deformed the steel surface beneath their feet and left the debris scattered everywhere. The bodies had been removed. Someone was washing their blood off the deck. She had to turn away.

Other than that, though, the ship appeared to have made it through the storm. There was some damage to the lower sections of the hull, near the cargo hold area, but miraculously, most things survived unscathed. Her beloved art collection had been spared. Anastasia exhaled a breath she felt she had been holding for hours.

It took the rest of the morning to find Pavel. By then, panic had set deep into her bones and seeing him brought a joy powerful enough to render her momentarily speechless. Anastasia simply put her arms around her husband and held him, her head nestled into his chest.

"Why are you out here?" she asked, as she finally pulled away from Pavel and took note of their surroundings. They were in an isolated area of the top deck. Anywhere else, she'd call it a remote corner, but there were no proper corners on the ship, it seemed.

"Just thinking, *ma chérie*," he said quietly.

She looked at Pavel's face. He looked haggard, as if last night had taken years from him.

"Are you all right?" she asked gently.

"I'm tired. So tired. I was helping the crew with the mast."

"My hero." Anastasia smiled proudly.

"No, nothing like that," he said, shaking his head, and there was such sadness in his voice that she felt it in her own heart.

"You haven't slept all night?"

"I'm afraid not."

"Come back to the cabin and rest, dear." Anastasia took his hand. "You need your rest."

Pavel let himself be led, like a child, and when she tucked him into bed, he obediently closed his eyes, but sleep wouldn't come to him for a very long time.

Whatever things they might have said to each other were left unsaid, as if by a mutually arrived upon tacit decision. These were matters beyond words. And in the end, what did it matter? They were together, they were safe, They could live with the unsaid.

CHAPTER 17

BEFORE

NEW YORK DIDN'T seem real to Anastasia. It didn't *feel* real. After years of fresh starts and new beginnings, she had found herself in a place that felt entirely alien. She couldn't imagine ever belonging here.

It was simply too removed from life as she knew it. Too shiny and new.

The country had recovered well from the Great Depression, and their WWII victory had boosted the nation's morale even further. Everyone was just so … happy. Yes, that was it. Everyone was so preposterously happy.

Anastasia shared this observation with her husband, and he was bemused by it.

"You'll find that Americans are very attached to their happiness," he told her. "They have even enshrined it into their constitution."

What strange people, she marveled. It was as if they had never encountered real life, or at least real life as she knew it.

SHORTLY BEFORE THEIR landing in New York, when there was still a blue stretch of the Atlantic Ocean between them and their new destination, Pavel said, "I crave a proper fresh start, darling, don't you?"

"What do you have in mind?" she asked, intrigued.

And so it came to pass that they boarded the ship as the Rostovs and departed it as the Koshmaroffs. The change was easy enough to make—all foreign names sounded the same to the local authorities. She remained Anastasia, though in time, even that would soon prove too polysyllabic for the Americans, and he became Paul.

"Now when I publish my novel, I shall be one and the same," he said, contentedly.

If she were honest with herself, she didn't love the change. She had become accustomed to being a Rostov. But then, it didn't seem to matter to her all that much, and it mattered a great deal to Pavel—Paul now to everyone but his wife—and so it was done.

In a way, it was rather amusing too, like sharing a private joke that the rest of the world was not allowed in on. In polyglot Europe, someone would have likely picked up on it—the French, certainly, as the two words were very close. But here, everyone seemed conveniently monolingual and perfectly incurious.

"Watch out, America, the Nightmares are here," Anastasia announced, smiling at her husband. He smiled back, the only man to understand her rather dark, occasionally sardonic, sense of humor. What was marriage, after all, but a world for two—*le monde à deux*.

THEY DIDN'T STAY long in New York, much to her relief. Pavel was dead set on California. He'd been corresponding with a man there and was eager to meet him, at last.

They took the 20th Century Limited to Chicago, transferring there to the Super Chief, which got them to Los Angeles. Both trains were the height of luxury travel, comfortable and elegant. Both, she found out, were known as "Trains to the Stars" and favored by magnates and celebrities alike. But there was no one she recognized, and one recognized them either. The anonymity was wonderful. One could simply sit back and watch this vast, strange country roll past their windows.

AS MUCH AS Anastasia didn't take to New York, she found the West Coast to be delightful. It was still unreal, but in a different way. There was nothing real about it at all, and no pretense either—the place seemed to pride itself on its artificiality.

Unlike New York, it didn't try to emulate the great European cities. And it was spectacularly sunny all the time. The sunshine penetrated your skin, right down to your bones. It was insistent. Unignorable. You couldn't help but give in to this irresistible feeling and the purely somatic joy of the place.

"I feel as if I've stepped into a postcard," she told Pavel.

He smiled. "It might be just the effect they were going for."

They settled in Pasadena.

"It means *of the valley*," Pavel told her. A nice name, there was a melodic quality to it. Originally a resort town, it had been a major staging area for the Pacific theater of war and had since become a major technological hub.

NASA's Jet Propulsion Lab was here, and the man they came to meet was one of its founders.

It was an unusual sort of interest for Pavel, and she wondered if maybe it had to do with his businesses.

But then she met Jack Parsons and understood.

Parsons, "*Just call me Jack*"—no formalities here in the new world—was a devoted Thelemite and an old friend of the late Crowley. She wasn't sure how strong that friendship had been or how long it lasted—there was something in the way Jack talked about it that made it seem like there had been challenges—but the connection was plain to see.

Anastasia found Jack to be a strange, seemingly contradictory, combination of a brilliant scientist and an occultist. He seemed equally passionate about both. By now, she had been indirectly around the occult for years and knew enough to have a superficial conversation about it and contextualize certain ideas. She didn't approve of it, per se, nor would she ever consider jumping aboard, but her level of engagement proved perfectly fine for everyone involved.

Jack was electric. There was a magnetism to him. He flirted relentlessly and talked a mile a minute— the kind of man who went at life's buffet with a voracious appetite.

"My family toured Europe in the late nineteen-twenties. I'm trying to remember if I might have met you then or seen you somewhere. Of course, I was only a child, but I'm sure you would have made an impression." Jack told her, ever the charmer. Compliments came naturally to him, but then he'd seamlessly switch to something dizzyingly scientific.

Movie star handsome and strikingly intelligent, he was absolutely bursting with ideas. In a course of the same conversation, he'd go from discussing rocket propulsion methods to advocating communism to expounding on his occult experiments.

The latter was of particular interest to Pavel and was just strange enough to interest her too.

Inspired by Crowley's novel *Moonchild*, Parsons and his friend Hubbard conducted a series of magick rituals designed to manifest an individual incarnation of Babalon, the archetypal divine feminine being. There was also an attempt to conceive a child through magick. The end result produced no child, but Parsons declared that they did successfully transform one Marjorie Cameron into Babalon, The Scarlet Woman of Crowley's writings. Jack had subsequently married her.

To Anastasia, it sounded positively mad. She could not wait to hear Pavel's take on it.

THEY WERE STAYING in a rented house by the beach, and whenever she looked around, Anastasia was reminded of the warm and sunny Torquay. Later that night, when they got home, Pavel told her of Crowley once confiding in him about being displeased with the experiments at the time. The old man had considered Jack a promising disciple and loathed to see him go. The subsequent use of Crowley's writings for Jack's own purposes was akin to a slap in the face.

Pavel also didn't think much of Jack's friend, Hubbard.

"Jack's a madman, but a genius, that's a reasonable balance," he stated thoughtfully. "But Hubbard is no genius. He has ideas, but they are mostly in the realm of science fiction. He isn't a man to set the world on fire—he's more likely to start a cult or something. He can, at best, be Jack's amanuensis."

She knew that there was a strangely incestuous connection between the two men. A certain sordid aspect to one of them marrying a wife of another, allegations of statutory rape. The details were vague, but it was something distinctly déclassé.

"Jack would write to Crowley, raving about Hubbard, telling him how much he was in line with Thelemic teachings, but Crowley was convinced Hubbard had Jack under his spell somehow," Pavel had provided by way of explanation, reluctant to rehash the scandalous past.

In time, Anastasia came to understand that her husband shared Crowley's opinion. Funny how the ghost of the old man still haunted their lives. Pavel adored

Jack's company and found an endless source of inspiration in their conversations, but Hubbard remained a constant bone of contention between them. So much so that Pavel began to talk of leaving Pasadena.

Anastasia suspected that her husband hadn't taken to The Golden State with the same enthusiasm as she had. The sunshine simply didn't hold the same appeal to a man devoted to darkness.

"Turns out California's state motto is Eureka," she shared with Pavel, bemused upon discovering the fact. "It's a place practically designed for you to make the most ingenious discoveries."

Her husband was unfailingly polite about his growing discontent, for he knew she was happy here. Popular, even. Anastasia's art collection was the talk of the town. The Koshmaroffs were known locally as the exotic émigré couple with the talking parrot. You could see the ocean from their windows.

"Why do you love it so much?" Pavel asked her once, gesturing at their expansive views.

Anastasia knew exactly what he meant. They both had every right to be traumatized by the sea.

She considered her answer, finding the perfect words to express her feelings. "It's like being at the very end of the world. Or rather, at the very edge of it. Seems like the most logical place to land, after all we've seen and everywhere we've been. One can forget about the rest of the world here."

"You're a poet, *ma chérie*." Her husband smiled and kissed her hand. But Anastasia knew that although he may like her words, he didn't agree with them.

"NASTYA, DARLING, COME see my newest acquisition," Pavel beckoned one day.

She did, genuinely curious. He had, after all, always expressed interest, if at times only polite, in her art.

The objects presented before her were a quill and a notebook. Her husband appeared to be beaming with pride at the sight of them. Anastasia looked at him questioningly, and he was all too happy to provide an explanation.

"These were said to have belonged to Sir Isaac Newton himself."

"Ah." She nodded her understanding. "Collectors' items, then."

"But so much more too, darling." Pavel clasped his hands in excitement.

"I'm familiar with Newton's works. Did he commit the secrets of gravity to his notebook first? Is that its value?"

"Actually, though not widely known, Newton had a strong interest in alchemy. He spent years trying to figure it all out."

"Alchemy?" She raised her eyebrow. "Turning things to gold?"

"Only on the surface, my darling. There's so much more to it, really."

"Go on, tell me," she said, knowing her interest would delight him.

"Well, it is believed that alchemy originated in Egypt around the time of King Hermes. Its first document was The Emerald Tablet of Hermes, the thing Europeans would later consider to contain the secrets of prima materia."

"Which is?"

"Which is the primal substance from which all matter originates. The Hermetic Corpus texts, attributed to Hermes himself, became the basis of Hermeticism—a philosophical, spiritual and, yes, magical, tradition."

He paused as if gauging her reaction to all of this.

Anastasia found her husband's passion endearing, if somewhat abstruse.

"And then?" she prompted.

"And then, the Greeks got curious and proceeded to incorporate their elemental sciences with Egyptian knowledge. The Greek word for Egypt was Khemia. When the Arabs, during their occupation of Egypt in the seventh century got interested too, they added al to Khemia, resulting in alchemy. The Arabs brought it to Spain in the following century, and the rest of Europe became obsessed."

"And the gold?"

"Oh, but the gold was only some of it, *ma chérie*, and the only thing people seem to associate with alchemy now. There was, in fact, so much more. Some of it was purely practical experiments—essentially the origins of modern chemistry. And some of it indeed became the metaphysical quest for immortality and yes, gold, among other things, though it was used largely to fund further research."

"Fascinating. And I'm guessing you are of the latter camp?"

"Well—" Pavel smiled, spreading his arms wide "—there are plenty of chemists out there already."

She smiled back, finding his enthusiasm delightful. "This quill and notebook. What can they do?"

"Well, it's been said that the notebook can hold secrets."

"Like a diary?"

"In a way, but one where the entries can be imbued with more intentionality. The secrets these pages can hold may only be revealed to certain recipients."

Anastasia trailed her fingers along the notebook's cover. "So soft. Is it vellum?"

"Either that or human skin," Pavel joked.

His deadpan delivery threw her, but only for a second. After all these years, she was mostly used to it.

"I'm sorry, darling." He pretended to bow his head in shame, if only to amuse her. "I'm sure it is most likely vellum. Though, to be fair, some of the ancient volumes on the darker arts were allegedly made of ..."

"No." She lifted her hand in protestation. "I don't want to know."

He acquiesced with a mock-serious expression and a finger to his lips.

"And what of this quill?"

"Ah, the quill is meant to be an inspiration. What writer couldn't use more of that?"

"In that case, I am delighted you were able to acquire these objects," Anastasia said, meaning every word.

AFTER SEVERAL REVISIONS, Pavel finally secured a publisher for his latest novel.

"They are in New York," he mentioned cautiously, searching her face for a reaction.

"But we do not have to be there, do we? Surely, they can publish the book without your presence."

"I know, I know." He hesitated before pressing on. "But I would like to be there, darling. It is a place of writers and the intelligentsia. This is a place for beatniks and surfers. The sun bakes their brains into mush all day."

"I love it here," she said simply.

"I know you do," Pavel assured her, kindly." I've thought about it. So much. There's an ocean there too, you know. We can be by the ocean there, just as you like. I've made inquiries. There's a place, Long Island. It's just as it sounds. There's plenty of land for development. We can build a house right on the water and still be near New York. Think of all the culture. All the plays. All the art."

In the end, Anastasia didn't put up much of an argument; letting her husband win. She simply didn't have it in her to fight; she valued accord too much. Besides, he was an old man now. Paul Koshmaroff had gotten rid of Pavel Rostov's Tolstoyesque beard, and his clean-shaven face made him look considerably younger than his age, but still ... So many years had passed them already. Who knew how many they had left together? She wanted them to be happy.

"Diego will never forgive us," she told her husband with mock seriousness. "He loves it here."

"Eureka," the parrot screamed from his perch in affirmation.

"I shall endeavor to win back his good graces," said Pavel, sincerely.

They knew, without acknowledging it, that he was talking about more than the bird.

And so it came to pass. Another move. Another change. They said goodbye to the increasingly erratic Parsons and the steadily irresistible Pasadena and left for Long Island, New York.

CHAPTER 18

BEFORE

Her husband's latest book was good. Anastasia thought it might be his best one yet. The plot revolved around a failed magician who goes into politics and has to resort to an entirely different manner of trickery. The novel was clever, funny, witty, and, toward the end, it got dark in a perfectly delicious Faustian way. It was completely unlike anything he'd written before. She read it twice and was excited for the world to love it as much as she did.

Now that they were back on the East Coast, Anastasia spent her time overseeing the construction of their new house, which seemed to grow like a mushroom in the rain, while Pavel did promotional readings arranged by his publisher.

The book wasn't the easiest sell—the American audience was too sunny by nature for dark fiction. She didn't know if her husband could single-handedly change that, but he seemed thrilled to try.

Once the build was complete, Anastasia took great delight in furnishing their new house. The clean lines of spacious rooms, with large windows and the promised ocean views, lent themselves easily to any style of decor.

There was a huge boom happening in home design. After decades of heavy, plain furniture, there was now a new movement—slick minimalism: chairs that contoured to your spine, teak wood tables and shelving units, and upholstery that featured bright modern colors. It delighted Anastasia, and she bought a number of pieces for their new place. Pavel was just going to have to like it. She did make sure to buy the couches and chairs with taller backs; otherwise, her giant of a husband would tower over them, making it seem like children's furnishings.

Only his office was done in a different style. In it, time stood still. The desk was a massive production of heavy oak, the bookcases were solid and glass-fronted, the rug was Persian, like the ones they used to have back in Europe.

On a pure whim, Anastasia bought her husband a rocking chair to relax in. He had mentioned once having a similar one in his childhood home—a gift, imported by a family friend from Western Europe. She thought he would enjoy having one again, picturing him relaxing in it after a long day of writing or maybe just prior to sitting down to type, rocking and coming up with new ideas. The chair was placed near the desk, by the window.

Pavel loved all she had done with the house, especially his office. Or at least, he said he did and was very convincing about it. Their home was finished, his book was selling reasonably well. It seemed like the perfect time to sit back and enjoy it all, yet she found her husband disappearing into his studies more and more. And thus, she knew without asking that his pursuit of magick wasn't over.

"Do you remember Otto?" he asked her one day, seemingly out of nowhere.

Of course, she did, poor doomed Otto and his impossible quest.

"I've been thinking a lot about him lately," Pavel said. "His obsession with The Holy Grail. Could he have been just like me, thinking it to be a magickal object? Was he hoping to draw the magick from it?"

It was a rhetorical question, she knew, but still …

"How would that even work?" Anastasia inquired boldly. "Hypothetically, how would the objects contain magick?"

Pavel looked at her curiously. It wasn't the sort of thing she'd ever asked him.

"Well," he started, thoughtfully, "magick is ritual, will, and intent. When focused, in a concentrated form, it can, in theory, be poured into a receptacle. It's only a matter of having the right components and practice. Think of it as cooking, if you will. There are ingredients, spices, preparation, and so on."

This was a rather amusing example, as both of them were quite useless in the kitchen. They usually had hired help and when they didn't, they simply ate sandwiches and fruit.

She considered his explanation. "So, the goal would be to, say, pour magick into this chair and have it do what? It would still be a chair, no?"

"Yes, but it would also be transformed; it would have potential other uses. To follow the food analogy, it would become more than a mere sum of its parts. It would be imbued with something ..." he trailed off.

"Something," Anastasia prompted.

"Something," Pavel finished, reluctantly, "like a soul."

"And these ingredients? Are they all the regular things you'd find in a witch's cupboard?" she jested, trying to lighten the mood.

"Not quite." He smiled. "Not for the really potent spells."

"And what do those require?"

He sighed and looked at her, hesitant to answer.

She met his eye, expectantly.

"Those, *ma chérie* ... those tend to work best with blood."

PAVEL BOUGHT THEM a telephone. "Two-thirds of American households have one," he announced, like a TV advert, presenting it to her ceremoniously.

A bulky, heavy thing made of black bakelite, it clashed with everything they owned and was thus relegated to Pavel's office.

"Who will we call?" Anastasia asked her husband, shaking her head.

"Who will call us?" he said, smiling. "The possibilities, my dear, are endless."

They did receive a phone call one day not long after. Jack Parsons was dead. Marjorie was nearly hysterical as she relayed the devastating news. She implied that it was a paranormal experiment gone wrong. Later, there was talk of a potential suicide. The death was officially written off as a work-related explosion. A tragedy, either way. Beautiful, wild Jack was gone. He was only thirty-seven.

Anastasia knew that Pavel was affected by this more than he let on. Every death seemed to him like a personal reminder to hurry up, that his time was limited. Whenever he intimated this to her, Anastasia didn't know what to say. The passing of the years didn't particularly scare her. She'd rue it in the moment—upon finding her first grey hairs or first wrinkles—but, overall, she was content with it all and resigned to growing old contentedly by his side. It was only their age disparity that scared Anastasia—now that they were both older; she feared there would come a time when she would be left all alone.

They talked about this now and again, whenever they could bring themselves to breach the subject.

"It's what I'm working on, *ma chérie*," Pavel told her. "So that we shall never be apart. So that you shall never be on your own."

To avoid causing her undue sadness, he promptly added, "Besides, you'll never really be alone. We both know Diego is going to outlive us both."

"You bet," piped in Diego, the only one of them whose American accent was flawless.

THE FOLLOWING SUMMER, their house flooded. They were able to save most of their possessions, but the experience was too reminiscent of another water-related trauma, and they were reluctant to remain on Long Island. Still, going someplace else sounded unbearably tiresome. There were only so many times one could start over.

"I think the Atlantic Ocean hates us," Anastasia told her husband, only half in jest. "We should have stayed on the West Coast."

"But we are East Coast people now, darling. And I've found a perfect place for us," he said. "Right here in the great state of New York."

"Not the city, I hope. It has gotten so loud and busy."

"Oh no, it's upstate. A lovely drive through the country and a peaceful estate already awaiting us."

"I don't know, dear," she prevaricated. "It sounds terribly provincial."

"It's quiet, peaceful, and far from the ravaging waters of the Atlantic." Pavel smiled. "You'll love it."

"I really didn't want to have to move again." Anastasia sighed, leaning into his open arms.

"Last time, darling," he told her, pulling her closer and kissing the top of her head. "Last time, I promise."

CHAPTER 19

AFTER

THE TELEPHONE

T HERE'S A TIME in the morning when sleep has left you and the world hasn't
claimed you yet, when your mind still hasn't caught up to your body, and your
body still hasn't caught up to your life—the perfect liminal state of being, brief
gone too soon as wakefulness steals it all away. It's my favorite time of the day. In
those fleeting moments, I am young and strong, and my beautiful wife lies beside
me; the sunlight stirs her awake, and she turns to look at me, to smile at me. And
then I open my eyes, fully awake, and there I am—an old man, alone in a bed made
for two, with nothing for company but pillows worn flat and memories worn thin.

My name is Johnny Smith. I am seventy-eight years old. I've lived in this
town for most of my life; I was born here, and I am content to die here. Everyone
I've ever loved is here too. All dead but for my baby sister Lucy, who at sixty-eight

is, of course, no baby. I'm older now than I ever thought I'd be older than either of my parents were when they died. To my everlasting regret, I have outlived my wife, my beautiful Ellie. I've also outlived four dogs and five trucks, though I think this latest, seemingly indestructible, tank I'm driving may outlast its owner. All my dogs had different names and all the trucks had the same one, with numerals after it, so this is now Buck Six. And I guess, as they say, the Buck stops here. I named it and its gas-guzzling predecessors after a wild mustang I used to know—he bucked and wouldn't ever settle down. Don't know why I thought that sort of unruliness would be good to bestow upon a personal vehicle, but there it is. I don't know why I'm thinking about it so much now. It doesn't really matter. I'm retired now, and Buck Six is just here to get me from point A to point B, home to grocery store, cemetery, and so on.

Maybe I'm thinking about my truck so I don't have to think about Ellie. It never works, though. She's always on my mind. It's been three years now that she's passed, the longest three years of my life. It wasn't sudden, her death. There was time to prepare, as they said. But what they don't tell you is that there's no way to prepare for a thing like that. You can't get ready to lose the love of your life. You can't possibly look at the endless solitude stretching ahead and accept it as your own. Until it's there, and you're stuck in it. You can get the paperwork in order, sort out the logistics, sure, but that means nothing in the end. You will never be ready.

Didn't think I'd last much longer after I buried my Ellie, but here I am, still alive. Still visiting the modest, as per her request, headstone in the cemetery with *Eleanor Smith, Beloved Wife* etched on it. Still talking to her ghost. Still missing her.

I've been thinking a lot about my life lately—the way it unfolded, the sequence of events—imagining it as a book. I suppose everyone's life is like that.

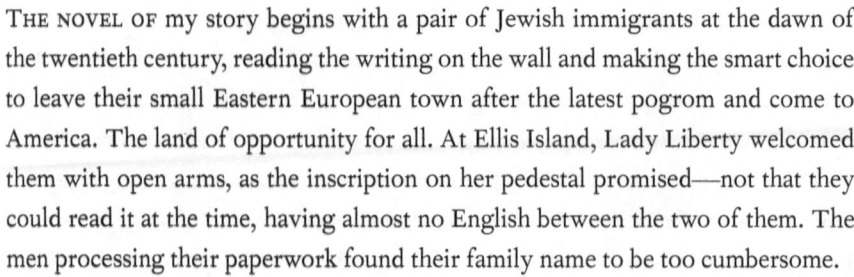

THE NOVEL OF my story begins with a pair of Jewish immigrants at the dawn of the twentieth century, reading the writing on the wall and making the smart choice to leave their small Eastern European town after the latest pogrom and come to America. The land of opportunity for all. At Ellis Island, Lady Liberty welcomed them with open arms, as the inscription on her pedestal promised—not that they could read it at the time, having almost no English between the two of them. The men processing their paperwork found their family name to be too cumbersome.

"What is good American name?" inquired my father, determined to make the best first impression in this new country.

"Smith," they replied.

And that's how my family became the Smiths, or so the story goes. It may be apocryphal. It's possible that all along, during their long journey across the sea, my parents had planned to disassociate themselves from their origins as much as they could, deciding to assimilate from the very beginning and thoroughly. They may have always wanted to be Smiths—shiny and new, not the people who had left behind everything they knew to get away from the ugliness and hatred of their old lives. They never spoke about it and never told our sister and me our original surnames. As far as we knew, we were always The Smiths.

It was the most incongruous of names for a pair of immigrants who barely spoke any English and had distinctly non-colloquial customs and preferences, but their attitude was pure American dream from the get-go. My father worked himself to the bone, as did my mother. As he began to slowly, ever so slowly, improve his lot, my mother stayed at the same job, in a shirt factory. Opportunities were different then, sadly limited. Nowadays, women can do just about all the same things men can and more. Both my late wife and my baby sister have outdone me professionally, with Ellie's career as a high school English teacher and my sister being an in-demand child and adolescent psychologist. I'm only a handyman. A Mr. Fix-It. JohnnyFixIt, actually, that's what it's always said on all my trucks. It's all I've ever been happy doing.

But there I go, digressing in what should be a linear narrative. My Ellie would have had something to say about that, and she knew these things—always had a book or three going, right up until her last days, when I took over reading them for her. She told me that a novel should flow like a river. Whatever tributaries, whatever obstacles might come up, there should always be a uniform direction.

And so, the river of my life was about to spring up. My parents had finally saved up enough to have a child and, less than a year later, had themselves a bouncing baby boy. They named me John, presumably guided by the same logic used in choosing their surname. What's more American than John? I guess they didn't know their new country's history that well though, because there already was a John Smith, a pretty famous fella, prominently featured in it. Once I learned all about him in school, that's when I became Johnny. And Johnny I've stayed all these years, despite being much too old these days for such a youthful moniker.

There's a popular movie actor now named Johnny. I'm wondering if he's going to keep it that way when he's old like me. Then again, I don't suppose actors age like regular people. Just look at Newman or Redford—Ellie's favorites. I couldn't tell you how many times we watched *Butch Cassidy and the Sundance Kid* together, even if I wanted to. In fact, it was the first movie I ever bought for her, a birthday present I remember scoring particularly high on. Anyway, those two are still as handsome as ever.

But there I go again ... oh, how the mind drifts when it's idle. The river of my life might flow in one way, only forward, but my memories all go in the opposite direction—back, back, back.

So, where was I? Oh yes, my parents had their bouncing baby boy. My father was doing well in his new business, so well that my mother was able to quit working and stay in their new apartment—a step up from tenements of their early years in New York—to take care of me. And then The Crash came. That's how they always spoke of it, The Crash. 1929 ruined my parents, like it did so many others. Whatever fortuitous timing magic they had used to get out of Europe when they did and to make all their smart life choices since—it failed them that year. All they had was gone. My father was crushed. He took his family away from the city that had promised so much and then turned the tables so brutally, to a small town with a time-forgotten appeal he deemed safe. Here, he believed, they would be insulated from the vagaries of fate. Here they could start anew. Again.

It never happened for them, though. Not the same way. I have a theory that you only get one shot at greatness per lifetime. In any chosen field, that is. You get lots of chances, mind you, but only one with a potential outcome of greatness. You get one great love, one great job, one great friend. The rest will be good, if you're fortunate enough, but never the same.

And so, my father never got a second chance at greatness that New York City had wasted. He became a janitor at a local school. The same place where my mother, after having my sister Lucy—"the happy surprise" as they'd call her— would eventually work too, as a lunch lady.

My parents went on to live a quiet, unassuming life in a small, neat house with a small, neat yard. I don't know if they were happy. People didn't discuss things like that back then, not like they do now, the notion that my sister has made her entire career out of. But they must have been content enough. Especially when the Nazis began stirring up trouble in Europe, making my parents realize just how perfectly timed their move to America really was.

They didn't want me going to war, but how could I not? A young, somewhat aimless man with high ideals and no direction. A patriot with a zeal of a fresh first-generation convert, I was raring to go. And so, I went. Fought. Survived.

The man who came back was recognizably the same Johnny Smith, only now with traces of premature grey at his temples. The scars I brought back were all on the inside, I was one of the fortunate ones. But I still get nightmares from my war days. Funny that, how the brain processes things. Lucy says it's trauma. She explains it, using her college words and her textbook notions. I listen. It doesn't help with the nightmares, but it's good to understand the whys and hows. Gives one a perspective.

Ellie was always interested in things like that and got me interested too. That woman gobbled up knowledge the way most people do pie--in a pie-eating contest. She and Lucy would talk for hours. This and that. I suppose Ellie always wanted to have more education than she did, more than just a junior college. Had she been born later or maybe to a wealthier family, she'd probably have five degrees, Ivy League and all, lining our walls. As it were, our walls were lined with shelves, full to bursting with books of all kinds, and she was just as smart or even smarter for it. The smartest person I've ever met, my Ellie.

Me, I was never much for reading. In school, the letters had this terrible habit of refusing to arrange themselves into proper words. It was years, decades, before I learned a proper term for this: dyslexia. During the war, when the rest of the fellas would pass those beat up ASE paperbacks around the barracks, I'd take one, try to read it, and wait to overhear someone who had already finished it to find out the plot. One Ellie understood the problem, she helped me with some practical advice, and got me up to speed. Though she never made a reader of her caliber out of me, nowadays I do get through a daily newspaper, a monthly *National Geographic* magazine, and an occasional noir novel with no problem.

That's how we did most of our traveling, Ellie and me. Through *National Geographics*, TV programs, and so on. Should have done more, I suppose, but there was always the expense of it to consider. Plus, I'd seen much of Europe, from behind the barrel of The Garand during the war, and didn't care to relive the experience.

We went places, though, saw the Great Lakes, Niagara Falls, and both oceans. Yellowstone and Mount Rushmore. All the great tourist destinations. The traveling tired me out in ways a twelve-hour workday never could, but the look on Ellie's face made it all worth it. Awe, I suppose it was. Awe at things greater than ourselves. I understood it then. A truly humbling experience. But, unless you count the very border of Canada, we never left the country together. All the exotic destinations remained on printed pages or TV screens.

I don't know if I regret it much; there are many other things that would come ahead of that in the great regret queue.

Kids, for one. That's a major one. We never had kids. Tried and tried, but after three miscarriages and one stillborn, we agreed to quit trying. The heart can only take so much.

And so, it was always just us. And a dog. Four dogs to be exact, though only ever one at a time. Different breeds, each, but somehow it always seemed like just another reincarnation of the same dog—large, shaggy, excitable pups with generally agreeable personalities and voracious appetites. As far as four-legged companions go, you couldn't ask for more. And we sure loved our dogs.

Life wasn't always easy, but it was good.

ELLIE HAD SOME inspirational quotes printed out and framed in our—well, mostly her—home office, and one of them said, "The past is never dead. It's not even past." I never quite knew what Faulkner meant by that, but now I think I'm starting to finally get it. The past seems as real to me as the present these days and sometimes even more so.

Maybe the trick to understanding things is just waiting long enough to gather the right amount of experiences.

Anyway, how the mind meanders ... One image, one thought can send me rambling down a memory lane. So where was I? The war?

Coming back after the war and adjusting to civilian life was both difficult and easy. Easy because there was instant respect for you as a person—nothing like a war to build and prove character. Plus, there were G.I. loans and things like that. The difficulties ... Well, you didn't go talking about those, not when you had the good fortune to come back in one piece anyway. So, I tried college upon my return, and sure enough, the letters were still as unruly as ever. Higher education didn't seem to be in the cards for Johnny Smith.

My father knew someone who lined me up with a job in sales and so that's what I did. Sold all sorts of things: typewriters, vacuums, encyclopedias once. My heart wasn't in it, but it got me out of my head and put some money in my pockets. And anyway, my heart was busy in those days, pining for the pretty girl down the street, never seen without a book.

Finally, through a friend of a friend, I managed an introduction. The rest, as they say, is history. But that implies smooth sailing, usually, doesn't it? Well, it wasn't smooth, I can tell you that much. Eleanor Walker did not fancy herself with a young man like me. She probably wanted a college professor kind of fella, tweed and elbow patches. But in the end, if it wasn't my charm, my six-foot frame, or my Caddy, then my sheer persistence must have won her over. When I'd ask her about it later, she'd always say, "You made me laugh, Johnny. You always made me laugh."

"So not my fancy footwork on the dance floor? Not my James Dean hair?" I'd joke. "I could've been a tone-deaf oaf with two left feet and a combover, and you wouldn't care?"

"Guess we'll just never know," she'd say, smiling. "Too late now; we're stuck with each other."

Boy, did she make getting stuck sound good.

IN THE EARLY days of our marriage, I was on the road a lot, selling this or that, putting miles on the Cadillac and wrinkles on my forehead. The nightmares held me down at night something awful, and it got so I couldn't sleep away from Ellie at all. I'd call her every night from whatever motel I was at after a long day, weary and restless in a strange bed, and we'd talk until I fell asleep. "Tell me a story," I'd say, and she always did, whether it was something she had read in a book or simply made up. It never failed to calm my mind.

It was murder on the bills though, long-distance calls like that. After a while, it started to eat into my commissions in an unsupportable way, so we talked about it, and I came back. Sold the Caddy, got a truck, and became a one-man repair service.

Those days, it was easier to start a business. All you needed was some ambition and drive. Once I built up a reputation for myself as reliable, resourceful, and reasonable, business became steady and stayed that way. There was nothing JohnnyFixIt couldn't fix. He'd do it in a timely manner and wouldn't charge an arm and a leg for it. Good business all around.

Through that job, I got to know just about everyone in town. If I didn't know them directly, I knew someone who knew them. It was a nice life. We were part of our community in a meaningful way. It was good to belong somewhere so completely.

Time passed. My parents died, quietly just as they had lived, within months of each other. They were too young, really, if you went by years alone, but something about them was always older, as if their souls were irrevocably crushed by the great upheavals of their lives. Which is just fancy talk for saying their disappointments aged them and ushered them into early graves.

Lucy and I buried them, side by side, in the Fairview Cemetery, which I admit is an aptly named final resting place, for the vistas its hilly location provides are indeed quite lovely. For years, I didn't visit their graves very often. Now I do, because it's the same place I buried my Ellie, whom I go to see every chance I get. I bring a small folding chair and stay for hours, talking to Ellie, missing the two-way direction our conversations used to flow. How I wish she were here to tell me a story.

DIGRESSED AGAIN, DIDN'T I? Nothing but memories competing for a spotlight in my mind.

Here's one: I remember the day the Koshmaroffs moved to town. Or I thought I did, but now I can't seem to fix a date, a month, or even a year to it. All I remember with certainty is that it was an unseasonable day—nippy, grey, and rainy—incongruous with whatever the calendar said or the weatherman promised. A terrible day for a move.

I was driving to a job and saw a procession of Chevy pickups with covered truck beds pull up to the old house on the hill. The place had been sitting abandoned for as long as I could remember and likely required plenty of renovation to make it habitable. I made a mental note to call in on the newcomers and introduce myself.

And so, I did. Waited for a nicer day, put on one of my better shirts, and headed up that way. The trucks were gone by then, of course. There was only one car in front of the house. But what a car. It made you stop and stare. Maybe even whistle quietly.

I knew cars, and I recognized this one. 1946 Alfa Romeo 6C 2500 Freccia d'Oro. Golden Arrow. I had only ever seen one in a magazine before, but a beauty like that was impossible to forget. Sheer perfection of Italian engineering, that. Of course, I wasn't too keen on Italians that soon after the war, but you couldn't deny this car. It was as close to art as I ever saw a vehicle come.

A woman who answered the door had a beauty to her too, but of a severe, forbidding kind. If people were seasons, she was winter. Her hair was so tightly pulled back from her face that it made her features appear sharp enough to draw blood. Her dress was black and modest.

She waited for me to explain myself. There was an imperial grace to her, a quality difficult to describe very much out of place in our small town. It would have been perfectly appropriate to one of the abandoned castles I'd seen in Europe.

I introduced myself, offered my services, and was summarily dismissed. They needed no one, she explained in a stilted but grammatically perfect English with a heavy, cut-glass accent. Her husband was perfectly able to take care of the house.

And that was that, our one and only interaction for years. I don't recall ever seeing them around town. If they ever left their house, I never heard of them socializing locally. They seemed to have been content in their isolation, getting their groceries and sundries delivered as needed.

Ellie said, not unkindly, that the pair of them reminded her of the Addams Family cartoons, living all by themselves in that house on a hill. Only they seemed to have no kids to provide them with warmth and shenanigans. The Koshmaroffs were alone, like us. But unlike us, they had no community to belong to and seemed to revel in their solitude. Gossip aside, no one really knew them or seemed eager to change that.

And then Mr. Koshmaroff died. Or, technically, disappeared. It was a huge deal around here, nothing like that had ever happened before. People either lived or died. They certainly never just up and vanished into thin air. The rumor mill went into overtime, but in the end, no one was the wiser. There was an investigation, but the local sheriff could only do so much. No body was found. No suspects were established. No foul play was brought to life. Eventually, Mrs. Koshmaroff was declared a widow in absentia. There was a talk of how this was done for insurance money. But talk was all there was.

Mrs. Koshmaroff began to make infrequent appearances in town, going to the law office or the shops. It was almost as if, after all this time, she had finally decided to check out the town she had chosen to live in. Always in widow blacks. But then again, maybe that was just her favorite color.

It was on one of her rare visits to town that we met again. She approached me while I was stocking up on supplies at the Main Street Hardware, decades before giant home improvement box stores would put them out of business.

"You are Johnny, yes?" she said. "I remember you came to our house once."

"Yes, Mrs. Koshmaroff, I remember you too."

"You must come. There are repairs that need to be done, and I'm afraid my husband is no longer able to take care of it."

Funny way of phrasing it, I thought. She could have said her husband was no longer around to take care of them. But semantics—one of Ellie's favorite words and areas of interest—had never been my strong suit, and I was glad for new business.

I showed up at the Koshmaroff estate the next day and was immediately taken aback by the state of things. There was a lot of work to be done, things that appeared to have been neglected for years.

It went like this: she'd tell me what needed to be done, listen to my suggestions, select an option or let me choose what was best, and leave me to it. I don't know where she went in that huge house or what she did with her time. All she had was a fancy parrot for company. Diego. A chatter and a charmer, but still only a bird.

Occasionally, I would hear her speak to another person. Since we were the only two people in the house, I presumed she spent a lot of time on the phone. Most of what she said wasn't in English.

Now I know that in theory, as a first-generation immigrant, I should have been able to converse with her in Russian. I even thought about it, figuring that maybe it would make her feel less alone or something. But truth be told, my Russian was rusty at best. I knew some words here and there, but it had been ages since I last used it conversationally, not since my parents' deaths. Lucy and me, we were all American, we were the Smiths. And we only ever spoke English to each other. I didn't think Mrs. Koshmaroff would have found whatever clunky, cobbled-together conversation I could have offered her very enticing.

So I didn't ever let on that I recognized her language. In fact, sneakily enough, I sometimes tried to make out the things I'd overhear her say on the phone. It was only an odd word here and there, and it never made much sense. I swear some of it was about magic or death or secrets. Or maybe I wasn't translating it right.

Ellie, understandably curious, would ask me about it, but then she'd also chastise me for intruding upon the old lady's privacy.

Old lady was how we referred to her, though she wasn't that old. Older than me, I suppose. Maybe old enough to be my mother. It was tough to tell. There was a timeless quality to her that rendered such categorizations null and void. She still pulled back her hair off her face just as severely as I imagined her younger self did, and her features and voice were just as sharp. Her carriage was ballerina straight, and her manners and mannerisms spoke of a bygone era. She would call me a young man, unfailingly. I don't think she ever addressed me as Johnny after our initial conversation at the hardware store, not once. I couldn't quite imagine her using diminutives at all.

And I'd only ever call her Mrs. Koshmaroff, although there was one time when an uncharacteristic current of nostalgia moved her to tell me her given name. It was Anastasia, she said, which I thought was beautiful. "But here in this country people call me Ana," she added. "Because the English language is so lazy."

She wasn't wrong, of course. I couldn't think of anyone I knew whose name wasn't either short by nature, abbreviated that way, or turned into some kind of nickname. Me being the prime example of that. But I also thought, *Who are these people who call you Ana? Who would dare to be that familiar?*

I didn't say that, of course, pleased by her confidence. The house needed a considerable amount of work, and she seemed to be able to afford it. She quickly became my number one customer, and we ended up spending a not insignificant amount of time together.

Her telling me her name was the start of something for us, like a thawing. From then on, she'd tell me things about herself now and again and have conversations with me outside of the strictly necessary word exchanges regarding the repairs for the day. It wasn't a friendship by any means, but it was a form of companionship— something the woman must have needed direly, since she seemed to have no one outside of the person on the other line of the telephone.

I never asked her about that, not directly. And indirect questions she ignored or swatted away like dust motes. Whoever she spoke to on that grand old relic of a phone remained a mystery.

Ellie and I would speculate about the unknown caller. The old lady had become a frequent subject of our conversations, her mystery irresistible. Oh Ellie, how I miss our conversations. What I wouldn't do to talk to you some more, to hear your voice again.

I WORKED FOR Mrs. Koshmaroff until the very end. I was in my seventies by then, and she'd still call me a young man. By then, she had me move her bed to the office, so she could live there full-time. I guess she drew comfort from being around her late husband's things. There was a portrait of her that I was asked to move from one wall to another, away from the sun—the woman in it recognizably the mistress of the house, only decades younger. She looked like a movie star or something. How cruel time was to take that away from someone. But then, time took everything away.

I remember telling the old lady of Ellie's passing. She offered me her condolences, and it was the most emotional I'd ever seen her be.

"It is a terrible thing to outlive a loved one," she said to me, speaking from experience, I figured. Her voice heavy with the weight of it and quiet. "It is such a lonely, terrible thing."

She had outlived her husband for decades. She lived an awfully long time. Nearly a century. I can't imagine doing that without Ellie. Don't want to imagine it. Three years has been long enough. In fact, when Mrs. Koshmaroff went to her reward, I knew that was the time to hang up my toolbelt. There is such a thing as doing something for too long. Living too long, working too long. What's it all mean if there's no one with you to share it? I've been ready to follow Ellie into the next adventure the way my parents followed each other, but it hasn't happened yet. I'm still here, biding time, waiting. Waiting.

<hr />

I WENT TO Mrs. Koshmaroff's funeral. Her lawyer organized it. It wasn't well attended—mostly gawkers and some morbidly minded, gossipy old biddies. And then, I went to her estate sale. I don't rightly know why. Mostly I think I just wanted to see one more time the house I spent so much time keeping upright. Maybe I was looking for some sort of closure. You can get closure with inanimate objects, I believe. Never with people, though, not really.

I didn't want to buy anything. "Just browsing," I said to the salesperson in charge. But then I saw that old telephone that Mrs. Koshmaroff—Ana—had spent so much time on and something just clicked. A nameless want surfaced.

"How much for this?" I asked.

"Oh, that item actually isn't for sale," the salesperson told me. "I have instructions here that it is part of a will. It was left to Mr. John Smith."

It took me a second, for it had been so long since I was John and not Johnny. Then I shook my head, biting back a smile. The old lady would have it her way until the end.

The salesperson eyed me politely but impatiently, eager to move on to potential paying customers.

I introduced myself, showed ID and everything, all very proper, and left the house with a heavy old beast of a rotary phone. *Some inheritance*, I mused. And yet it felt right somehow. When I gathered the phone from its permanent place on the desk, I thought about unplugging it first, but someone, presumably the salesperson, must have already taken care of it. I didn't even see a plug around. In fact, the more I thought about it, the more I realized that I couldn't recall ever seeing it plugged in, though it must have been, of course.

When I got home, I placed the phone on the kitchen table. It didn't look right sitting there. The black bakelite bulk of it didn't fit in with Ellie's bright, homey decor. I moved it to the office desk. Ah, that was more like it. I plugged it in and, to my surprise, got a dial tone. Boy, they sure built things to last back in the day.

I looked at the phone for a while, thinking of how I had no one to call, and then I went back to the kitchen to make myself a solitary sandwich.

THE PHONE RANG for the first time two days later. In the evening. I remember it interrupting a nature documentary I was trying to stay awake for. When I picked up the receiver, there was static on the line, too much static for the voice to get through.

It rang again the next night and the night after that, the static fading each time, and the voice of the speaker coming in more clearly. After a few days, I could hear it was a female voice. It even sounded familiar.

After a week, I could hear that it was Ellie.

Now, I know that doesn't make any sense. And I know, given my age, this account makes me a prime candidate for senility. Yet it was her, I could swear it.

Years ago, on our way back from Niagara Falls, Ellie and I stopped over in some quaint town to eat and rest and ended up in an antique shop right next to the diner. Ellie saw an old watch she just had to have. It didn't work, but she was sure I could fix it.

I couldn't. The cogs wouldn't line up right, much like the letters refused to back in my schooldays. The obstinate little thing defied the great JohnnyFixIt. I huffed and puffed, but eventually gave up. The watch got relegated to a shelf of one of Ellie's many bookcases and forgotten about. Until a couple of years later, when Ellie heard it ticking. She took it down and sure enough, it was working like it never stopped. She set the correct time, and the watch kept it.

All I wanted to do was take it apart and figure it out, but Ellie said, "Leave it, Johnny. It's a miracle. You shouldn't question miracles."

And so, by the same logic, I find myself carrying on phone conversations with my beloved three-years-dead wife every night. It doesn't need to make sense to feel right.

I've moved the phone to my nightstand now. There's no working plug there, but it doesn't seem to matter. Having it right by the bed makes it easier to fall asleep while talking. Ellie's death brought back my long conquered and forgotten insomnia, but I'm back to sleeping soundly once again.

In fact, it's getting to be that time of the night now. The phone is about to ring and, when it does, I'll answer, and I'll ask my Ellie to tell me a story.

CHAPTER 20

BEFORE

IT WOULDN'T BE the last place they lived in, Anastasia decided, not if she had something to do with it. But it would do for now. Provincial barely covered it; this was positively—what was that silly American word?—Podunk.

A nothing of a place.

The house itself, imposing enough to qualify as an estate, sat on top of the hill, overlooking the town.

"The intersection of the ley lines here is most auspicious," Pavel declared proudly, rubbing his hands together, as they stood outside the house, taking it in.

Ah, so that's what it was all about. His latest passion project. She had learned enough about it to be conversant on the subject, but the entire thing seemed too far-fetched even for her adventurous thinking husband. Imaginary lines that ran that across the world, connecting important sites. Lines that the ancient civilizations apparently recognized and strategically built structures upon.

"So, your Mr. Watkins led you here," she said, holding back her skepticism.

In the 1920s, Alfred Watkins wrote the book on ley lines. Anastasia had read some of it and found it to be an intriguing abstract concept, but not enough to base relocation decisions upon.

"Maintain an open mind, my dear, I beg of you. I've done so much research on this, above and beyond what Mr. Watkins has originally conceived of. Did you know that ley lines are a significant part of Māori culture?"

"I didn't, but I'm glad you didn't move us to New Zealand," she quipped.

"But I hear New Zealand is lovely this time of the year." Pavel smiled. "Please just see inside the house first, dear, before you judge it. The place is wonderful, and I'd like to be forgiven in this lifetime."

She didn't think it was wonderful per se, but it was, indeed, nice, if too large. They had to hire help just to maintain it. It felt grand in a bygone European way, all too wrong for this young country so obsessed with egalitarianism.

They kept to themselves and didn't have much to do with the locals. Occasionally, they took long drives amid the endless rows of trees in what she referred to as Pavel's toy car. Her husband's one proper indulgence, the Alfa Romeo had been shipped over from Europe at a considerable expense.

Pavel continued his work, promising her he was closer than ever. She read. Occasionally he'd drive her to the station, and she'd take a train down to the city to see an art exhibit. Anastasia expanded her collection very slowly, acquiring only the pieces that truly spoke to her, frequently to Pavel's utter bewilderment.

"This is art?" He'd shake his head at her latest. "It looks like a floor covering from a studio where the art was made."

"And this is just a color," he'd say about another piece.

"At least it isn't a urinal," she'd counter.

"At least," he agreed.

Occasionally, Anastasia wondered idly about the mythical lines their new house allegedly stood upon. How easy it was for a mind to trick itself into seeing and recognizing patterns. Once upon a time, people looked at the stars above, imagined lines connecting them, and came up with constellations. People always wanted to believe there was more to this life, none more so than her husband.

She gave him a typewriter for his next birthday. An imposing dark metal antique, which had to be delivered by a bear of a man who worked for the shop.

"Where do you want this beast, ma'am?" he asked, the local accent distending his vowels.

Anastasia had him place it on Pavel's desk. Pavel was in the city that morning, on yet another object acquisition trip. There were fewer of those now. He was concentrating more on the possessions at hand. She wondered what it would be this time. Some of his objects were so terribly ordinary. She missed the faux Fabergé's originality. Sometimes she wondered what kind of magick such things could store, and which ones would be changed while others remained perfectly ordinary. Would he supernaturally empower his beloved car? Why, wouldn't that be something?

It was funny to think how accepting she'd come to be about all of it. There was her husband, a charming giant of a man of good education and social standing, a writer, a thinker ... and an aspiring magician.

Anastasia had ignored that aspect of him for so long, dismissing it as a character quirk, and now that it had become a definitive driving force behind him, she had learned to live with it. She had even made efforts to understand it. Some of it she found genuinely amusing, like the way he personalized his new typewriter. There was a childish charm to it, but a charm, nonetheless—a youthful whimsy.

"A nightmare machine, darling?" she asked, reading the words on the black metal frame.

"Sure, why not?" Pavel smiled mischievously.

Another day, he played her a recording of something she hadn't heard in years, the haunting sounds all but forgotten, left behind in another life, music from a different time and place.

"Remember this?" he asked her. "You told me you liked it once."

Znamenny chants. Of course she remembered. She couldn't believe he did. She couldn't believe there was a recording of it. What a world.

It wasn't until Anastasia had read Pascal and learned of his famous wager that she was finally able to process the seemingly divergent notions she had about her wonderfully complicated husband. An eccentric or a magician? Who was to tell? Why not believe? Philosophy boggled the mind but did wonders to help frame one's thinking.

"I think the time is near, *ma chérie*," he told her one evening over tea. "I believe I must start my final preparations."

She looked up at him slowly, taking a great effort to control her suddenly shaking hand.

"Pavel ..." she started, uncertain of what came next but wanting to say something, to prove him wrong.

"If I wait any longer, I shall be too weak," he said reasonably.

This she couldn't argue with. The last few years wore heavily on her husband, as the aging process he had always dodged so easily had finally caught up to him, making up for lost time.

"This won't be the end. You mustn't think of it as such. It'll merely be a transition."

She couldn't help it; she felt her eyes brimming with tears and hated it.

"No, no, please, no, darling." Pavel came over and kneeled before her with considerable effort. "This isn't a cause for sadness. It's ... I've had it all figured out. I'll come back, I promise you."

"I don't want this," Anastasia said, steadying her voice and adding a measure of steel to it. "I don't want visitations from the astral plane. I don't want to have to contact you through a séance. I want you, here, with me. For as long as we have left together."

"But it is so short," he protested, taking her hand. "Too short. Theres almost no sand left in the hourglass. I wish I had met you sooner. I wish we had more time together. And now we will. It is the only way, darling, don't you see? You won't be my caretaker. We won't watch each other wither away. We will perpetuate as equals: young, strong, happy. We will share a life, a soul, an eternity."

She pulled her hand away. "And what am I to do after you leave? Just wait here? Alone? Indefinitely? Or follow you to the grave like a pharaoh's devoted wife?" Anastasia felt herself getting angry. Tears often made her angry, for she cried very infrequently. She used to say that the fire had burned away her tear ducts when she was seventeen.

"You won't be alone," Pavel said firmly. "When the time is right, you shall join me. I'll find a way. And then we will have all the time in the world."

"But that's too much time," Anastasia whispered so quietly that she didn't think he heard her.

In the end, they chose not to argue. They'd had too many perfectly genial years together, and it would be a shame to mar the denouement of it all with disagreement.

They spent their last days together companionably, reliving their happiest memories of their strange, peripatetic lives.

Pavel had made all the arrangements with their lawyers, he assured her. There was nothing for her to worry about. There would be plenty of money left, plenty of security. There were some simple logistics to discuss, but she didn't plan on going anywhere anyway. By then, she had gotten used to their house on the hill. She'd stay and wait. It was the least she could do.

Anastasia didn't think the wait would turn out to be as long as it did. Their last night together, chosen by Pavel, based on some mythical properties, was quiet and happy. They had the cook prepare all their favorite dishes. They sampled all of them and, sated, sat together on the front porch, watching the stars come out.

Pavel took her hand. "I want you to know," he started quietly, "that the happiest moments of my life, the times of pure joy and pure solace, were all found by your side. I didn't know ... I don't know what I've done to deserve your love, but it has been the greatest privilege of my life to be deemed worthy of it."

A tear slid down his cheek. Anastasia had never seen her husband cry. She watched it shimmer in the moonlight for a moment, then kissed it away.

Pavel smiled at that. "I've studied magick from the world over," he continued. "But none have rivaled you. None have rivaled us. And I will use all I've learned, I will pay any cost, go any distance, to have more of this. I promise you I'll return to you. We will be together again. In this life and the next."

There might have been more after this, more tears, more confessions, more of this uncharacteristically- maudlin-for-them scene, but she banished it from her memory. Anastasia edited her perfect moment with Pavel and held on to it, gathering her resolve for what came next.

It would be years of solitude with only Diego for company. Years of waiting.

CHAPTER 21

BEFORE

Wait—any wait—has a structure to it. At first, you're cautiously eager, but patient. Next, you begin to veer into impatience. And eventually, after a long time of nothingness, you drift into indifference.

Anastasia's wait lasted too long. The morning after the perfect evening they shared, she woke up and found her husband gone. He took the car as he said he would, drove off, and left it at a local spot infamous for suicides. For all the world to see, it looked like her husband was simply an old man who had gotten tired of waiting for death and decided to depart on his own terms. It seemed perfectly plausible.

There was a note he left for her with only three words in his firm cursive.

это не конец.
This isn't the end.
The message was and always would be for her eyes only.

YEARS OF SILENCE sporadically interrupted by a chatty parrot followed. Anastasia had dismissed the cook; sandwiches and fruit would have to do. She couldn't bear company, she found. Even the maid came by less and less; at first, once a week, and then only once a month. Without other people in the house, the passage of time became a strangely nebulous thing. Occasionally, Anastasia ventured to town. The visits to the supermarket were just about tolerable—the place was large enough to offer a semblance of anonymity.

The house, it seemed, had been held together by some of Pavel's magick all that time. Now that its owner was gone, the place appeared determined to go with him, steadily dilapidating all around her.

She had to hire a local Mr.Fix-It. True to his name, he was able to take care of the house's numerous needs and even became a regular fixture at the estate, always working on one project or another. There was a nice, calming presence to the man. To her surprise, she didn't mind having him around.

Outside of that one connection, Anastasia knew she was becoming an eccentric figure. The old lady Koshmaroff. Who always wore black. Who seldom left the house. Whose husband had disappeared. It would have been easier to be eccentric in the city, passing for a fashionable recluse, perhaps. But in a small town, there was only one word to describe a woman like her—a witch. It amused Anastasia to think that, while, unlike Pavel, she had no magic of her own, in the end, she would be the one known as a witch.

It took years for her to officially become a widow. Pavel was declared dead in absentia. She was now the sole owner of the Koshmaroff estate and everything in it. It was simpler this way for legal purposes, her lawyer assured her.

IT WAS ONLY after she had finally stopped expecting any miracles and settled into a quiet slide into oblivion that the phone in Pavel's office rang. Through the deafening static of that giant and, by now, antiquated apparatus, she made out the faint, tentative voice saying, 'Nastya?'"

"Pavel," she breathed out, afraid that anything louder might shatter this illusion.

"At last, my darling. There you are." His voice was coming in stronger now. "Didn't I tell you I'd call?" he joked.

"You did," she said, a tear quietly making its way down her cheek. "A long time ago."

"Nastya." His tone became worried. "What year is this?"

She told him.

There was a long silence on the line.

"Oh no. Oh no, no, no. My darling, I am so sorry, so very sorry. It felt like perhaps a month on my end at most. I've been trying to reach you this entire time. In essence, it was a matter of finding the right frequency."

Anasia held the receiver so tightly that her knuckles turned white, but the words wouldn't come. There were so many things to say, so many questions to ask. But talking to him felt simply too surreal for something as mundane as a regular conversation.

Pavel must have sensed the hesitation in her silence, and so he spoke. He told her about his new lease on life, his quest to find her, his plans. He sounded like a much younger man now, so full of energy, so vital. They talked late into the night.

And so it began, the phone would ring, and they would converse for hours.

Sometimes, even Diego joined in, spouting delightful polylingual nonsense.

If the maid was around or Johnny was fixing something in the house, Anastasia would switch to Russian or French. Americans, it seemed, were all reliably monolingual and proud of it.

The more they talked the more her mind and her heart began to open to the magick she had scorned, disbelieved in, or laughed at for so many years. Incontrovertible proof had a way of changing one's views.

IT TOOK SEVERAL more years for Pavel to successfully manifest himself. She came into his study one day and found him rocking in the chair she had bought him so long ago.

"What do you think?" he said, leaning back with his hands behind his head, a picture of relaxation.

"I think it's an excellent way to give an old lady a heart attack," she said, but couldn't maintain the frown—she was too happy to see him.

Her husband wasn't quite solid nor was he particularly transparent. It was some in-between state that, in the right light, made him look almost entirely real. Anastasia tried touching him, and her hand went right through. It felt like putting a hand through dense winter fog.

"Still working out the kinks, as they say." Pavel smiled mock-ruefully. "Nearly there."

But it was enough. More than enough, really, it was almost perfect. It reminded both of them of their days during the war, spent cooped up together, their world pared down to the bare essentials and each other.

"*Le monde à deux*," he whispered.

"You remember?"

"I remember."

"I'VE LEARNED A new trick, *ma chérie*," he told her one evening, barely able to contain his excitement.

"Show me.".

"Pick an age."

"Ah ... Forty."

And just like that, Pavel transformed himself into a man who came to her birthday party and gave her a green talking bird. Anastasia gasped. Delight won over shock.

"Twenty-five."

He changed again, becoming impossibly young—much younger than she had ever seen him, but still recognizably himself.

"That mustache." She raised her eyebrow, smiling.

"At the time, I thought it was dashing."

"I'm sure it was."

"Honestly, it was rather itchy. I was glad to get rid of it."

"You make me feel like such an old lady."

Pavel changed back immediately to the age he had been when he left. And then to the age she was now.

"Look, we are of the same vintage, at last," he said.

"The wonders never cease."

"Wonderful," chimed in Diego. "Wonderful."

FROM THAT POINT on, they communicated in two ways. When Pavel would exert too much energy on his various, often unmentioned, endeavors, he'd call on the phone. Otherwise, he'd show up in person, as it were. Either way, she had the pleasure of his company—someone to talk to, someone to dream and reminisce with.

Their peripatetic lives were terribly busy and involved for so long that, after a while, the details would often slip through her mind like sand through fingers. She found it to be more and more the case with age. It was nice to have someone to verify the minutiae, because, after all, what was life but: an accumulation of small things?

One day Anastasia was going through a shelf of drawers and found an old, damaged clock that she absolutely could not account for.

Was it one of her husband's mystery objects? She waited to ask him.

"Ah, that," Pavel said, when next he came to her. "I do remember it. Found it in the aftermath of a fire once."

"What fire?"

"People burning things," he recollected grimly. "The same things people burn throughout history: books, art, ideas."

"It still works," she noted.

He nodded. "Sometimes it does. It was the only thing I could save that day. One small thing to set free amid the flames."

"And does it have—" Anastasia hesitated momentarily "—any other purpose?"

"Darling." Pavel smiled charmingly. "To paraphrase a disagreeable lady poet we once knew, sometimes a clock is just a clock is just a clock."

He had been steadily at work convincing her to join him, but Anastasia couldn't quite let go. She was unable to explain this reluctance, this fundamental fear of leaving the only plane of existence she had ever known, even though the evidence of the next one was right in front of her.

"Why, darling?" he would ask.

She tried her best to explain that she was afraid to get lost somewhere in the weeds of time and space, the way he did those first years.

AND SO, LIFE went on, day after day, year after year. Anastasia got older and older, and her husband adjusted his appearance accordingly. They were happy in each other's company, and the world outside passed by like a distant dream.

There were wars, none of which, they agreed, could measure up to the first two. There was a man on the moon, which delighted them both to no end. There was strange new technology that put information right at the tips of your fingers. The phones lost wires. The cars gained and lost bulk. Movies came to people's homes.

She had Johnny buy her a television set and help her set up cable reception. She and Pavel spent countless evenings watching movies. They didn't care for the TV shows. Americans, it seemed, required guidance on humor, and so their comedies came along with tracks of laughter, cueing people in on the jokes.

The two of them had become observers of this world and not participants, a role that suited them both to a tee. Years marched on. A slow steady procession of days, months, seasons—all but a mere ruffle through calendar pages.

CHAPTER 22

BEFORE

THEY NEVER STOPPED having the conversation about her joining him. There were only pauses—long pauses. Deep down, Anastasia knew it was inevitable, yet she continued to put it off the way one would delay leaving a fun party to go to bed. Even if it wasn't all that fun, sleep was never the winning option—dull nothingness at best and bad dreams at worst.

The promise of the potentially exciting future was simply not enough to take one away from a perfectly tolerable present. It was easier to continue as things were than to risk losing it all.

But entropy was determined to have its way in the end. The present turned increasingly less desirable as Anastasia's body weakened. Her mind held steady, but the sheer weight of the accumulated years upon her shoulders was becoming too much to bear.

Her quality of life—the term she heard bantered around on television all too frequently—was diminishing, and there was no coming back from it.

By then, Pavel had made a breakthrough. He discovered the next step in their evolution, such as it were. It took ages, but finally, he had figured out their return to the mortal plane. No longer a theoretical possibility, he promised he could make it a reality. And Pavel always kept his promises.

There were almost no more excuses left for Anastasia. If her husband's plans and ideas sounded far-fetched, well, she could live with it. There was no need to understand every single detail, because, in the end, all magic, much like love, required a great deal of faith.

DIEGO WAS THE first to go. Having outlasted any reasonable life expectations nature had imposed on him, he nevertheless got old in the end. Too old to trill, too old to chat. Too old for anything other than a slow, silent wait for death. Anastasia found it unbearable. She found the silence unbearable. And so, with a heavy heart, she made a deal with Pavel.

One day, when she woke up, the cage was left open and empty, with nothing but a faded green feather on the bottom. She cried like a child. She didn't know there were that many tears left to her, not after so many years and yet ...

Pavel appeared and consoled her, promising they would all be together again. "A parrot shouldn't take as long as a person," he told her. "Give me time," he said. 'I promise."

It took a year. Nothing, in a grand scheme of things. When Anastasia heard Diego again, when she saw him again, she knew her time was close. The thought didn't scare her as much anymore. She turned it over in her mind and saw only its shiniest facets. It had crystallized like a dream, and there was nothing brighter.

"Would I also have to disappear the way you did?" Anastasia asked her husband worriedly. "I think I may be too old to pull it off."

"Nothing as dramatic as that, my love," he assured her. "All you'll have to do is fall asleep. When you wake up, I'll be waiting for you on the other side."

Anastasia thought of all the people she knew, all the ones she had outlived. None of them likely had an exit plan like hers. She simply needed one last gust of courage beneath her sails.

It came in the shape of an old friend—a vintage bottle unearthed in the basement. The green fairy and she would dance together one last time.

It would be in Pavel's writing studio. On the eve of her ninety-ninth birthday. She was determined not to be a century old, that sounded simply impossible. Curious how of all the things in her strange and long life, *that* was the impossible one.

By then, she had been living in the office/writing studio full time. At her request, Johnny had set up the bed for her there and moved her portrait onto the wall opposite the desk, away from the sunlight. Both Pavel and she loved having it there. It was a striking reminder of the past, which Pavel swore wasn't dead or even past.

She looked at it now. The young woman with icy blue eyes looked back at the old lady, reduced by age, took in her grey hair, her wrinkled paper-thin skin, and found her wanting.

Anastasia knew exactly what age she would choose to be when the time came.

"Are you ready, darling?"

"Ready," she said. They'd rehearsed all the practicalities for years now. Nothing was left to chance. Whatever came next, however it came to pass, they were beyond the bounds of morality. Such were the exigencies of immortality. Such were the costs of love.

Anastasia picked up the glass of dancing green liquid and downed it at once. The delicious burn warmed her very soul, it seemed.

Slowly, she lowered herself in his chair to wait. It wouldn't be long now. She thought she could feel her husband's arms around her. The sensation of coming home after a long and winding journey enveloped her, suffusing her with perfect peace.

"This isn't the end," he whispered as the darkness came for her. "This is the beginning. This is the beginning of forever."

CHAPTER 23

AFTER

THE DIARY

Stop whatever you're doing right now," says Dan, his voice slightly louder than it ought to be, given all the modern advancements of telephone technology.

Only a few years ago, I would have hung up. And it would have been funny. Not just because of my friend's penchant for melodrama and hyperbolic conversation launches, although I never once remember him doing the conventional "Hey, how are you?" but also because I would have taken his command literally. Which is just amusing in and of itself.

But no, I wouldn't do that now. I know all too well how it would play out—he would just call back. So, I do in fact stop reading the book I've been enjoying, splay its belabored spine out on my nightstand, and say, "What's up?"

"The old lady Koshmaroff has finally kicked the bucket," he says, breathless with excitement. "And they are having a frigging estate sale over at their place. All those secrets, all those goodies for anyone to see and buy."

Okay, this is a huge deal. For him, anyway. Dan has been fascinated by the Koshmaroff family ever since he found out about them, years and years ago on an abortive dare. He has been obsessed with all things scary, creepy, gothic since middle school and never met a conspiracy theory he didn't like. He has all these ideas ...

And I know I should be supportive now. I just have to summon the energy to do so.

You see, Dan and I have been friends since we were kids. My parents bought the house next to his parents, and that was it. Though initially it may have been a friendship of convenience, soon enough, the proximity factor was overshadowed by genuine shared interests. From then on, it was Dan and Dave forever. Double D in school. Daniel and David to our much-beleaguered parents whenever they had to chastise us for some cleverly orchestrated prank. Good times were so good. And then they were over. High school ends, people change.

They don't change that much, mind you. Both Dan and I still work in the same supermarket. Only he continues stocking shelves, while I'm an assistant manager now and taking night classes in a community college two towns over, with the hope of doing something more with my life. I still haven't decided what that something might be yet, but I've been feeling the constraints of this town more and more with each passing year. And Dan, for all his grand ideas, never does. Even living in his mother's basement, clichéd as that is, doesn't seem to bother him. To him, it's home.

I can never tell if he hasn't noticed we're growing apart or has and chooses to ignore it. Either way, he is exactly the same Dan he's always been. And if I'm not the same Dave, well, whose fault is that? Is it fair of me to take it out on him?

Not like I have lots of other friends. I know people, sure, but it isn't the same. There's no one I can spill secrets to or ask for a liver donation if I needed it. There's no one like Dan in my life. For better or worse.

Yes, he may be an absolute lunatic. Yes, he has, on numerous occasions, tried to persuade me that the moon landing was a setup. Yes, he may be completely and utterly convinced that the old lady Koshmaroff is the Romanov Princess Anastasia, who survived the massacre and ended up hiding out in our Podunk town. He has evidence for this theory of his too: age matches up, there's the accent, and her first name is indeed Anastasia—something he had once espied in her checkbook at the supermarket checkout. And so, to him it makes perfect sense that she would come live out here, in the middle of nowhere, in a creepy old house on a hill. After all, who would ever suspect the truth?

It's exhausting to try and reason with that. Usually, I don't.

I know what's coming next too. One way or another we are going to the Koshmaroff estate sale.

A KID IN the candy shop probably isn't the right analogy. I mean, that is how Dan is acting, but this place is just too far off the mark. It's too bleak, too depressing, too gloomy.

I always thought this house didn't fit the town. It just sits atop a hill like a peeling star bauble atop a dead Christmas tree. There's nothing like it around here. Nothing for miles that I'm aware of. Does every small town have their creepy old house on a hill, or is it just all the horror movies Dan and I have stayed up watching over the years?

I've never wanted to set foot here, but not because, like most people in this town, I believe it's haunted or anything. To me, it has always looked ... sad. The kind of sad that you can't just visit and walk away from, the kind that permeates your skin and comes with you when you leave.

Dan is loving it, though. To him, it's a treasure trove. He is a man on a mission here, hunting down evidence for his crazy theory. I don't know what to do with myself, so I check out other shoppers. It's a diverse bunch. There's a guy absolutely losing his shit over something that looks like an overdecorated egg. An old dude checking out what seems to be an actual quill.

The Koshmaroffs obviously had money, at least once upon a time. And this, for all the world to see, must have been their fairy tale castle. There are things here that are probably worth a lot of dough. Or maybe less so, given the state of them. Things from a world long gone. And now their owners are gone too. If objects were alive, they'd be orphans. But now there are just ... what? Discards?

Dan has spun the Koshmaroffs saga for me often, and it only gets more elaborate with time, mixing facts with fiction. I don't think that giant book of Russian Folklore has helped matters any, but hey, at least he's reading. So yeah, I've learned secondhand all about the Romanovs and their tragic fate and Rasputin and all that. And, of course, Dan's obsession—the youngest Romanov daughter,

Grand Duchess Anastasia. "Not Princess," as Dan likes to correct me. We've watched an entire documentary on her infamous impostor, Anna Anderson. I don't know why someone would bother with a thing like that. Just another attention-hungry person. Everyone wants their fifteen minutes of fame.

I'm not sure if attention's what Dan is after. It seems to me that he genuinely wants to solve the mystery. But then again, I can't imagine him turning down a chance to espouse his views on national television, bright lights and all, if given a chance.

In the years since, I have often wondered what it must have been like for Dan to go through life believing the things he did, searching and researching proof for some elusive truths of his imagination. And the only thing I've ever come up with that made sense is that it must have made him less lonely in this world. So what kind of friend does that make me?

"Check this out," Dan says in a genuinely reverent tone that echoes slightly amid the tall walls of the Koshmaroff's estate. "The library." It's the Holy Grail for him, the place where he thinks all the secrets are hidden.

To be fair, it is a nice library. Gloomy like the rest of the house, but nice. Dark wooden shelves are positively groaning under the weight of heavy tomes. I imagine the same heaviness in the very atmosphere of the space, pressing down on us. A glance at Dan reveals that my friend doesn't share my discomfort.

So, I look at the shelves closer. Some of the books' titles feature what must be Cyrillic writing, some are French, but a good many of them are in English.

I don't recognize any of the names. Dan seems to, though.

"Crowley. Blavatsky. Dee. Swedenborg. Gardner," he whispers to me. "All the greats."

"Who are they?" I feign interest.

"Great occult authors. People who tried to figure the world out. People who knew magick."

I know he means magic with a "k." I've seen him write it down before, and I can hear it in his voice now. Dan is a fanboy struck with awe.

"Are you gonna buy any of them?" I ask.

I have no idea what things cost at estate sales; but I imagine them to be expensive. This is a far cry from the garden variety sidewalk sales my mom occasionally drags me to, mostly so I can serve as a mule for her random crafting finds.

"Nah, man. What I'm looking for is special. It won't be labeled. Nothing like that."

I'm not sure how to take it. Maybe it's a tacit acknowledgment that, for all his interest, Dan can't afford any of it. I hope he doesn't hit me up for money. I make two dollars more than Dan hourly, a fact I've stupidly told him once and have regretted mentioning ever since.

To my relief, he doesn't ask, just continues browsing. As I wait, I start thinking about a tricky homework assignment due next Wednesday. I begin to actually compose the essay in my head when Dan slaps me on the shoulder hard enough to send me stumbling.

"Whoa, whoa, sorry." He holds up his hands. "Are you okay? I didn't mean to … Just got so excited. Look at this."

I look. It's a leather-bound book. The leather has seen happier days. There's a small metal lock on the side. It's shiny, not a flake of rust. Weird. Must have been added on at a later time.

To me, it seems like a fancy notebook or maybe a diary. I've seen the type, pretending a tiny lock can keep their secrets safe.

"It's her diary," whispers Dan with the same profound awe in his tone as a person sighting a Sasquatch in their front yard.

"How do you know that? Maybe it was her husband's diary."

"Nah, the dude died, allegedly." Dan punctuates this with a raised eyebrow, meaning he probably has a theory about that too. "Been gone for decades. And this thing has been recently handled. I can tell."

"Well, maybe she handled it recently on account of missing him."

"No, no, man, it's hers." Dan's got that look. Logic be damned. He's chasing the high of discovery now.

It's getting late, and I have no desire to argue.

"Well, go ask what they want for it," I tell him. "I'll meet you outside."

"Sure," says Dan and disappears, diary in hand.

Outside looks grey. I can't remember if the forecast promised rain. I look at the house and wonder if this is all there is. All the dreams, hopes, and desires of the people who have lived here, all the things they have lovingly accumulated over the years—now just fodder for the idle curiosities of collectors and weirdos. Maybe the pharaohs had the right idea, getting their possessions buried with them. There's something distinctly unsavory about leaving it all behind in this manner.

Dan emerges from the house, empty-handed. "Let's go," he says.

We walk. He's booking it, so I adjust my speed. The Koshmaroff estate recedes behind us to a Bates Motel silhouette against the darkening sky.

"So, you didn't get it?" I ask. Maybe the salespeople had some privacy-based boundaries or scruples after all.

Dan stops, smiles, and opens the flap of his windbreaker. The diary is there, snug against his worn-out *The Truth is Out There* T-shirt. The tagline from his favorite—no surprise there—and one of the all-around best shows on TV. Something we can both agree on, and not just because agent Scully is a total babe.

"Wait. Dan, did you pay for that?"

He grins. "Sure. But more along the line of a five-finger discount."

"Not okay, man" I feel genuinely ticked off." It's like stealing from the dead."

"That's the best way to steal," Dan counters. "No real victims."

"The money might have been going toward her relatives or friends or something."

"Nah, man. She had no one. No kids. No pets. Nothing. No one ever visited."

I'm not sure how he knows that, but it sounds about right. Surely, if anyone ever visited the old lady, outside of the repairman and the occasional grocery delivery person, someone would know about it. Small towns are like that.

"It still seems wrong," I say, but lacking real conviction. The entire thing has left me weirdly drained. I just want to go home.

"Wanna come over and check it out?" Dan asks. "I've got beer."

Of course, *that* he'll spend money on.

"Nah, man. I got schoolwork. I should probably just go home and get on that."

"Party pooper." Dan sighs exaggeratedly for comic effect. "Your paltry mind isn't ready to unravel the mysteries of the universe."

He may be right, but we part ways at the intersection, and I leave him to his discoveries.

THE NEXT SHIFT we work together is Tuesday. I figure in the intervening days Dan has learned all there is to know about the old lady Koshmaroff from her diary and moved on to other things. He's been really into ancient aliens lately, ever since reading Von Daniken. Now he's convinced this theory has all the makings of the next great TV show.

When I see Dan, he looks ... haggard. Who knew that word even existed in my vocabulary? But apparently, there it is. My English lit professor would be proud. Dan's normally pasty—he calls it his "basement complexion"—but the circles under his eyes are distinctly more pronounced, his hair is a mess, and his uniform shirt looks slept in.

"You okay, man?" I slap him on the back and joke, "Old lady diaries keeping you up at night?"

He gives me an indecipherable look, shakes his head, and walks away. This is odd, but not distractingly so, not on a hopping day like Tuesday. I busy myself with inventory and orders. Hours pass. We take a break together like we always do when our shifts line up.

I have some leftover pasta with meatballs that I nuke in the breakroom. Dan's got his customary PB'n'J sandwiches. The guy can eat obscene amounts of them and never get tired. This time, there's a modest stack of three in front of him. And a large red apple. Brain food, as he refers to it.

"So, seriously, though. What's up with you?" I say, digging in. Whoever says pasta doesn't reheat well hasn't had the right pasta. The trick is not to make it too delicious the first time; that way there's no noticeable difference the next day.

"I can't get in," Dan mumbles into his sandwich.

"What?"

"I can't get in. That stupid lock, I can't undo it. It's like some Fort Knox shit."

"Have you tried just busting it open?"

"Yes, genius. That and every other thing you're going to suggest next. I've tried it, and it didn't work. I've even tried lock picking. Nothing. Nada. Zilch."

I want to make a joke. There are so many jokes to make here. But the guy looks genuinely upset. So I try being a good friend instead.

"How about I come over after work tonight and take a look at it? Maybe all you need is a fresh pair of eyes."

For a second, Dan looks like he's going to snap at me, but then he seems to rethink it and simply nods. "Yeah, sure, that'd be great, man. If all else fails, there's a freshly rented VHS of the new *Candyman* with our names on it."

"It's a date," I tell him, and he steals a meatball from my lunch container.

WHEN DAN'S RIGHT, he's right. I didn't believe him at first, unable to imagine such a tiny lock putting up this much resistance. But here we are and, short of a blowtorch or a chainsaw intervention, the damn thing is well and truly stuck.

"Told you," Dan says with something like resignation.

"Maybe it's got a magic spell holding it locked."

"Maybe." He takes this more seriously than intended.

"Yeah," I follow up in a mock-grave tone. "And we just need to break the spell. Like dip it into borscht or something."

"Oh, fuck you, man," he says, but there's no fight in it.

We watch the movie. It isn't as good as the first one. Or the second one. But it's entertaining all the same.

We get good and wasted on cheap beer. The hours get away from me. There's no proper daylight in Dan's basement, a fact that is partially intentional. The place is like a freaking casino—it exists outside of time and encourages you to make stupid decisions. Meaning we try the lock again. And again. Dan goes after it with scissors and makes a production of it. It's funny, so I laugh. I'm still laughing when he cuts himself. Predictable.

"All slapstick ends in blood," he decries theatrically, before using a dirty T-shirt from the floor pile—Dan does not believe in laundry baskets—to staunch the blood.

"Oh shit, you got blood on the diary too," I notice.

"Here." He throws me another T-shirt from the same general vicinity. "Clean it up."

I do. Then I go off in search of a first aid kit for his injured finger.

Once Dan's patched up and I'm sobered up, I leave. I even rewind the VHS before I leave and drop it off through the overnight return slot on the way home. Me, the ever responsible one.

DAN IS STOCKING shelves the next morning at the supermarket, while I'm trying to sort out a messed-up bread order, and we are both regretting last night's beers. Maybe not the beers themselves, but the quantity consumed. Well, at least I do. I'm hydrating aggressively to make up for the damage done. We haven't had a chance to talk yet, only nodding to each other in passing. I like to present a serious face at work. Makes me feel more mature or something. That and the collared shirt.

We take our fifteen-minute coffee break together. The sludge that comes out of the breakroom machine isn't quite coffee, more like coffee-adjacent, but it's free, and free tastes right.

Dan looks like a kid with a secret to spill.

"What?" I ask. I know he wants me to.

"I opened it," he says.

"You did?"

"Well," Dan prevaricates. "It opened. By itself. I mean, I don't know. I woke up, and it was unlocked."

"Weird."

"Weird," he agrees. "Maybe you did something to it while cleaning it last night."

"Maybe."

We sip the sludge.

"So?"

"So?"

"Don't be coy, dude. What does it say?"

"Well, here's a thing ..." Dan starts.

"It's in Russian, isn't it? You can't read a word of it, right?"

"Well, first of all, naysayer, *nyet*, it isn't. It's in ... it's like ... it's like coded or something. Can't make head or tails of it. I'm going to the library after work to get some books on ciphers."

"Hey. Whatever gets you to the library." I raise my coffee mug in mock salute.

"You just wait and see," Dan says with the arrogant smirk of a true believer. "You just wait and see."

WEEKS PASS. WEEKS during which Dan's already somewhat lackluster work performance turns truly abysmal. Even his attendance, usually fairly reliable—the guy always took the showing-up-is-half-the-battle thing seriously— becomes spotty. Then he stops showing up altogether. As the assistant manager, I have to have a talk with him, and I dread it.

As a friend, I miss Dan. Didn't think I would, but I do. I miss the cheesy horror flicks and the crazy ideas discussed over cheap beers. I miss the subterranean basement man cave with its throwback seventies décor, consisting of all the furnishing rejects from upstairs, courtesy of Dan's mom. I even miss his deceptively comfortable couch—butt-worn, shit-brown, cigarette burned, but home to the best naps I've ever had.

The way we sort of reconnected after the estate sale set back the clock on the growing apart thing for the time being. And now this … It's weird.

The last time I visited, Dan's mom, Mrs. Malson—"Call me Janice." "No, thank you."—told me he wasn't home. I didn't believe her. This time I won't be turned away at the door, and I won't take a lie for an answer.

Turns out I don't have to. I go in prepared for a battle that isn't there. Mrs. Malson is home and appears to have started her happy hour early. She just nods at me and lets me in. Ever since Dan's dad hit the midlife crisis head-on, bought a sports car, and started banging his secretary, eventually moving out to live with her, Dan's mom has taken to lounging around in kimonos and drinking cocktails at all hours of the day. The woman radiates loneliness. She's even tried flirting with me a few times; at least that's what I think it might have been. Super uncomfortable, no matter how many times you've seen *The Graduate*. But today the coast is clear.

I head to the basement. It's closed but unlocked. Drunk or not, Mrs. Malson is good about privacy.

"Dan?" I poke my head through the door and shout into the basement. "You down there?"

No answer, but I can hear him shuffling around. Mumbling too, it sounds like.

I take a chance and descend, deliberately hitting every creaky spot on the stairs so as to not startle him with the suddenness of my appearance.

The first thing I notice is the smell: unwashed body, general staleness, and something else I can't quite put a finger on. The next thing is Dan himself. He comes into view, and he looks like shit. His hair is sticking up, thick with grease. His shirt looks like it hasn't been changed or even taken off in a week. Remnants of past meals encrust it. They also litter a lot of the available floor space. All other surfaces are covered in papers and books. The walls are covered in taped notes. Strange music is emanating through the surround sound.

The place is creepy in a way I haven't encountered before. Serial-killer creepy. It looks like somewhere John Doe from *Se7en* would hang out.

There are so many questions I want to ask but what comes out is this, "What are you listening to, man?"

"Znamenny chants," Dan answers, like it's a totally normal musical choice. Like I'm supposed to know what that even is.

"Which is?"

"It's these chants from the Russian Orthodox tradition. She listened to them as a child. She missed them."

"So you translated the diary?" I ask. Oh good. Maybe there's a perfectly rational explanation for all this madness.

"Yes and no."

"Meaning?"

"I know what it says now."

"That sounds like more of a yes," I prompt him.

"I can't read it, but I know what it says," Dan clarifies before finally making eye contact. "She told me."

The last three words permanently destroy any hope I might have had of being able to rationally sort this all out.

"She *told* you?"

"She speaks to me. She told me her whole life story. For a long time, she was sad. But I don't think she's sad anymore. She wanted me to know, I think. She wanted someone to know."

"Dude," I say in what I hope sounds like a calm voice of reason, "you're not making a lot of sense. Did you take something? Are you on something?"

As a rule, Dan stays away from anything harder than pot and booze. There have been occasional ventures into heavier highs: a time he took acid and thought the public pool was hiding Atlantis, the one coke adventure that left him up for three days trying to learn ancient Sumerian, things like that. Party anecdotes. All left in the past, or so I thought. But maybe not. I mean, that would explain this entire thing. Maybe he's finally gotten his hands on some peyote he always talks about.

"No, no. I ... nothing." Dan shakes his head. "I don't need that. Not now."

Fuck.

"Is she speaking to you now?"

"No. You're here."

"So she's shy? Like a shy ghost?" I can feel myself getting angry, and I'm trying to control it.

"No. It's just that you're not ready to hear her. You're not ready to know her secrets."

"And you are?"

"Yes. Yes. I bled for it. I opened the door." There's such a serene expression on Dan's face, none of his usual jumpy energy. He looks like the guy who peered behind the curtain and liked what he saw. Like maybe that glimpse revealed something that made perfect sense of the world for him.

"Look, why don't we get out of here," I offer. "Take a shower and change, and then we'll go to Paulo's and get some pizza. It's your favorite. And then maybe we can rent a movie, come back here, clean some of this shit up, and watch it? *Stir of Echoes* is out. You liked the book, remember?"

This is it, I think. *Please say yes. We'll do all those things and write this weirdness off as indigestion or something and never speak of it. Please. I don't want it to be something else. I don't want to have my friend go crazy.*

Dan looks at me like he can read my mind. Like he regrets he cannot accommodate my wishes.

"I'm sorry," he says simply. "But it's too late for all of that. There are things I need to do now, and I need to do them alone."

And then he turns away from me, dismissing me. And I understand with a terrible finality that, at long last, our friendship has come to an end.

I KNEW I should have done more. Even then I knew it. And it has haunted me in the years since. But it was just all too much at the time. Too much in a way I didn't want to deal with and couldn't even begin to process. Should I have had Dan sanctioned? Taken away in a straitjacket, locked up until he stopped hearing voices of dead old ladies? Maybe, but I wasn't ready to make that kind of a decision. He had a mother, I reasoned. She could take care of all that if push came to shove. Dan wasn't dangerous and didn't appear suicidal. He was just off his rocker, and frankly, considering all his esoteric interests over the years, it made a certain kind of sense. Either way, I walked away.

I know now it all sounds like excuses, and I no longer want to excuse my behavior—I want to take responsibility. But, of course, it's much too late for all that.

I tell myself that things have a way of working out. And they do. Only not in a way you ever imagine.

There's one thing that really gets to me even after all this time, a splinter in my brain. That day, on the way out of Dan's basement, I stole a glance at the diary and saw only bone-white pages with nothing on them.

DAN DISAPPEARED SOON after that. He was, of course, long fired by then, but the news still found me through the grapevine. They said he just took off and left. Dan, the guy who never seemed to venture much further than his mother's basement, had somehow left town. Before me. I, the ambitious one, stayed behind. It was ironic ... or something.

I never heard from him again. Mrs. Malson would come into the store from time to time, her selections more and more dominated by alcohol, bottles clinking and sloshing in her shopping basket. I heard she had liver troubles. Eventually, it killed her.

I finally got my degree. It took longer than I anticipated, but there were setbacks along the way and plans gone awry. With the ink on my diploma still wet, I landed a job in finance and moved to the city. For a while, everything went well. Life was finally beginning to take the shape I had always dreamed of. There were some good years, great ones even. And then the market collapsed. One by one I lost my job, my condo, and my girlfriend. In that order, like some kind of a terrible domino effect. There was nothing to do, but pack up, put my tail between my legs, and go back home.

My parents were retired by then and eager for company. I tried to put a good face on my depression for their sake. I got my old job, believe it or not. It didn't help my depression but gave me something to do all the same.

Once, I unthinkingly drove past the old Koshmaroff estate. Made me shudder. It still stood upon that hill, proud as a monolith, forbidding as a tomb. Time could batter the place, it seemed, but not destroy it.

I was far enough away, but there was this feeling, like something had reached out across the distance with its icy tendrils, grabbed me, and made my heart seize. I had been avoiding going anywhere near the estate ever since—not an easy task in a town this small.

And then, one day, the hyperactive rumor mill of the work's breakroom informed me that the estate was getting a new owner. Someone had bought it and was moving in.

I couldn't believe it. Who'd want that place? Some eccentric magician? A lunatic occultist? A freaking cult?

I had to, *had to*, know. So much so that on that very same evening, I took a walk across town and up the hill, to the one place I never wanted to visit again. Fate seemed to have other ideas for me, I mused, as I stood in front of the Koshmaroff estate, remembering a time gone past and my happy, mischievous friend with his newly stolen treasure.

I didn't ring the bell, but the new owner must have seen me from one of the windows. He came out to greet me. Tall, straight-spined, well dressed, with slicked-back hair and a nice black suit, my old friend looked like a hip, successful undertaker. Or maybe it was just the house framing him that way.

"Dave," he said, not unfriendly. "Long time, no see."

"Dan." I couldn't find any more words, so I just nodded.

"I heard you were back in town." His voice was deeper than I remembered and more refined. "We both are now. Seems like this is the Rome all roads lead to."

"A depressing thought," I finally managed, aiming for sarcasm, not bitterness.

"Oh, I don't know. I kind of like it here. I've traveled all over, and this has always felt like home."

"Where did you go?" I asked. "Where have you been?"

"Here and there. France, Italy, Greece. Russia."

"Russia," I echoed, surprised, impressed. My old friend had traveled further than I ever did.

"Yeah, great place. So much to see, so much history. I spent years there."

"And now you're back. Here." I gestured to the house.

"And now I'm back. Here." There was an easy pride in my friend's voice. "I came into some money and wanted to invest into local infrastructure."

"Right." I nodded again like it made any kind of sense. Like any of it ever did.

"Supper is ready, dear," emanated from somewhere in the house. I couldn't see the speaker, but was intrigued by the melodic and strangely accented feminine voice. Dan smiled like a man hearing his favorite song.

"I'm sorry, I don't mean to hold you up," I said, realizing the time. "I'll go. It was good to see you again."

"Nonsense." Dan's hand landed on my shoulder in a warm, friendly manner. "Come on in, stay for supper. We'll catch up. You'll get to meet Mrs. Malson."

I dreaded lifting my feet past that threshold but found myself somehow unable to decline the invitation. Time slowed down, events unfolding with the pace and logic of a dream sequence. Or maybe a nightmare.

"Welcome, welcome," I heard a parrot trill in my direction.

"Ah, that's Diego. Our dear feathered friend. He's somewhere around." Dan made a nebulous gesture with his arm toward the dark interior.

I heard the flapping of bird wings, a strangely-familiar hypnotic music playing in the background.

"Ana, darling. Set the table for one more," my old friend exclaimed with a game-show-host enthusiasm, ushering me inside. "We have a guest."

CODA

(BUT FIRST...)

ARE YOU ABSOLUTELY mad? What is this? What ... ?"

"You must help. Anton, please. Look. She is bleeding."

"Is this ... ?"

"Are you sure you want to know?"

Deep sigh.

"Place her on this table, Ivan. Hurry. Undo these corset stays."

"I'm sorry, I'm sorry, I didn't know what else to do."

"It's too late for apologies now, brother."

"She was still alive, Anton. I couldn't just ... do nothing."

"You did nothing and worse for many years for those terrible people."

"I can't apologize for that. I had to follow my convictions."

"Your convictions have led you to an abattoir, Ivan. Or what did you call it? A House of Special Purposes?"

A quiet sigh. "The Ipatiev House."

"No, brother, a slaughterhouse. Do you know what that makes you?"

"I didn't do it, Anton. I didn't do *this*. My gun ... I said my gun jammed. You couldn't see in all the smoke from the gunpowder."

"The good news is I can stop the bleeding. A lot of this blood isn't even hers. The wounds are surprisingly superficial."

"The corset must have taken the brunt of it. She wore another corset originally."

"Help me, Ivan. Here, hold this down."

Silence, heavy breathing, sounds of work, lifesaving efforts.

"How did you do this, Ivan? Did no one see you?"

"A priest had come before the ... There was a robe."

"They didn't notice?"

"It was madness, Anton, pure madness. I've never seen, never imagined such a thing."

"And I thought you've become accustomed to murder, brother."

"Not like this." A violent shudder. "Never like this."

Shaking, crying now.

"They wouldn't die, Anton. The children wouldn't die. The jewels had offered some protection. It took more effort, making the soldiers angrier. They shot the boy, stabbed him, put a bullet in his head. They bayoneted the girls. There was so much blood, so much blood ..."

"All births are bloody, Ivan. And your people's republic will be born awash in blood."

"I know, I know, you've said it all before."

"And how it galled you then, my dear revolutionary brother."

"And how it scares me now, Anton."

Pause. Bandages. Water.

"You may recall that I studied the repair of the mind, not the body."

"But you know both. You're helping her now."

"She'll need much more help than this, Ivan. Your people will come looking for her, won't they?"

"No."

"No?"

"No."

"Explain."

"There was a girl of a similar age. A cousin. Somebody. I switched the bodies and the corsets."

"Very crafty."

"It wasn't planned. I was desperate. I felt compelled to save her."

"When she wakes up, what will you say to her, brother?"

"Me? Nothing. I won't be here. I need to get back before they notice me gone."

"Back to that, Ivan?"

"What choice do I have? If Yurovsky notices, I'm done for."

"Leave then. Go now. Disappear. Save yourself as you saved her."

"I can't, Anton. There's nothing for me out there. My soul is covered in blood, and I must pay for it. My sins are too heavy to lug around."

"I thought you gave up your faith."

"Today was a rude awakening."

"She's stable now. What shall I tell her when she wakes?"

"I had hoped you could hypnotize her."

"Oh, is that all?"

"Isn't that what you learned under that man. What was his name? Gérard something."

"Gérard Encausse."

"Yes, him. The secrets of the mind he taught you, Anton."

"At the time, you said they were party tricks."

"I was wrong, brother. Wrong about so many things. Perhaps you can forgive someday. But she doesn't have the luxury of time. You were always a loyalist, a tsarist. Help her now and preserve their bloodline. It's the most anyone can do for that family now."

"I can't tell her who she is. She won't be able to live with it."

"So tell her a story. You used to be so good at storytelling when we were kids."

"I can ... Maybe I can tell her she is someone else. A happy child from a happy family. I can invent a tragedy less terrible than the one she has lived through."

"How would it work, Anton?"

"Imagine, if you will, a wall. I shall put up a wall in her mind. In many ways, her life will start when she wakes up."

"Where will she go?"

"I know of some families, loyal tsarists like me. One of them will take her in as their own daughter. I shall arrange this."

"Thank you, thank you, brother."

"This isn't for you, Ivan."

"I know."

Pause.

"What will you tell her then, brother? How will your story begin?"

"I'll say ... I'll say there was a fire."

"And she'll remember nothing of her life at all?"

"Not if I build this wall just right."

"It seems unfair she should lose all of herself, doesn't it? She has already lost so much."

"Well, then, perhaps she can keep her name. Yes, that and nothing more. Which one is she?"

"Oh, I should have said. Anton, meet the Grand Duchess Anastasia Nikolayevna."

"Anastasia she shall stay then. For all her life to come. Now go. I'll wait here with her. Make sure no one sees you."

"I am in your debt forever."

"Forever is a long time, Ivan, try to stay alive that long."

"Goodbye, brother."

"Goodbye."

THERE'S WORK TO be done. So much work. Anton has never thought that all his learning, all his skill would be put to the test quite like this. Not just the misunderstood and frowned-upon science of the mind, but the darker, more mystical secrets of it too. Until now, it has always been regarded as something a party trick. He has never had to rely on it to save a life.

Now he is determined to do his utmost for the girl before him. *Save a life, save the world*, he thinks, but there's no world left to save. The world as he knows it is rapidly disappearing in a whirlpool of blood and gunpowder.

Anton doesn't know that he will never see his brother again, or that he himself will be gunned down by an angry youth in a torn Red Army coat only a few months from now. In this mad world, all he has are his convictions. He believes this revolution will bring no peace, no fairness. He believes that this vast and troubled land will never know true fairness and peace. He believes that socialism will fail, how can it not?

Anton remembers the ceremony conducted by Rasputin himself not too long before his death. The years ahead were glimpsed then and found wanting. It was the will and the promise of the Mad Monk, perhaps an act of revenge for what was to come. But for now, the future, bleak as it may be, is still in the future, looming unknown. Saving this life is the one thing—the only thing—he can do now.

AFTER A LONG while, the girl comes to with a start. She opens her eyes. They are the bluest of blue.

"What ... what happened?" she asks. "Where am I?"

"There was a fire, Anastasia. But you are all right. Your parents are on the way to get you. Here, have some tea."

The man seems kind, and she accepts the tea. Her mind is in a fog, but she feels remarkably calm. She waits.

"Anastasia," she repeats her name to herself and likes the sound of it. Soon, the rest of her memories come. They are of a happy comfortable pastoral life in a large house with a loving family.

How nice, she thinks, *this life.* She wishes it would last forever.

THE END?

AFTERWORD

DEAR READER!

You made it all the way to the afterword and stuck around. Thank you.

This novel being out in the world, read and enjoyed, is my dream. Thanks for helping me make my dream come true. Being a dream-come-true maker looks good on you!

If you liked *Estate Sale*, please take a moment to review it on Goodreads and/or Amazon and/or a platform of your choice. Or shout it from the rooftops. I'll hear you, and I'll appreciate you.

I wrote this book during the lockdown, on a shared computer, in a shared tiny studio apartment. It was a labor of love. I poured all of me into these pages, all my passions, all my interests. My goal was to write a book I'd want to read: original, exciting, clever. And sure enough, every time I revisit *Estate Sale*, I'm very pleased with it. Immodestly so. I just don't want to have to edit it anymore. This new edition has been all kinds of spruced up with six thousand words added.

Please note that I have done my absolute best to stay historically accurate, but facts and magic (let alone, magick) can be slippery, so I apologize for any inaccuracies.

This book may be my baby, but unlike other children, it didn't take a small village to raise. Only a few dedicated people helped me along the way. So here's some gratitude where gratitude is due:

To everyone I've met online and in person who buys, reads, reviews, and promotes my work—THANK YOU! Without you, I'm just a writer which is to say a weirdo scribbling tall tales in anonymity. With you, I'm an author. A proper storyteller. Thanks for being there.

To Clay McLeod Chapman, Douglas Wynne, Seb Doubinsky, Jethro Wegener, Arthur Shattuck O'Keefe, and Suzie Lockhart, many thanks for your kind words about *Estate Sale*.

To Justin Sanz for giving my book such a gorgeous cover. I used to worry about having a cover that wouldn't do my book justice. Now I just hope my novel lives up to its cover.

To Chelsea Sanz for the lovely inside "object" art.

To Arthur Shattuck O'Keefe (again), for doing the most exhaustively thorough BETA read/edit and infinitely improving my novel. Be sure to read his book, *The Spirit Phone*, for more historical occult-flavored shenanigans.

To Davida De La Harpe Golden for the final copy edit and steadfast encouragement.

To Michael Marshall Smith, for everything.

To Atticus Morton, my wonderful patron of the arts, for his unwavering faith in my writing.

And last of all and most of all, thank you to my beautiful wife, Chelsea, without whom this would all just be atoms and letters. Thank you for making me a better person and a better writer, for always telling me to look up, for infusing my world with magic. For everything. Thank you. Every word I write is for you. Forever.

ABOUT THE AUTHOR

Mia Dalia is an internationally published, CWA-nominated author of all things fantastic, thrilling, scary, and strange.

Her short fiction has been published online by Night Terror Novels, 50-word stories, Flash Fiction Magazine, Pyre Magazine, Tales from the Moonlit Path, carte blanche magazine, Jaded Ibis Press, Weird Wide Web; in print anthologies by Sunbury Press, HellBound Press, Black Ink Fiction, Dragon's Roost Press, Unsettling Reads, Phobica Books, PsychoToxin Press, Wandering Wave Press, rebellionLIT Press, Bullet Points Vol. 3, Critical Blast, Off-Topic Publishing, Exploding Head Press, Sinister Smile Press, DraculaBeyondStoker Magazine, Mystery Magazine, Headshot Press, Nightshade Press, WonderBird Press; Crystal Lake Publishing, WriteHive, and more, and featured in narrative podcasts such as Zoetic Press' Alphanumeric, Sudden Fictions, and Tales to Terrify.

Mia's work has been selected as Tales to Terrify's top ten best stories of 2023, shortlisted for the Crime Writers Association's Daggers Award 2024, and praised by authors and editors such as Michael Marshall Smith - "One of the best novels I've read in years", Stephen Jones - "horror tour-de-force", Clay McLeod Chapman - "every flip of the page leads its readers deeper into uneasy dream", Neil Sharpson, M.R. Carey, A.C. Wise, Ian Rogers, and more.

She is the author of the novels *Estate Sale* and *Haven* (CamCat Books), novellas *Tell Me a Story*, *Discordant* (Anuci Press) and *Arrokoth, Do You Know The Muffin Man?* (Spaceboy Books) and the collection *Smile So Red and Other Tales of Madness* (Anuci Press).

Find her online at:

Official website:	https://daliaverse.wixsite.com/author
Twitter:	@ Dalia_Verse
FB:	DaliaVerse
Instagram:	@daliaverse
More:	https://linktr.ee/daliaverse